THE GARDEN CLUB GANG

Neal Sanders

The Hardington Press

The Garden Club Gang is a work of fiction. While certain locales and organizations are rooted in fact, the people and events described are entirely the product of the author's imagination.

Also by Neal Sanders

Murder Imperfect (2010)

*To the memory of my late aunt, Virginia Hallman (1917-2006),
who would never have done any of the things described in this book.
Or at least I don't think she would have.*

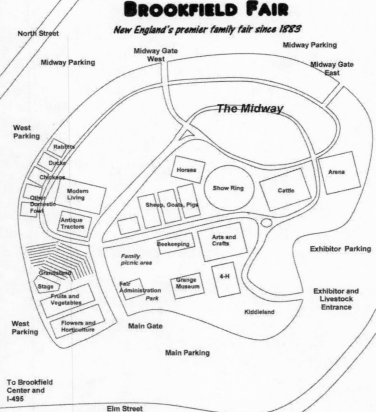

Map of the
BROOKFIELD FAIR
New England's premier family fair since 1883

North Street

Midway Parking

Midway Gate West

Midway Parking

Midway Gate East

The Midway

West Parking

Rabbits

Ducks

Chickens

Other Domestic Fowl

Modern Living

Antique Tractors

Horses

Show Ring

Cattle

Arena

Sheep, Goats, Pigs

Beekeeping

Arts and Crafts

Family picnic area

Grandstand

Stage

Fruits and Vegetables

Fair Administration Park

Grange Museum

4-H

Exhibitor Parking

Exhibitor and Livestock Entrance

West Parking

Flowers and Horticulture

Main Gate

Kiddieland

Main Parking

To Brookfield Center and I-495

Elm Street

THE GARDEN CLUB GANG

1.

The idea of robbing the Brookfield Fair did not spring full-grown from the minds of the four women. The concept of knocking over the gate receipts – or even an awareness of the phrase 'knocking over' – took time to take root. It did so in a series of small events, some of them personal, some of them shared. It is likely that, had those events not occurred within such a brief time frame, there might never have been a realization that such a feat was possible.

If there was a moment when the first seed was planted for what would become the Garden Club Gang (as they would call themselves), it was at another smaller fair, just a month earlier.

Eleanor Strong, age 62, stood in front of the flower show entries at the Barnstable Fair on Cape Cod. In her view, none of the four entries in the 'Delight in the Dunes' category merited a blue ribbon.

"They're pitiful," she said to Alice Beauchamp, who had agreed to accompany her that day in mid-July. Gesturing dismissively at the entry that had garnered the blue ribbon, she said, "There are six well-established elements of floral design and the person who put this together knows nothing about any of them. What this amounts to is a big pile of flowers in this year's 'in' color. It's fair to say this person knows squat about anything other than how to say, 'charge it to my account'."

Eleanor leaned over and peered at the entry card. *Priscilla Lewis, Back Bay Garden Club.*

"What Ms. Lewis has," Eleanor said, standing up straight and erect, "is three hundred dollars to throw away on flowers. Pile them high and thick enough, especially the exotic and expensive ones, and they'll give you the ribbon."

Alice was silent. She was listening to her friend, but her thoughts were elsewhere. *Three hundred dollars for flowers*, she thought. *Three hundred and seventy-five dollars would get me to Denver to see the birth of my first grandchild.* She had looked up the fares on the internet. She had contemplated clicking the mouse to make the purchase. But she didn't have even remotely that much extra money in her checking account and it would take months to scrape together the fare by scrimping on food or turning off the air conditioner for the summer. And, by then, the fares would have certainly gone up. *The only way I am going to get to Denver is to ask my son to send me the airfare, and that would mean asking that wretched harridan of a woman he married.*

She shivered at the thought, which in turn caused her foot to start throbbing.

Alice was nine years older than Eleanor and her health was reasonably good. She had Medicare now, but the twenty dollar co-pays at the HMO had deterred her from getting her toe taken care of. The toe was one of those annoying things. A hammertoe, they called it. It would only be day surgery and then a week off her feet, but five or six visits to the doctor before and after the operation meant at least a hundred dollars in co-payments.

She ignored the throbbing of her toe.

Eleanor noted the silence. She ought not to have mentioned the money. She knew Alice lived on her late husband's social security and the paltry funds they had accumulated despite all the saving over thirty-six years of marriage. Eleanor knew her friend's financial condition and berated herself mentally for raising such a delicate issue.

But she looked at the flower displays that substituted volumes of expensive blooms for finesse. It wasn't fair. Rich women who lived in the Back Bay entered competitions seventy miles distant with their Platinum American Express cards as their primary credential. Eleanor had studied floral design for fifteen years and could create things of beauty from what grew in her own yard.

What we need to do is to win the lottery, she thought. *Or rob a liquor store.*

What Eleanor said was, "Let's get a hot dog. My treat."

* * * * *

At that same hour in a drab, beige windowless consultation room at the Dana Farber Cancer Institute in Boston, Paula Winters absorbed the dismal news she had just been handed.

"It has spread," her doctor said, simply. "I can't sugar-coat it."

The doctor's words were spoken softly and with empathy. It did not make them less difficult to bear.

Paula's physician was a highly respected oncologist. Dr. Melissa Peterman's credentials were impeccable and she was universally considered to be on the cutting edge of breast cancer treatment. Twelve lymph nodes had been biopsied. Cancerous cells had been found in four of them.

"This is Stage III, not Stage IV," Dr. Peterman said. "There's no identified metastasis beyond the breast. But we need to discuss aggressive treatment options."

Paula was still fixed on those first three words. *It has spread.*

A lumpectomy had been the course of action recommended by a different specialist eighteen months earlier, and had been followed by an extensive course of radiation treatment. That was back when the cancer was termed Stage I and Paula was assured that the ten-year survival rate was 95%. Until a month ago, the checkups had been clean. Then, an examination had been what her previous doctor called, 'inconclusive'. That led to the search for and meeting with Melissa Peterman.

Suspect cells in four out of twelve lymph nodes indicated an aggressively spreading cancer and one that could be stopped only with surgery. Moreover, it was possible that even surgery would only slow the cancer's spread. It was mid-July. Paula thought, *I could be dead by Christmas*.

And, with that thought came a flood, not of fear, but of regret. *What in the hell have I done with my life?* she thought. *What have I really accomplished in fifty-one years?*

In Paula's view, everything she had ever done had been the 'safe' choice. The choices, in turn, had been dictated by her parents, by society and by her husband, Dan. She had gone to the safe state college, gone into the safe profession of nursing, married the man her mother approved of, and left nursing after Dan's career took off. Her two children were now out of college and on their own. But upon Julie and Perry's graduation, Dan had dropped his bombshell: he wanted a divorce. A few weeks after the divorce was final, he married a sweet young thing from his company, a woman only a few years older than Julie. A blonde, pretty girl with dazzling white teeth, slim hips and an MBA from the Wharton School.

And Paula was alone.

Melissa Peterman, aware that her patient's mind was elsewhere, had stopped talking.

Paula looked up at her. "What happens if I decline treatment?"

"The cancer will spread at its own pace, accelerating as it goes." The doctor's words were spoken in a way that was clear and unmistakable in its meaning.

"But all we can really do is slow it down," Paula said. "We can't cure it."

Doctor Peterman chose her words carefully but spoke strongly. "I have many patients who were where you are two and three years ago," she said. "They're still here, living active, vital lives. And there are new drug therapies coming to market that are very promising."

And what shape are those two- and three-year survivors going to be in after five years? Paula thought. *Are they still in remission or are they living from one round of chemo to the next?*

"I need time to think," Paula said.

"We will need to move quickly," Dr. Peterman said, emphasizing 'quickly'.

I've *never been white-water rafting,* Paula thought. *I've never gone bungee jumping. I've never even traveled on my own. Lord, I've never taken anything like a risk in my entire life.*

* * * * *

At a CVS store in the suburban town of Hardington that same hour, Jean Sullivan waited with growing impatience for her photos. Two teenaged boys manned the check-out counter, trading snickers with one another as they scanned items. A girl of about twenty whose purchases had included a box of tampons had just exited the store and the two boys were elbowing one another, their conversation too muted to be understood but the leering looks on their faces were unmistakable.

"Excuse me," Jean said. "Are my photos ready?"

One of the boys glanced over at the photo desk. "It'll be a couple of minutes," he said. His voice betrayed a lack of sincerity in what he said.

"That's what you said ten minutes ago," Jean countered.

The one boy shrugged, his dark hair flopping into his eyes. "What can I tell you?"

Do they treat their own grandmother this way? Jean thought. The boys had gone back to an animated conversation about rock groups on tour. Jean wondered if finding the store manager might be the solution to her problem. It had been half an hour. Surely the photos were ready by now.

She glanced down the aisles, looking for anyone in a shirt and tie who might be a manager. But it appeared decision-making authority in the store belonged to these two teenaged boys. A woman, probably in her early thirties with a four- or five-year-old in tow, put her purchases on the counter. The boys efficiently checked out the woman, showing a degree of deference as they did. *A woman close enough to their mothers' age to command attention*, Jean thought.

Five more minutes went by. Neither of the boys made any effort to check the photo printer.

I am invisible, Jean thought. *I am sixty-six years old, and therefore, I am invisible.*

And then an idea occurred to her. *If I am invisible, I may as well use it to my advantage.*

Jean, a slight woman standing just an inch over five feet, walked to the far end of the counter. The two boys were elbowing each other again, their attention drawn to a buxom teenager, apparently a classmate, who was crouched down looking at cosmetics in an aisle twenty feet away. Jean calmly went through the pile of prints that had accumulated in the photo printer's output tray. She selected the six prints that were of her grandchildren, emailed to her that morning by her daughter and son-in-law.

She found an envelope and dropped the photos into the sleeve. The envelope went into her purse. She thought for a moment about paying for the photos, but decided that the store should be made to bear some consequences for hiring such oafish, disrespectful children.

As Jean left the store, the two teenaged boys were still watching every movement of the girl in aisle two.

* * * * *

The next day, at the pre-meeting social hour of the Hardington Garden Club, Jean Sullivan showed the photos of her grandchildren to Alice Beauchamp.

"They're getting so big," Alice said with genuine appreciation. "They must be seven or eight."

"Eight," Jean said with pride. "The twins' birthdays were last month." Jean also knew Alice's financial predicament and so did not say that she had sent her grandchildren the clothing the twins wore in the photos.

Paula Winters wandered over to see the photos being passed back and forth. Though more than fifteen years younger than Jean and twenty younger than Alice, Paula felt a special kinship to the pair. They were all without spouses and they were *gardeners*. Some people joined the club just because they had idle time on their hands. Others were content to sit through programs on lavender hand creams and ointments that were poorly disguised sales pitches. Like Paula, Jean took care of elaborate perennial beds at her home. Alice, she knew, maintained a large plot for vegetables in the town's community garden.

Jean noted Paula's pale appearance and wondered if it was health-related. Paula's bout with breast cancer a year earlier had been well known within the club.

Eleanor Strong joined the group, carrying a slice of coffee cake and mug of coffee. Though she had no children of her own, she made appreciative noises upon seeing the photos. She, at least technically, was still married. Her husband, though, had been confined to a nursing home for the past year. Ten years her senior, his Alzheimer's had progressed to the point that at-home care was no longer possible and he recognized her only intermittently.

The four women spoke of children and grandchildren until the meeting was called to order at ten o'clock. At noon, they found themselves leaving at the same time, walking out into the searing heat of a New England July day.

"Anyone interested in lunch?" Paula asked. "I'm pulling

tomatoes out of the garden by the bushel basket and I've got enough chilled gazpacho to feed an army, plus some good bread."

It had not been a planned invitation. Paula did indeed have an excess of tomatoes and had converted several dozen of the surplus into gazpacho with the intent of giving it away, though at the time she did not know to whom. The idea of lunch simply occurred to her on the spot. Also, while she had no desire to share her most recent diagnosis, she wanted to hear the sounds of voices other than her own in her home.

The three women accepted the impromptu invitation.

It was over lunch that Jean first vocalized her belief that she was invisible to all but women of her own age.

"I've been thinking about it for the past day," she said after recounting her experience in the drug store. "After a certain age, we disappear. It's as though the human mind has been trained to filter us out and ignore us. It wasn't just those two teenaged boys, either. The same thing happens in grocery stores all the time. I can be at the delicatessen counter at Stop & Shop and wait forever. In a clothing store, no one ever asks if they can help me."

The other three women nodded their concurrence. Jean was the shortest of the four and her hair was a distinctive silver. Eleanor, who remained a blonde, stood a head higher than Jean and weighed perhaps fifty pounds more than her friend, said that she, too, had to raise her voice to get anyone to notice her. Even Paula, younger by more than a decade than anyone else in the room, had to agree that she, too, had passed the point at which she could count on being noticed.

"I was guilty of it," Alice said, nodding her head. "At the bank, I'd see the men first because they were usually taller. Then the young people because they were noisy. Then the younger women because of their clothes and because they frequently had children with them. The little old ladies came last. They got lost in the background."

The women spooned their soup, taking in Paula's large house with its impeccable furnishings. The invitation was an unusual one, for Paula had seldom invited people into her home, and even less so since the divorce.

Paula brought out a tray bearing four glasses and a bottle of white wine. She offered it to the other women.

"Wine doesn't agree with me," Jean said.

"Oh, I couldn't," Alice said. "I have to drive."

"I never drink during the day," Eleanor said, holding up her hand to ward off the bottle.

"Well, I'm having one," Paula said, and poured a glass. "It's a hot day and a cold glass of wine seems right." Having a glass of wine on a hot July afternoon was her first act of living dangerously.

The other women watched Paula pour the wine, take an ounce of it in her mouth and roll it around, her eyes closed and a smile of satisfaction on her face. Their resolve quickly melted. The first bottle was emptied and then replaced by a second.

"Have any of you ever been hang-gliding?" Paula asked of the three women when all had had a second glass of wine.

There were looks of bewilderment around the table.

"Went sky-diving?"

They shook their heads.

"Would you if you could?" Paula asked.

The others looked baffled, but Jean spoke up. "I could do those things. I went for a ride in a bi-plane when I was a little girl, which I realize today was quite a dangerous thing. Paula, are you talking about things that involve risk, or things that are foolish?"

Paula asked her to explain the difference.

"There are things that offer a thrill, but that involve some degree of risk," Jean said. "You mentioned sky diving. Parachutes are safe. But if yours is the one parachute in ten thousand that doesn't open, it means almost certain death. People who ride motorcycles are more likely to be killed in accidents, but people still ride them. They trade the risk for the pleasure it brings. Hang-gliding, though, seems to me to be not so much a sport as a kind of Russian roulette. I read that some percentage of hang gliders are killed every year regardless of their level of experience. It's like driving on an expressway at a hundred miles an hour. It's courting death for no reason other than some momentary thrill. It's foolish, pure and simple."

"Then leave out the foolish things," Paula said, pouring more wine. "Would you do something risky – providing it appealed to you – just to be able to know that for once in your life you had not taken the safe choice?"

Once again, as she had at the garden club meeting, Jean wondered if health was somehow at the core of Paula's odd questions.

Eleanor spoke up. "I think about Phil and all the things we didn't do." Phil was her nursing-home-confined husband who could no longer make choices for himself. "He wanted to start his own business but we – no, I – decided it was too risky. We never had children because any pregnancy for me would have been a high-risk one. Looking back and knowing what I know now, I'd gladly have taken those chances."

The others were quiet for a moment. Then Alice spoke. "We never took risks. Especially not financial ones. John insisted on putting our money in savings accounts and savings bonds. He said he didn't know what the stock market was going to do and he didn't trust it. Look where it got us."

The others were stunned by this simple declaration. Alice never spoke of her finances though it was clear to everyone that she was in an increasingly precarious position. She had sold her home following her husband's death and now, after a disastrous relocation to Florida, lived in Hardington Gardens, a subsidized apartment complex for low-income seniors.

Jean felt it was her turn to speak. "We weren't brought up to take risks. We were brought up to be mothers and housewives and helpmates. Risks were something men took. Risks were something we were taught to avoid. Al was a wonderful provider, but he was taking the biggest gamble of all – smoking all those years. When he died, I had to learn everything he did, and that meant doing everything with the least degree of risk. Yes, I wish I – and we – had done something for the thrill of it. Because now, I can't afford to take chances anymore."

"I thought about robbing a liquor store yesterday," Eleanor said. The others laughed. "Now, that's taking a risk."

The others wondered why Paula, who had raised the question of risk-taking, did not volunteer her own thoughts on the subject. But it would have been poor etiquette to ask their host such a question. They finished their gazpacho and remarked that it was wonderful. The second bottle of wine was drained. And then they departed into the hot afternoon.

* * * * *

Paula thought about what she had heard as she picked up dishes after lunch. They were four women, friends who shared a common interest in gardening. Now, she knew they had a second thing in common: they all regretted what they had not done. It had been a remarkably frank conversation.

Upon returning home from her doctor's office, Paula had made a list of things she wanted to do. It included going on an African veldt safari, seeing China and Australia, sailing a boat by herself and going whitewater rafting down the Colorado River. Unlike the three other women, Paula could afford to do these things. Dan wanted out of the marriage so desperately that he had given up most of their assets plus a share of his business. The money provided a more than adequate income for Paula's needs.

What she had not been able to do was to manage her cancer.

Paula had been on the verge of telling her friends of the new prognosis. Instead, she listened to the stories of risks not taken and decided not to. For the other three women, the future was constrained by money. They lived on fixed incomes and those incomes did not keep up with their cost of living. Paula felt that Eleanor, Alice and Jean were wonderful friends but they could not relate to her longing for adventure and her fear that time for that adventure was running out.

Paula left her kitchen and went to the downstairs half-bath. There, she stood in front of the small mirror over the sink and examined herself. Her chestnut hair was still thick and shiny. The color now came from sessions at a salon but her hair had always been one of her best features. Her face was lean, like the rest of her body. Her nose was small, her pores tight. She was, overall, still an attractive woman. But she saw a pallor in her skin and the dark circles under her eyes that makeup could not hide. *The face of a woman with cancer. The face of a woman who has been told how she will die*, she thought.

She thought of the years she had devoted to her family. She had been the sole breadwinner while Dan got his business started. *"We were brought up to be mothers and housewives and helpmates. Risks were something men took."* Jean had said that, Paula recalled. Dan had taken the career gamble – albeit one softened by the guarantee of her nursing salary. But then, as soon as Julie and Perry were out the door and safely beyond the psychological damage of a parental divorce, he had come home from a business trip and said he was in love with someone else.

Dan had abandoned the security of a corporate job to, in his words, roll the dice for a bigger payoff with his own business. He had explained what he wanted to do and why, and Paula had gone along with the decision; supporting him both financially and emotionally. Once the risk paid off, though, he had found someone younger and prettier with whom to share the second half of his life. The announcement had been so unexpected – so out of the blue – that Paula had never fully recovered from it. Six months after Dan's remarriage she had found the lump in her breast.

The end of the marriage and the possible end of her life, all in the same year.

What was it Eleanor had said? *'I thought about robbing a liquor store yesterday.'*

Now, that was a risk.

2.

"What are my options?"

Paula was in Dr. Melissa Peterman's small office. Paula's MRI scans and pathology reports were spread across Dr. Peterman's desk. Books on the diagnosis and treatment of cancer – seemingly all with black spines befitting the grim subject – filled a bookcase. Incongruously, a print of Mary Cassatt's *At the Opera*, with its young, glowingly healthy woman in a pink evening gown, was the lone wall adornment.

Dr. Peterman, a tall woman in her fifties with salt-and-pepper hair in a no-nonsense bob, pressed her fingertips together. "A modified radical mastectomy of the right breast, going as far as necessary into the muscle under the arms to get ahead of the cancer. Radiation to target anything else that seems suspicious. We get it all and then we watch."

"How long would I be incapacitated?" Paula asked.

"You could be on your feet three weeks after the surgery, assuming you opted for simultaneous breast reconstruction."

"Is that 'on my feet' driving and taking care of myself or 'on my feet' able to get to the bathroom with someone holding me up?" Paula asked.

Dr. Peterman nodded her understanding. "It's surgery. Muscles and scar tissue need to heal." Full recovery would take two to three months."

"And the post-surgery therapy?"

Dr. Peterman opened her hands. "You've been there. You know how much you can take. This would be no different."

Paula thought of the days spent in a stupor following treatments. *Can I go through with that again? And would I just be buying a few months?*

A long silence was broken by Paula's final questions. "How long can I wait? What's the longest amount of time you can give me before I go under the knife?"

Dr. Peterman's brow furrowed. "Why?"

"Let's say I wanted to live life one last time. Let's say I wanted to go bungee jumping or see Yellowstone or go look at zebras in Kenya."

Dr. Peterman nodded her understanding. She pulled out the MRIs and examined them using a magnifying glass. "As long as you recognize that the real answer is that this surgery should have taken place a month ago, and that I could have you in an operating room next Tuesday morning, you could have two weeks."

"What if I asked for two months?"

Dr. Peterman shook her head vigorously and put down the films. "You're giving the cancer free rein. It could pop up anywhere in two months."

"One month?"

"Same thing. You don't need two months to go bungee jumping, though I appreciate what you're saying and why you're saying it."

"You said two weeks," Paula pressed. "Two weeks was OK. Now you're saying that between two weeks and five weeks, this cancer is going to metastasize all over my body?"

"Two weeks was generous," Dr. Peterman countered. "I also said next Tuesday."

"You can have my body in five weeks," Paula said. "Maybe even four weeks. If five weeks is too long, I'll just accept the death sentence and save the insurance company the money for the surgery."

Dr. Peterman looked at her patient closely, seeking a clue to the source of this unusual request.

"Depression is not uncommon in diagnoses like this," Dr.

Peterman said. "I can prescribe something for you that would alleviate..."

"No," Paula said, shaking her head. "This isn't depression. This is a kind of a wake-up call."

Another silence, then, "What exactly are you going to do in four or five weeks?"

"Live," Paula said. "I'm not sure exactly how. But I'm going to have an adventure and take some risks before I die."

* * * * *

Jean Sullivan continued to ponder the previous day's luncheon and its odd subject matter. She also re-played in her mind her experience in the drug store.

Paula would raise those questions only if she was questioning her own mortality, she concluded. *These are end-of-life questions; summing-up questions. Someone who is in their early fifties and healthy does not ask about risks not taken.*

Jean reached for her phone.

* * * * *

"We need to help her," Jean said.

Eleanor and Alice sipped coffee in Jean's living room, having responded to Jean's invitation to meet to discuss their friend.

"You mean more than sending flowers, I assume," Eleanor said.

"I mean finding a way to help her, whatever that is," Jean said.

"We could invite her over for dinner," Alice offered.

Jean shook her head. "Paula needs more than a dinner. She needs a reason to live."

"I could murder that rotten ex-husband for her," Eleanor said. "That ought to make her happy."

"Be serious," Jean said. "What can we do for her?"

"We should start by taking her to the fair," Eleanor said. "It's full of life. Lambs, piglets, baby sheep. It's refreshing."

The three agreed that, though it was far from a solution, it was at least a beginning.

* * * * *

As the other three met at Jean's home, Paula perused the internet from her family room, looking at everything from excursions to China to whitewater rafting trips. She had printed out a dozen pages, but had also come to a disconcerting conclusion: *going on an escorted vacation to an exotic place is not the same thing as having an adventure. And, going with a group that thinks they are somehow living dangerously because they're sleeping in tents instead of five-star hotels is worse than going somewhere alone.*

She continued to click through sites offering thrilling adventures, but she also kept coming back to Eleanor's off-hand remark from lunch. *"I thought about robbing a liquor store."*

Committing a robbery would certainly be taking a risk. It would also be foolish. Bank robbers almost never got away with their crime. Packets of dye exploded when bags were opened. Tracking devices secreted in among the bundles of currency showed police exactly where the thieves were driving or hiding. Liquor store owners kept guns and were not afraid to use them. At least that was the case in movies and on television.

But neither was jumping from a bridge with one's feet tied to an elastic cord the answer to her desire for that 'thrill of a lifetime'. On the whole, it was a stupid concept: a few seconds of uncertainty followed by the reassuring feel of the cord breaking the fall. And if the cord failed to hold, it would be a few seconds of terror followed immediately by death.

The true nature of the thrill, she decided, had to be as much in the anticipation as in the execution. There must be risk, but the risk must be mitigated by skill. The better the preparation, the lower the risk.

Do it, but don't get caught.

She was not certain why her mind kept coming back to Eleanor's remark. On the surface it had been simply a glib, throwaway line. But it had struck a respondent chord inside Paula. She could envision planning such a thing...

The phone was ringing.

"We're going down to the Barnstable Fair tomorrow." It was Eleanor speaking. "We'd love for you to come with us."

Without knowing why, Paula accepted.

* * * * *

The other women were right: the fair was fun. While development pressure had reduced agriculture on Cape Cod to a handful of small, specialty farms, its presence at the fair was reassuring. The women sampled honey from a beekeeping exhibitor, marveled over a display of intricately hand-stitched quilts and watched experts find ribbon-worthy differences in the judging of seemingly identical sheep.

In open, airy sheds well away from the noise of the Midway, baby lambs and goats nursed from their mothers. Freshly hatched chicks peeped and blinked at their first encounter with light. A dozen piglets vied for milk, their mother laying, seemingly exhausted, on her side.

There is re-birth, Paula thought as they paused at various exhibits. *There is new life. I will get through the surgery and I will get through the chemo and I will have another chance.* She said none of these things aloud, but the others noticed the change in her spirits. They had done the right thing.

Their wanderings brought them to a barn where the fair's long history was displayed. Paula stood before the fair posters and memorabilia and put her hands on ancient agricultural implements. *Things endure*, she thought. *And so shall I.*

As they left the fair museum building, an armored truck

backed into a parking space perhaps fifty feet away. The women watched as two men went inside a one-story cinder-block building identified as the fair's headquarters. They emerged two minutes later, each carrying two duffel bags, presumably filled with money. One of the men opened the back of the truck with a key and the two men hoisted the four bags into the body of the vehicle. Three minutes from the time the truck arrived, it departed.

"Well, that was fascinating," Jean said.

"You get used to it," Alice said. "At the bank, we'd have trucks carrying in money all the time. They've got a routine."

"Like at the Brookfield Fair," Eleanor added. "The building where the flower show is held opens right up against the administration building. Every afternoon at five o'clock, that truck would roar on in, belching diesel fumes everywhere. Like to have made me sick."

"How did you know they came every day?" Paula asked.

"I babysat the exhibit for three years running," Eleanor said. "Excuse me – I was a 'docent' for three years. Same questions every day, most of them having to do with where are the rest rooms. And, having to keep little kiddies' hands off of the flowers. While their mothers stood right beside them saying, 'now Tiffany, don't touch the flowers,' and not doing a darned thing about it while their precious little…"

"Now you've got her started," Alice said.

"Well, these people just don't care," Eleanor said, defensively. "They could tear apart an arrangement and their parents wouldn't blink an eye. But lay a hand on the little brat, much less slap one on the fanny, and those same parents will start screaming for the police."

"Is there a flower show here?" Paula asked.

Eleanor pointed to a tent a hundred feet away. "Over there."

"Do we have time to go in?" Paula asked.

"If you do, you'll *really* get her started," Alice said.

The tent, perhaps thirty feet on a side, held both horticultural entries and the flower show entries. Near the entrance, two elderly women sat in chairs. One worked a crossword puzzle, the other read a book.

Paula took in the surroundings, feeling her pulse racing. "Tell me what goes on in here," she asked Eleanor.

Surprised by the interest, Eleanor obliged. She pointed at the series of arrangements. "This is a standard flower show. 'Standard' means the show adheres to a set of guidelines developed by a national council and the entries are judged by a defined set of rules. To start with, there are at least four entries per class. If there aren't four entries, they aren't judged. Every entry is evaluated by accredited judges, meaning they've gone to flower show school for umpteen years and won blue ribbons in competitions like these. There are 'sections', which are a group of classes. There may be five sections or there may be twenty. There's a different set of requirements for each section and the exhibits are judged against how well the entrant met the requirement while showing creativity."

"Or conspicuously spending money," Alice added.

Eleanor ignored her and pointed to the other side of the tent. "The horticultural entries are also judged, but there's no defined number of spaces. People bring in their best lily or rose and the hort people classify it. You may have a hundred hosta entries or you may have three."

Paula listened carefully, attempting not to appear too excited. She took in the tent, imagining that it opened onto the fairground administration building rather than a display of lawn tractors as this one did.

"How do you volunteer? I mean, to be a docent at these flower shows?"

Eleanor shrugged. "The fair only runs three more days. I suspect they've already got the people they need."

"I meant the Brookfield Fair."

"Oh," Eleanor said. "I guess I'm just on the list of people willing to work the fair. They always call around the second week of August."

"Well, when they call this year, tell them I'm interested, too," Paula said.

* * * * *

Paula spent the evening on the internet researching the Brookfield Fair. It was always held the third week in August. While not the biggest in the region – that honor belonged to the Topsfield and Big E Fairs – it had drawn 120,000 people the previous year. Admission was twelve dollars per person. The fairground map was on the website and, true to Eleanor's description, the 'Flowers and Horticulture Building' was adjacent to one labeled 'Fair Administration'.

She thought about what she had seen that afternoon at the Barnstable Fair. First, almost everything had been done in cash. The admission booth took credit cards, but families handed over twenty-dollar bills instead. Concession stands all dealt in cash, probably the better to conceal their earnings from the IRS. In a world of credit and debit cards, the fair was a bastion of cash changing hands.

Second, the fair was full of people in constant motion. One more person in motion following a robbery would not be noticed.

The scene of the armored truck from the fair played in her head. One truck, two men. That it happened so quickly meant the money from the fair was already in bags inside the administration building, awaiting the truck.

"Every afternoon at five o'clock, that truck would roar on in, belching diesel fumes everywhere," Eleanor had said.

People with a routine, Paula thought.

Am I really thinking about robbing a fair?

Paula paused. The idea had seized her. She could not remember ever being so excited about something. Family vacations to Europe had been contemplated with much less fervor. Working with her attorney during the divorce, when her future financial security was at stake, had not stirred her like this.

And then Paula thought of Dr. Peterman's words when she said she could not have surgery for four weeks. *"Depression is not uncommon in diagnoses like this..."*

Paula shook her head. *No. Not depression. This is The Thing. This is the risky thing that I need to do. When it is over I am going to undergo surgery and chemotherapy from which I may never recover. And if I do recover I may be a shadow of who I am today.*

Paula printed out the map of the fair. Well into the evening, she wrote ideas on a pad of paper. Some thoughts were underlined, a few more than once. The heaviest underscoring belonged to these points:

Jean: women of a certain age are invisible

No one will suspect a woman of committing a crime like robbery

Robbing is easy – getting away with it is hard

* * * * *

The next afternoon – Saturday – Paula was again at the Barnstable County Fair, this time alone. She sat by the administration building, reading a book. At 4 p.m., an armored truck pulled into the drive and parked in the same spot as the day before. Two men – they may have been the same ones from Friday – got out of the truck. One was young, in his thirties and in good physical shape. The other was probably in his mid-40s and carrying a bulge of fat around his midsection. She saw them glance quickly around at the people nearby. One of the men's eyes passed over her without pausing.

She saw that they wore guns.

The two men went into the building. *I could get into the truck while they're inside*, she thought. In under a minute the men were back outside, carrying five bags, one more than on Friday. One put his bags on the ground and unlocked the back of the truck. *I could just run by, scoop up a bag, and disappear into the crowd*, she thought.

The bags went into the vehicle. The driver went to his door and pressed a button on his key ring. Paula heard the unlocking of the doors. *Nope, I'm not hiding in the truck.*

The armored vehicle's engine started and the driver shifted into gear. Paula looked at her watch: two minutes from start to finish. *They trade speed for heavy security.*

She stood where the truck had been and tried to imagine an escape route. She would be carrying at least two heavy bags. Around her was a throng of people, spilling off the macadam sidewalk and onto the grass by the booths and tents. If she disappeared into a tent, was there a way out the back? If she ran for a gate, could she outdistance two guards? How much would two bags of money weigh?

I have four weeks to find out, she thought.

For an hour she explored getaway paths and hiding places. She could sprint to the tangle of the Midway and ditch the cash-filled bags among the equipment bins, then retrieve them at her leisure before the fair closed. She could race into the 'Modern Living' shed that housed the vendors with their tacky jewelry, overpriced 'miracle' cooking implements and massage chairs. The duffel bags would go behind a curtain and she could transfer the money to a backpack, possibly to be taken out to her car in several trips.

Paula weighed each possibility, knowing that she had several weeks and as many dress rehearsals as needed to get it right. Her mind raced with possibilities and she felt almost lightheaded at the possibility of what she was planning.

Endorphins, she thought. *Planning a crime is activating my brain's pleasure center. Who would have thought it possible?*

* * * * *

On Sunday, the closing day of the fair, she again drove to Falmouth and positioned herself on the bench at the entrance to the administration building. This time, an old man was also seated on the bench, wheezing.

"These fairs, they take it out of you," the old man said as she sat down.

What if there's someone there on the day of the robbery? she thought. *There can't be an eyewitness.* She gave a non-committal response and opened her book.

"My grandkids love these fairs," the old man continued. "Of course, they don't have to shell out three bucks for a stick of cotton candy. Neither do their parents. I get invited along so I can pay the bills."

He's not going anywhere, Paula thought. *The armored car is going to come and go and he'll be there, gabbing away. What if there's someone like him at the Brookfield Fair?*

"Do they know where to find you?" Paula asked.

"They'll find me when they run out of money," the old man said. He continued wheezing. "You here with your kids?"

Paula smiled and shook her head. It was nice to be mistaken for someone with fair-aged children. "Friends," she said, and picked up her book and began reading conspicuously.

The armored truck came two minutes later. The old man was still wheezing at her side, ready to provide a full description of her had this been the day of the robbery. As before, the two guards scanned those in the vicinity and, as a day earlier, Paula did not merit even a second look. The two men walked briskly into the administration office.

Paula closed her book and stood, counting the seconds. At thirty seconds, she began walking toward the back of the truck. As she got to within ten feet of the truck the door of the administration building opened and the two men struggled with six bags. Paula slightly altered her course. Without ever looking at the two guards, she intersected their path about ten feet from the back of the truck.

"Excuse me, lady," one of the guards said, fumbling under the weight of the bags.

"I'm terribly sorry," Paula said, looking up at the guard who had spoken. "I didn't mean to be in your way." She quickly backed up two steps and the guards passed.

The men did not glance back at her. Instead, one guard dropped his bags at the back of the vehicle and took out his key. Paula continued to stand in the same spot, just six feet from where they began putting the bags into the truck. Only when they were finished did the second guard glance back at her, a look of annoyance on his face.

"You need something?" he asked.

"I was just trying to decide what to see next," Paula said.

"Yeah," the guard said. He walked around to the passenger side of the truck. A few seconds later, the armored car's engine started and it pulled away.

Paula stood in the same spot as the vehicle left.

I might as well be invisible, she thought.

3.

For several days, Paula tried not to think about her plan. She attempted to dismiss it as an errant thought, a ludicrous idea that had been born of the crushing news of the recurrence of her breast cancer. She went back to reading reviews of safaris, trying to convince herself that one to Kenya to see the annual giraffe migration – and which still had a space available – was the answer to her need for a life-affirming adventure.

Paula called her daughter, Julie, in Alexandria and asked if she might come down the following weekend.

But by Wednesday she was back to examining her map of the Brookfield Fairgrounds, and Thursday morning, she drove the twenty-two miles to the site.

Fairs have been a New England tradition for more than a century and a half. Until the 1930's they were considered the best means of displaying new agricultural implements to farmers in widely dispersed areas, and hundreds of fairs were held annually in the six New England states. Rural families found fairs to be a common, end-of-season meeting ground where they could compete for the best pies, the biggest pumpkin or the fattest calf. The Depression killed many fairs and the suburbanization of the region after World War II meant there were far fewer farms. By the 1960's, only a handful of fairs – ever larger and now focused on nostalgia and family fun rather than the sale of tractors – remained.

Outside of New England, regional fairs consolidated into state fairs which became huge enterprises, while smaller district and local fairs disappeared into history. Either by a quirk of geography or a collective reverence for simpler ways of life, a handful of New England fairs not only lived on, but thrived.

In the second decade of the twenty-first century there was a fair circuit consisting of the same Midway rides and food vendors setting up shop for nine or ten days, then moving to the next site. The Barnstable County Fair was one of the first, the Fryeburg, Maine and Topsfield, Massachusetts Fairs closed out the fair season in early October. In between, a half a dozen fairs competed for the attention of parents intent upon introducing their children to close-up views of cows and ducks or, conversely, parents showing off their children's horses and riding skills. At some fairs, elements of a long-vanished rural America were resurrected: horse pulls, sheep dog trials and cow-calling. At all the fairs, sheep, goats and rabbits were judged. Also at every fair there was entertainment: superannuated pop musical groups belted out their hits for middle-aged audiences. Horse races gave suburbanites who would never venture near Suffolk Downs a taste of pari-mutuel wagering.

In the metropolitan Boston area, two fairs vied for visitors during August. The Marshfield Fair and the Brookfield Fair both claimed long histories and both had well-established, town-owned fairgrounds that were rented for other purposes year-round. Marshfield, on the south shore, drew attendees mostly from the arc of suburbs from Boston south to the Cape Cod Canal. Brookfield, in the northwestern suburbs, pitched itself to the prosperous suburbanites between Routes 128 and 495.

On the last day of July, the Brookfield Fairgrounds hosted an antique car show and Paula readily paid the ten dollar admission charge. She quickly passed by the displays of restored mid-1950's Chevy Bel Airs and headed, instead, for the fair administration building. It was located perhaps a hundred feet inside the main gate and she could easily see the route that an armored car would take to get to it. There was a wide, paved apron in front of the building to allow easy access for vehicles.

Just to the west of the administration building, as described

accurately by Eleanor and shown on the fair map she had printed
from the fair's web site, were twin buildings – permanent structures
rather than tents. One housed Flowers and Horticulture, the other,
Fruits and Vegetables. The Flowers and Horticulture building
opened toward the administration building and the entrance was
less than fifty feet from where an armored car would park. This
explained why Eleanor smelled the fumes from the vehicle so
readily.

The Flowers and Horticulture building and its twin were
simple, white barn-like structures. The building had no
temperature control and the heat inside was stifling. Based on
seeing the arrangement of the floral exhibits at the Barnstable Fair,
tables would likely be arranged around the perimeter of the room
with horticulture displays on tables in the middle of the building.
There were no storage areas in the structure but there was a rear
access door. Behind the building was an eight-foot cyclone fence
topped with barbed wire. The alley between the building and the
fence was perhaps eight feet wide. There was a similar, though
narrower alley between Flowers and Horticulture and Fruits and
Vegetables. Beyond that building was the Main Stage – the
amphitheatre where a stream of music acts, decades removed from
the charts, performed.

Paula walked her potential escape route. If she took the
money bags and then fled into the Flower and Horticulture
building, she would likely have to jump over or crawl under a table
to reach the rear exit, then turn right, sprint fifty feet and lose
herself among the crowd – if there was one – in the seating area in
front of the Main Stage. It was not a good prospect.

There was a small park in front of the Administration
Building, an oasis of trees and benches amid the packed dirt and
asphalt. To the east of the administration building was a building
shown on the map as the 'Grange – Museum'. Paula walked over

to it to inspect it as a hiding place following the robbery. The building likely housed a permanent exhibit because the door was locked. It was a more solid building with ample opportunities to hide a bag or bags. But what if she were seen stashing a duffel bag? She would be quickly caught.

The other two options were to flee into the heart of the fair or run out the Main Gate into the parking area. The first presented distinct possibilities. A broad stretch of asphalt curved toward distant buildings housing, according to the fair map, separate quarters for cows, sheep, goats and other animals. This stretch of road would be lined with booths offering the things people went to fairs to buy: funnel cakes, fruit-flavored ices, fried dough, and sausage and pepper sandwiches. She could easily slip in behind one booth, then zig-zag to another. She need not even run.

By contrast, trying to flee the fair through the Main Gate would be foolhardy. She would be running when everyone else was walking. She would be laden with heavy sacks while those around her carried balloons and packages. She could be readily spotted in the parking lot and the exits would be quickly sealed by fair security.

Paula walked the area for an hour, sensing opportunities and obstacles. As she rehearsed her steps, she made three mental notes:

I can walk up to the guards without attracting attention, but I cannot get the bags without finding a way to overpower or incapacitate those guards.

Once I have the money, I need to find a place to hide it because leaving the fairgrounds will not be possible.

Once the search for the robber has yielded no result, I will need to find a way to retrieve the bags without attracting attention, including a probable search of my car.

And, to these three points, she added a reluctant conclusion:

I cannot do this without an accomplice.

* * * * *

Paula flew to Washington, D.C. the following day to spend the weekend with her daughter. Julie, now 24, had turned a degree in Political Science into the start of a career with the U.S. State Department. Julie had grown into an attractive woman with her mother's brown hair and an intelligent face. While Julie considered herself little more than a glorified secretary in her entry-level position, her mother counseled patience.

"You have time," Paula said over lunch at a small French restaurant in Old Town Alexandria. "You don't need to rush things. Observe, file away what you see, and make special note of what works." To which she thought, *Sage advice whether you're contemplating a career or a crime.*

"Dad calls me every week," Julie said. "We talk. I hope you don't mind."

Paula gave her daughter her best smile. "Of course I don't mind. He's your father and nothing's going to change that. What happened was between the two of us. He left me. He wasn't happy. You and Perry were already out in the world."

"*He* left *you*," Julie repeated, emphasizing the first and last words. "He broke up our family." And then, in a softer voice, "Dad wants to know if I'd like to join him and Patty for Thanksgiving. They're going to Rome."

He wants to buy your forgiveness, Paula thought. *He's willing to bribe you with a trip abroad. The rat bastard.*

"What do you want to do?" Paula asked.

"Spend it with you," Julie said.

Thanksgiving, Paula thought. *On Thanksgiving Day I may be recuperating from surgery with half a dozen rounds of chemo still in front of me. Or I may be in jail. Or I could be in the last months of my life.*

"You should do what you want to do, dear," Paula said. "I'd love to have you join me. Do you know what Perry's plans are?"

Perry was her son, a year older than Julie. He had not, as they say, 'settled down'. The divorce had been harder on him. She had last received an email from him three weeks ago. He was in Oregon, or so he said.

Julie shook her head. "I'm not counting on him. But I was hoping you might spend Thanksgiving here, with me." There was a hopeful inflection in her voice.

The first time one of my children has invited me to spend a holiday with them, she thought. *The old order changeth.*

"I shall put it on my calendar," Paula said, smiling. "But you have the right to change your mind and go to Rome."

Julie smiled and took her mother's hand. "I'll make you Thanksgiving dinner."

Another reason to go through with the surgery, Paula thought. *And to live to a ripe old age.*

It was a good weekend, filled with museums and shopping. They talked well into the night about Julie's plans and aspirations, her romances – sanitized for parental ears, Paula suspected – and her friends. On Sunday afternoon, a few hours before her flight home, Paula told her daughter she would have a mastectomy in a few weeks time.

"I wasn't sure I wanted to go through with the surgery," Paula said. "After this weekend with you, I know it's the right thing to do."

* * * * *

If Paula was to have an accomplice, she knew it would have to be Eleanor. They were close friends, bound not by just their mutual interest in gardening, but by many other common bonds. For years they had shopped together, gone on house and garden tours, played bridge and shared dinners. Eleanor had been the first to invite Paula to dinner after the divorce. It was an act of thoughtfulness Paula would never forget. The day that Eleanor placed her husband in a nursing home, Paula was there, insisting on handling the painful logistics and then sitting with her friend through the long first evening alone.

Upon her return from Washington, Paula called Eleanor and invited her for coffee.

"It's too hot for coffee, but if you have lemonade, I'll be there in twenty minutes," Eleanor said.

How do you ask a friend to risk their freedom for a lark? Paula thought. *Do you ask it as a favor? Do you make it sound like there is a reward at the end of it all?* Paula set out a pitcher of lemonade and two glasses in her sunroom and wondered how to begin such a conversation.

If she says, 'no', this whole crazy idea ends here and I still call Dr. Peterman and schedule the surgery for next week.

When they were seated, Paula asked Eleanor if she remembered the conversation of ten days earlier about risks.

"Paula, that conversation has been reverberating around in my head ever since," Eleanor said. "You get into honest conversations like that about once a year and you want them to go on for a long time. That one didn't last nearly long enough for me."

"You said you had thought about robbing a liquor store."

Eleanor smiled. "I did, didn't I?"

"You never said why you had that thought," Paula prompted.

Eleanor took a long sip of her lemonade and stared out at Paula's garden. "The honest answer? I was thinking about Alice. We were at the flower show exhibit at the fair and I made some stupid remark about some people having hundreds of dollars to buy themselves a blue ribbon by stacking up piles of flowers. As soon as I said it, I saw this look on Alice's face and I wanted to staple my stupid mouth shut. She's really hurting, financially. A few weeks ago, I asked her about some article I had seen in the

Times and she said she hadn't been up to the library yet."

"Alice has subscribed to the *New York Times* ever since I've known her," Eleanor continued. "Sometime in the last few months, she dropped her subscription and now she reads it at the library. That woman worked the *Times'* crossword puzzle every morning before breakfast, and now she's reduced to reading the library's copy, and I bet they frown on people working the puzzle."

"So, as soon as I made the remark, I regretted it because she's the last person on the face of the earth I want to hurt," Eleanor continued. "But, it made me mad: she worked hard all her life and inflation has reduced her to living in those ugly, squat little apartments over by the town garage. I believe my exact thought is that we need to win the lottery, or rob a liquor store."

Paula absorbed what Eleanor said, held her breath, and then took the plunge. "What if I told you I was thinking about committing a robbery?"

Eleanor blinked, then took another long sip of her lemonade before answering.

"I'd ask you who you were planning to rob."

"You wouldn't say I was crazy?"

"You are my dear friend," Eleanor said. "I know you're not crazy. You'd only be crazy if you told me you were planning to get caught."

"I'm not planning to get caught," Paula said. "You'd seriously consider helping me?"

Eleanor drained her glass.

"I went to see Phil yesterday," Eleanor said. "Alzheimer's is supposed to be this gradual deterioration. Everyone warned me that when he first went into the nursing home there would be a noticeable drop in his cognitive abilities because, even with his condition, he's aware that he's in a nursing home. Well, that happened and it was certainly depressing."

"Then, he seemed to stabilize – albeit at that lower level – and I learned to live with that. But in the past two months, he has started sliding down further into himself. I can't say that he has recognized me since sometime in early June. He's like an infant, holding conversations with himself that only he can understand."

Eleanor looked out at the garden again. "He's gone, Paula. There's no pill or therapy that's going to bring him back. And so all the things we missed out on doing together – all the things we put off – are never going to happen. It's a really rotten joke. So, I put together Alice, widowed, sitting in an apartment where she doesn't even have enough money to keep up the subscription to the newspaper she's loved all her life; and me – a widow except they haven't held the funeral."

"I guess I'm in a funk, Paula," Eleanor said. "And, doing something to get me out of this melancholy is going to take more than taking up macramé or joining those idiots at the Historical Society. So, unless you've some *Thelma and Louise* stunt in mind where we drive off a cliff, you can count me in."

"But why *you*?" Eleanor asked. She gestured at Paula's large house and immaculate garden. "With all this to keep you busy, it doesn't seem to me that you're bored and, to be frank, you're obviously not hurting financially, either." Eleanor paused, and then frowned. "Unless you've had some bad medical news."

Paula paused, her mouth partly open. *Truth or lie?*, she thought.

"I realize I could get that bad news at any checkup," she said. "Being clean for eighteen months says nothing about eighteen months and a day or two years. And for the past few weeks, it has gradually dawned on me that in my life, I've never done anything unexpected. Never lived on the edge. Well, before I'm too old, I'm going to do something."

"So who are we going to rob?" Eleanor asked.

"Do you remember at the Barnstable Fair that afternoon, we saw the armored truck?"

Paula unfolded the map of the Brookfield Fair she had carefully concealed under her napkin.

* * * * *

The following morning, Paula and Eleanor were at the Brookfield Fairgrounds. The antique auto show had closed, and set-up was underway for an arts and crafts festival. The sight of two women wandering the grounds did not look in the least out of place. They could be inspecting booth sites or fetching material for their own display.

Inside the Flowers and Horticulture Building, Eleanor swept the walls with her arm. "There'll be tables all the way around the perimeter of the building for the flower show entries, with a double row of tables up the middle to hold the horticulture exhibits."

"What about the door in back?"

Eleanor shrugged. "It's an emergency exit. We always just left a space between displays for it."

"Is it kept locked?"

"Not if it's for emergencies. But I don't think that's the escape route." Eleanor led Paula outside the structure to the four-foot-wide walkway between the Flowers and Horticulture and Fruits and Vegetables buildings. "This is where we go. Fire codes are strictly enforced and nothing is allowed to be stored in this alley. In all my years of babysitting these exhibits, I only ever saw someone stack boxes in this alley once, and the person who did it caught holy hell in a matter of minutes. The fire marshals take the rules about clear exits very seriously."

"But everyone will see where I ran," Paula said. Her pulse had quickened when she heard the '*we*' in Eleanor's last statement but chose not to question her on it, or accept the implicit expectation that two people would grab the bags and, therefore, be liable if they were caught.

"Sweetie, if you're really serious about this, it isn't just a matter of grab and run," Eleanor said. "Like Jean said, we're invisible. But that's before we grab those bags. Once they're in our hands and anyone realizes what's happening, we're going to be very highly visible in a very big hurry. The police are going to turn this place upside down. We're going to need a hiding place that no one is going to spot, and we're going to need alibis."

Paula was quiet, absorbing the reality of Eleanor's assessment.

For an hour, the two women walked getaway routes, exchanging ideas about where they could run and where they could hide the bags. Eleanor pronounced each scheme 'half-baked'. Each one left too great a probability that there would be onlookers inside the busy fairgrounds. Paula could see that Eleanor was being logical, not negative.

At the end of the hour, Eleanor said, with finality, "We're going to need help. We'll need a hell of a diversion and we'll definitely need help hiding the money. Paula, like it or not, this just isn't a two-person job."

"How many more people are you thinking about?" Paula asked, her spirits falling.

"At least one. Not more than two. But first, we need a plan that makes sense but that is simple enough that we can all follow it without screwing up."

And so they went back to the parking apron.

"Step One is that we stay out of sight until we see the armored car arrive," Eleanor said. "That's actually the easiest part. I already know we can keep a close eye on this area from inside the Flowers and Hort Building, and we'll be there because we belong there. No one will be able to say, later on, that they saw us lurking." She looked up at the roof of the administration building. "No security cameras. Thank goodness for that. I hear those things are getting cheap enough that even a little outfit like this will be able to afford cameras pretty soon. If we're going to knock over the place, this is the year."

This year or never, Paula thought.

"Step Two is the diversion," Eleanor continued. "The diversion has to be big enough that everyone's attention is drawn to it rather than just looking around gawking. If a thousand people are just looking straight ahead, the odds are that a couple of dozen of them are going to be looking right where the robbery is taking place. We're going to need a doozy of a diversion." Eleanor's face was drawn up in a pensive look.

"Do you mean like an explosion?" Paula asked.

Eleanor shook her head. "We're not trying to hurt people; we just want to just draw their attention somewhere else for a couple of minutes. I'll come up with something."

Paula marveled at how quickly Eleanor had jumped into the planning for the theft. No, it wasn't just *planning* the theft. Eleanor appeared to be taking over the *execution* of the event.

4.

Alice Beauchamp, two months past her seventy-first birthday, sat at her small dining table, the humiliation building inside her. Before her was a three-page form. She had not filled it out nor did she want to, though she knew inside her that it was the intelligent and rational thing to do.

Outside the small window to the outside world, Alice saw only the stillness of a hot August afternoon. Her neighbors would all be inside, their air conditioning turned to a cool setting, their televisions turned on to a comforting program on one of the cable channels. Alice elected not to turn on the air conditioning and she had stopped paying her cable bill months earlier. Eventually, the cable company took notice and her serviced had ceased. The bill for her *New York Times* subscription, which had ballooned up to $195 every three months, sat on the table, unpaid. The newspapers had stopped arriving six weeks earlier.

How did I come to this? she thought. *How did I end up in this rabbit hutch of an apartment, unable to spend money on any semblance of an acceptable retirement?*

It had been a slow descent, she knew. One so imperceptible that she could point to only a handful of events that marked the changes in her life. John's death had certainly been the first. That had been sixteen years ago when she was 55. *You're not supposed to be a widow that young*, she had thought. *People are supposed to live into their eighties or longer.*

But he had died. And he had lingered long enough that the hospital bills had exceeded their insurance cap. That was the first calamity. The second was selling her home during the rotten market of the early 1990's. Despite its acreage it had fetched under $200,000, half what her children had persuaded her to believe it might bring when she first put it on the market.

Her plan had been to move to Florida and start anew, but she had hated the weather and hated the people around her with their cliques and snubs. It was like being back in high school. She was judged by how ostentatiously she wore her jewelry and whether her clothes were this year's styles. Being a born-and-bred New Englander, such displays were simply not done. Incredibly, it seemed that everyone knew the size of her bank balance and mocked her for her basic Yankee frugality. Nine months after moving to Delray Beach, debilitated by the humidity and unable to stomach her neighbors any longer, she sold her condo at a loss and returned to Massachusetts. Hardington had been her home for thirty years and it was here she would make her stand.

Her children could have helped. She had *expected* them to help. She and John had raised them and put them through college. Now they were out in the world but seemed to have forgotten who had made their lives possible. One of them – her son, especially – should have stepped up and offered to defray the cost of a new home. But instead they sent birthday and Christmas cards filled with reasons why they could not come to visit. Though they knew how she lived, as long as they did not have to see it first-hand they could pretend all was well.

Alice placed most of the blame on her son's wife, a bitchy, social-climbing snob who had forced Charlie to move to Denver six years earlier and now spent his money lavishly on a pretentious home and a Mercedes convertible. Alice had never seen the home because she had not been invited to Denver since the move, but she had heard it described in all its horrible detail by Charlie's wife in a gloating phone call. Why her son stayed with this woman, who had put off starting a family until she was nearly forty, was a mystery. Why he had married her in the first place was beyond her comprehension.

Alice still shuddered at the arrogance of the woman and at her son's lapse in judgment.

But neither had her daughter offered assistance. Debbie had not married well and had periodically asked for 'loans', then become petulant when Alice told her there was no money to give. Both children, it seemed, blamed their parents for not having all the things they wanted and took out their disappointment on her.

Having moved back to New England and becoming substantially poorer for her two moves, Alice had moved into Hardington's lone apartment complex. But she could not abide the unruly children in the hallways and the common areas. They mocked her cruelly for being elderly and alone.

There was an 'over-55' condominium project within walking distance of the center of Hardington but it was out of the question with her diminished nest egg and so she felt trapped. Then, this apartment in Hardington Gardens had become available. She found, not surprisingly, that she met the age, income and net worth requirements.

Now, in front of her was the ultimate indignity. For the past five years, she had volunteered, along with Paula Winters, at the Hardington Food Cupboard, where she arranged canned goods and frozen meat packages for the charity's twice-monthly distribution.

The paperwork in front of her was an application to become a recipient of the charity's largesse.

It had arrived in the mail, with no return address, sent to her, she assumed, by someone who knew of or sensed her predicament and wanted to help. But she had never accepted a charity of any kind and she did not intend to start doing so now.

Her reverie was interrupted by the ringing of the telephone. She had no Caller ID but neither was she expecting a call from anyone. She picked up the receiver warily.

An hour later, with the Food Cupboard application form safely stowed out of sight in a drawer, she poured iced tea for Paula and Eleanor.

* * * * *

"Your role would be simple," Eleanor said. "You would fall down and faint."

It had taken less than a minute for Alice to grasp that the circuitous questions being asked by her two friends were intended to feel her out for something illegal, and she instantly made the connection about the armored car transfer she had witnessed two weeks earlier.

"How much do you think we'd get?" Alice had asked.

Eleanor and Paula had looked at one another without answering her. It was obviously a question they hadn't anticipated. Paula took a small calculator from her purse.

"Their web site said they had 120,000 attendees over nine days last year," Paula said. "Let's say we make our move on the last Saturday or Sunday when the attendance is... let's assume 15,000. If admission is twelve dollars and three-quarters of the people pay in cash..." She pushed buttons, looked surprised at the answer, and pushed the buttons again.

"We could see $135,000 assuming cash is collected just once a day," Paula said.

"Split three ways, that's $45,000 apiece," Alice added, doing the math in her head.

"We could get caught," Paula warned. "All the planning in the world doesn't mean something can't go wrong."

Alice shook her head. "You and Eleanor are very smart. I'll bet you have this planned to the last detail. But even if we were caught, what would they do to us? What judge is going to put a seventy-one-year-old widow in jail? Now tell me about falling down and fainting."

"You're the diversion," Eleanor explained. "You're the key to helping us pull this thing off without being seen by two hundred people. You're going to be about a hundred feet from where the armored car will be. You grab your heart, you scream, you collapse in the middle of a crowd. That's all there is to it. Security comes to your rescue, there's a first aid team on the premises. You attract a crowd. They give you oxygen, you let them put on the mask. They offer to put you on a stretcher, you stall them and tell them you need to lie still for a few minutes. Your sole role in this is to attract as much attention as possible for about five minutes. In the meantime, Paula and I have grabbed the money and taken off, but everyone is around you or looking in your direction."

"How did you overpower two husky male guards?" Alice asked.

"We're still working on that," Eleanor said. "I'm thinking mace."

"Mace is good," Alice nodded, but there was a dubious sound in her voice.

Paula, who had also been thinking for several days about how to overpower the guards, added, "But we're open to suggestions."

"You'd need a lot of mace," Alice said. "Four or five cans. You'd need that many because it comes on those little vials designed to fit in a woman's purse. Can you even buy that in Massachusetts?"

"We have time to find out," Eleanor said, confidently.

"The places you'd buy it all have cameras," Alice added.

"So, three women go to three different stores," Eleanor countered. "No one would think that was suspicious."

"Except that every sale of mace for the past six months will get reviewed by the police." Alice was a huge fan of *Law and Order* and never missed an episode. She had been devastated by the death of Jerry Orbach and had never fully accepted the various detectives brought on to take his place. "And that's *if* you can buy it legally in Massachusetts."

Paula was beginning to understand the limitations of mace as a solution. "You don't like the idea of mace?" she asked Alice.

"I like the idea," Alice said, "but I keep seeing problems. Those little vials, especially. You have to have it practically in someone's face before you can press the button. By the time you've pointed your spray directly in one of the guard's eyes, they've probably gotten a very good look at you."

"You have a better idea?" Paula asked, "Or are you just saying it's impractical?"

Alice held up a finger. "You give me a minute." She rose from her chair and walked the few feet into the apartment's tiny kitchen. From a cupboard, she took down a large, clear plastic bag. Inside it was a large mass of something bright orange. She brought the bag to the table.

"I have a plot at the community garden," Alice said. "For three years, I've been growing these." She untied the bag and pulled out a long cord to which were attached several hundred dried, but still brilliant orange peppers.

"Habaneras," Alice said. "My taste buds aren't what they used to be and I use them to spice up my food. But you just get near these things and your eyes start watering. I bet we could make something so potent those guards wouldn't know what hit them. It wouldn't kill them. It would just get them to concentrate on getting these things off of them rather than catching whoever poured the stuff over them."

"You don't want to spray a vial of mace at those guards," Alice said with a serious look. "You want to throw a bucket of mace over their heads."

Paula looked at her friend in wonderment: was this the sweet-tempered woman who made small talk about gardening as they shelved food at the Food Cupboard?

"If one of you could lend me a food processor, I could grind the chili peppers into a dust, mix them with something like glue or oil that would stick to their skin and clothes…"

"We'll work on it," Eleanor said. "I'll get you a food processor. You're in charge of mace. But on the day we do this, your job is to faint."

"I'm going to be the best fainter you ever saw," Alice said, and beamed.

"There's just one more thing," Eleanor said.

"Yes?"

"There won't be three of us," Eleanor said. "We'll need a total of four."

5.

Jean Sullivan wiped the sweat from her forehead with her kerchief, cursing the mosquito that droned in her ear but refused to land. The August weeds were up in force and she had been working steadily in her perennial beds for what must surely be two hours. She had already taken a dozen buckets of debris to a pile deep in the woods where the weed seeds would never germinate.

She was only half done, and she knew that she would likely need to repeat the process in two weeks. She knew that if she did not, these aggressive August weeds would produce seed heads that would lie dormant in the soil until next spring, when then would burst forth by the hundreds to confound and demoralize her. Only by keeping current with the weeding – staying ahead of their flowering and bloom – could she have any confidence that next season would be manageable.

Moreover, as the early summer perennials reached the end of their bloom cycle, Jean saw the need in coming months to dig and divide them and she winced at the work ahead of her. The garden had always been hers, but in the early years, Al had provided the heavy labor, digging through the rocky New England soil to create new beds, mixing in the compost and peat moss and lugging the endless bags of lime needed to neutralize the acidic loam. Then, as the years of smoking took their toll, he cut back on his efforts, leaving her with the majority of the garden work.

One Sunday afternoon in September, four years earlier, she returned to the house after an exhausting afternoon in the garden to find Al in his recliner, dead of an apparent stroke, a meaningless football game blaring on the television.

As she worked pulling weeds, the conversations of two weeks earlier continued to be on some kind of an endlessly repeating loop. The other women had been honest about their thoughts on risk, she thought. Alice, especially, had been frank about money, something she almost never spoke of.

Thinking of her own contributions to that conversation, Jean knew she had lied, as she had lied by omission for years.

She had been truthful about Al's being a good provider and about her now being unable to take financial risks. It was what they expected to hear. It was part of the façade she had erected around herself and her thirty-seven years of marriage to Al. But she had held back, as she always did, when it came to the underlying truth of that marriage and her life. Because the truth was that she could not say she had ever loved Al, not even at the beginning. Al was a salesman and he had sold his merits as a husband to her with the same shallow charm he used when he sold industrial equipment to factories.

It was only after they were married that she saw him as he really was: a cruel man with a malicious need for control over everything – and everyone – in his life. Al had viewed their marriage license as a sales receipt and their wedding ceremony as a ritual formalizing his ownership of her.

Al Sullivan had been a bastard and she had sought to be free of him almost from the first.

For years she looked at other men and was pleased when they looked back at her. But she could never risk an affair. Al controlled the money, restricting her to an allowance which he counted out on the dining room table each week. He meted out money for gas and demanded she account for the miles she drove each week. He totaled the grocery receipts and questioned every miscellaneous expenditure. The more he exerted that control the more she chafed, hoping some man would notice that she was still beautiful and desirable and offer her a new beginning. She would have gladly had an affair or even left Al for the right man, but her husband ensured that it would never happen.

Even as the emphysema progressed and his heart weakened, he demanded to know where she was going and with whom. Their checking account was in his name only, which was as demeaning a lack of trust as it was a means of ruthlessly exercising power over her.

Which is why, on the day her husband died, Jean waited more than an hour before calling the paramedics. He wasn't breathing and his skin already felt cool to the touch, but she wanted to make certain he was really dead. Only when his skin began to turn to a pinkish gray did she dial 9-1-1.

With the benefit of four years of widowhood, Jean now knew divorce would have been her best option, especially decades earlier when there was a good chance of starting over and re-marrying. A court would have awarded her alimony and Al's mental cruelty provided more than ample grounds. But Al would have demanded custody of their daughter, Emily and, for thirty seven years, he drummed into Jean that she was both stupid and incapable of any independent action.

Unless she had another man to fall back on – a possibility Al's control made moot – she could not conceive of leaving. Jean's father had given her mother an allowance and her mother had repeatedly told Jean that a divorce would be a sin and a disgrace. 'A woman needs a man,' her mother had said hundreds of times. And so Jean stayed.

After the funeral, Jean discovered that Al's need for dominance extended beyond the grave. He had structured their finances so that, upon his death, the bulk of their funds reverted to a trust account. The trust paid the property taxes and utilities and gave Jean what amounted to an allowance. Should she remarry, the trust's assets would revert to their grandchildren for college educations. As a result, Jean lived principally on her social security.

When she wanted or needed something extravagant, like presents for the grandchildren, she was reduced to selling things on eBay.

But there had been some satisfaction in selling off all of Al's possessions. He would have unleashed one of his blood-curdling screams when she got rid of his treasured Ping golf clubs for a few hundred dollars. His prized Purdy shotgun had been sold off next. She hoped that there was a hell and that every time she sold something that had been near and dear to his heart, it was broadcast on some wide-screen television as part of his eternal torment.

But his things were long gone. Now, to give her children and grandchildren the gifts she thought they deserved, she was reduced to selling off her mother's jewelry and the heirloom furniture she had inherited from her family.

At sixty-six, men and beauty were a moot point. She still had her pixie-like figure, but there was no demand for women of her age. She had let her hair go to silver and she no longer dressed up when she was going out in public.

In a life of regrets, she had only one joy, Emily. Emily called or emailed her almost daily and the two were as close as a mother and daughter could be. Jean, at least, had broken the cycle in the raising of her daughter. *'Don't just marry for love,'* Jean had said. *'Marry a man who respects you. And wait to get married until you know that respect is real.'*

Jean also doted on her two grandchildren. Her living room and bedroom were filled with the twin's photos, cards, and schoolwork. Were it not for her daughter, her love for her grandchildren, and her handful of friends, depression might well have overtaken Jean years earlier.

Would she take a risk today?

Just point me in the right direction.

Which is why she was both surprised and pleased when she

saw Paula's dark green Volvo pull down her driveway. In the car, she could see, were Paula, Eleanor and Alice.

* * * * *

By the time they had outlined the plan to her, Jean's heart was racing. She had, at first, been unable to believe they were serious. Not because it wasn't appealing, but because their planning was so advanced and their time frame so short. Most of all, however, she was thrilled that she had been included to play a crucial role.

"Do you have a problem with being the getaway driver?" Eleanor asked.

"I just worry about lifting the bags into the car," Jean said. "The ones at the other fair looked fairly heavy."

This stopped the momentum of the discussion.

"She's right," Paula said. "We need to figure out how much each bag weighs."

Alice raised a hand. "Remember, I worked at the bank. Let's say it's $135,000, mostly in twenties." She closed her eyes and did some quick counting on her fingers. "That many bills would weigh a little over fifty pounds. Assuming it's in four bags, each bag will contain about thirteen pounds of money. The canvas bags each weigh about five pounds. Call it eighteen pounds per bag or seventy-two pounds all together."

"You know how much money weighs?" asked Eleanor, incredulously.

"We used to get in armored car shipments regularly," Alice said with a shrug. "I'd help unload them. I got to where I could guess within a few hundred dollars how much was in a bag just by lifting it."

The others were in awe of this skill. "You never told us anything about that," Eleanor said.

"It's not something you go around bragging about," Alice

replied. "I've also been thinking about getting the money from the drop point to Jean's car."

The plan – 'Step Four' in Eleanor's planning scheme (with Step Three being the actual theft) – had been for Jean to be in a wheelchair with a storage compartment rigged under the seat. Eleanor owned a wheelchair that her mother had used in her final years.

"If we're transferring four bags that weigh a total of seventy-two pounds, that's going to make it very difficult for Jean to use the wheelchair," Alice said. "It's a problem of weight distribution: she's sitting on top of the extra weight. If there's any kind of an incline, she'll just be stuck there, unable to move."

"We need to recruit someone to push her?" Eleanor said. "I think five people are too many."

"No," Alice said. "I was thinking of something much easier. I think a stroller would do the trick."

"I have a twin stroller," Jean offered. "That ought to be big enough."

"We'd need a baby on one side," Paula said. "You can't push an empty stroller filled with bags of money."

"I could offer to baby-sit for my neighbors," Jean said. "They've hinted often enough."

Paula shook her head. "Too complicated. I've heard about these life-size babies. Very realistic. The schools use them. I think I could get one. We'd put it in the stroller, let people think it was asleep."

There were murmurs of assent. The problem seemed solved.

Toward the end of the afternoon, Jean looked down at her feet to find her toe tapping. It was the kind of unconscious thing she did whenever she was especially excited and in a state of pleasant anticipation. The last time she could remember her toe tapping so vigorously was when she was in her family room, awaiting the arrival of the paramedics to pronounce her husband dead.

* * * * *

The first dry run of the theft occurred on the final day of the arts and crafts festival. While not as large an event as the Brookfield Fair, there were several thousand people in attendance, including a full complement of exhibitors set up inside the Flowers and Horticulture Building.

The four women came in three cars, just as they would need to do on the day of the robbery. The first question to be resolved was whether Jean, who drove a nine-year-old Plymouth Voyager minivan, should use her handicapped tag to park in the close-in area. "It will look funny if I don't," she said.

"And you'll draw more scrutiny," Eleanor countered. "More people will walk by you and look at what you're doing. It's better to use the general parking, even if it means pushing the stroller farther."

The second question was time of arrival. "The last year I did this, the armored car came at five o'clock," Eleanor said. "Shifts were four hours, starting at 10 a.m., 2 p.m. and 6 p.m. Paula and I will need to be here a few minutes before two." Speaking directly to Jean and Alice, she said, "I don't see a need for either of you to be here before a quarter 'til five. I especially don't want anyone looking inside a stroller and finding a doll. Nor do I want anyone remembering your faces. Alice, your job is to faint, right in the middle of the walkway. Jean, your responsibility is to wheel that stroller out of the fairgrounds. No one should be wondering why you're in back of the building, waiting around with a baby carriage."

"I've been thinking," Alice said. "When I faint, I need to take down someone with me. Preferably a toddler so that there will be lots of screaming."

"You do what you think is best," Eleanor said, warily. *How did Alice keep coming up with these ideas?* she thought.

All four women wore watches, all were synchronized to within a few seconds of one another.

At three minutes before five, Jean wheeled her stroller to a spot just behind the Flowers and Horticulture Building, out of sight of anyone along the central walkway of the fairgrounds. At exactly five o'clock, the presumed time the armored car would have driven through the main gate and now be parked in the apron, Paula and Eleanor picked up their canvas tote bags and began a slow walk from the entrance of the Flowers and Horticulture Building toward the spot where the car would be. A few seconds later, Alice began walking up the fairground main path away from the administration building. There were perhaps fifty people in the immediate vicinity who, had they been paying attention, would have seen this tableau unfold. That was a problem that would need to be addressed before the robbery.

Ninety seconds was allowed for the guards to get into the building, get their bags, and get back to the car. Paula and Eleanor waited under a tree in front of the administration building for the door to open. At the end of the ninety seconds, it was presumed the guards would be at the back of the armored car with one man opening the van's door with a key. The two women began walking toward where the van would be and, from their tote bags, extracted Mason jars. Unscrewing the jar lids as they walked, they approached the spot where, they believed, two men would be standing with bags of money. The imaginary contents of the jars went into the faces of the two imaginary men, who would immediately drop their bags and begin clawing at their eyes, trying to wipe away the stinging concoction that was now affixing itself to their faces.

At that moment, exactly two minutes after the armored car

would have parked, Alice selected a spot in the center of the walkway where, at this moment, two nuns in summer garb strode briskly toward the fairgrounds exit. Instead of the nuns, Alice imagined a young woman with a four-year-old in tow, holding his hand. All around her would be other people, hurrying from one part of the fair to another. She imagined clutching at her chest and shouting, 'Something's wrong', and then collapsing to the ground. As she went down, she would reach out and pull down the four-year-old with her. The child's mother would immediately scream, both at the sight of an elderly woman collapsing in the sun of such a bright day, and of her own child being smothered. The flow of traffic would be interrupted as people bumped into one another and two or three fell over Alice, causing more screaming. Everyone would stop to help, causing yet more chaos. It would be grand.

What Alice did instead was to blow a whistle, causing the two nuns to look back at her with annoyance.

Paula and Eleanor heard the whistle just as they reached down and each picked up two imaginary satchels, each weighing eighteen pounds. For this dry run, their canvas totes each held three bricks in addition to the Mason jar. The bricks didn't weigh eighteen pounds, but the five bricks required would have been too bulky. Paula and Eleanor now sprinted down the narrow alleyway. As they ran, they imagined that all attention was being directed to the shouts and screams emanating from fifty yards away.

A few people, sauntering toward exhibits or headed for the fair exit, looked with puzzlement as two women, seemingly for no reason, suddenly began a headlong dash from the parking apron toward the gap between two buildings.

At the end of the alley, they turned left where Jean waited with the twin stroller. The six bricks were quickly placed into the stroller, mostly on one side of it, and a blanket laid over the bricks.

Then, a rag doll, substituting for the life-size infant still being sought by Paula, was placed on the other side of the stroller and a blanket placed up to its neck.

Jean began pushing the now-heavy stroller toward the fairgrounds exit a hundred feet away. Paula and Eleanor opened the back door of the Flowers and Horticulture Building where they sidestepped a vendor's booth and found themselves occupying the spot where their chairs would be located when they monitored the flower show.

Paula and Eleanor looked at their watches. Exactly three minutes had elapsed.

By now, they imagined, people would have heard the cries of the guards and would be rushing to their rescue. They, too, might join the flow of curious people on the day of the robbery.

Instead, by pre-arrangement, Paula and Eleanor left the building and wordlessly walked to a picnic area north of the fair administration building where a handful of vendors sold foul-smelling food. They found a reasonably clean picnic table, wiped the benches with tissues, and sat down to wait for their companions. Within five minutes, they were joined by Alice and Jean. Alice was smiling broadly, Jean looked worried. Paula asked Jean if there had been a problem.

"A slight snag, but nothing that can't be overcome," Jean said. "I pushed that carriage right out of the gate and no one paid the slightest bit of attention to me. Just an old lady taking her grandchild out for a stroll. And the stroller wasn't difficult to push. I'll have no trouble with the satchels."

"The problem is the weight," Jean continued. "The stroller is designed to hold two children up to about thirty pounds each. We'll have more weight than that and, based on the fabric bagging just from the bricks, I need to do some heavy-duty reinforcing."

"That's what a run-through is for," Eleanor said. "Clear up

the glitches."

"Well, there's no glitch on my part," Alice said. "Fainting won't be a problem. I know exactly what to do. How was my timing?"

"You were about ten seconds late," Eleanor said, not sharing her enthusiasm. "And, my problem is sunglasses."

"Sunglasses?" Paula asked.

Eleanor took off her own sunglasses and wiped them with a handkerchief. "We're supposedly going to have stuff strong enough to temporarily blind anyone who gets any in his eyes, but as soon as I unscrewed that Mason jar lid, I started thinking, what if the guards are wearing sunglasses?"

There was silence around the table.

"Aim for the forehead," Paula said. "No one wears sunglasses so tight to their face they don't allow in some light. We'll also see them the day before and we'll know if we have to adjust."

The response seemed to satisfy Eleanor.

"My concern is that there were forty or fifty people coming in or going out through the Main Gate just now," Paula said. "That's too much traffic, and this is a smaller event that the fair."

Eleanor shook her head. "It's because this is a smaller event that there's more traffic right now. Everyone is parked in the main parking area and that's the only gate open. Every year I've been here as a docent, the main parking area was full by noon and they started parking cars in the Midway lot. When that fills up, they park them at the high school and shuttle them in. The only people coming in that gate on the day of the robbery will be people with handicapped plates and people who parked out on the highway somewhere and walked in."

Eleanor then pointed at Alice. "And, as for people going out the main gate, there's our secret weapon. I'm counting on us having a minute or more when this area is fairly well empty of people."

The answer made sense to Paula, but she had a second concern. "We also have the problem of people in the Flowers and Horticulture Building when we come back in through the rear door. People are going to notice."

"Unless we're carrying in something," Eleanor said. "I already thought of that. We'll be carrying watering cans to freshen up the exhibits. We'll have them outside by the rear door. We carry in the cans, fuss around for a few moments, then go back to our chairs. We're supposed to water the exhibits every afternoon, anyway. Anyone who sees us will assume what we're doing is part of our responsibilities."

Paula nodded again.

"What if paramedics insist on taking me to a first-aid tent?" Alice asked.

"What if they do?" Paula countered. "You'll have a racing pulse. They'll put it down to heat exhaustion."

"Maybe it's better if they do take you," Eleanor said to Alice. Then, to everyone, "What else?"

No one had a comment.

"This is too easy," Eleanor said. "Nothing ever goes this smoothly."

6.

For the next four days, the women met daily. The first afternoon was at Alice's apartment. Using Paula's food processor, she had ground a hundred of her Habanera peppers to a fine dust. To that mixture was added black pepper. Alice had added four cups of water to the grated peppers and, stirring continually, brought the liquid to a simmer, where the mixture took on an ominous, deep orange color. A small amount of liquid dish detergent was added to the liquid and stirred in carefully. The result was a concoction that one did not want to get too close to. Everyone's eyes watered and sinuses cleared as a tablespoon of the pepper juice was passed around Alice's kitchen table.

"I tried oil but it was too viscous," Alice said. "Wouldn't come out of the jar to save your life. So, I started experimenting and even went to the library to read up on the subject. I came up with diluted dish detergent. It will throw like slightly thick water, but stick to whatever it hits like glue," she said proudly. "I've been playing with the recipe for a couple of days." There was considerable delight in her voice.

"Have you tried it on anyone?" Paula wanted to know.

"There's no one I dislike that much," Alice said, shaking her head. "Unless someone wants to volunteer, you'll have to take my word that this stuff will incapacitate anyone who gets it in their eyes or on their skin."

Quick looks across the table indicated that no one wanted to volunteer.

"I think a quart jar full of the stuff is best," Alice continued. "You can surprise someone by throwing it in their face. A sprayer won't get enough on them."

"Did you try that, too?" Jean asked.

Alice tapped her head. "Intuition. Besides, if Paula and Eleanor go carrying around spray bottles, they're going to be noticed."

There was general agreement that spray bottles were not a good idea.

The second afternoon was at Jean's home, where she demonstrated her money-carrying twin stroller.

"It looks like a twin stroller, but it's a rolling money cart," Jean said proudly. "Same fabric outside, but everything inside is new. It's got a canvas lining and a set of three reinforcing straps across the bottom. Heavy duty thread on all seams and I deepened the well a few inches to ensure that the money satchels won't show. The sun visor comes down over the top and there's a zippered mesh for added privacy."

Jean began piling bricks into the carriage. In under a minute she had put in ten bricks. "This stroller will hold a hundred pounds, easily. I also converted the blanket and diaper bag into additional reinforced space. The plastic wheels have been replaced with metal ones. I've tested this puppy with a hundred pounds of paper, rocks and metal. It rolls like a breeze and there's no way this money is going to fall out of that stroller."

Everyone agreed it was a marvel of engineering.

On the third afternoon, Paula hosted the other three women for lunch.

"Is anyone having second thoughts?" she asked, uncorking another bottle of wine. "I feel like I've dragged you all, kicking and screaming, into this scheme."

Eleanor looked up from her Cobb salad. She took a drink of wine to clear her throat. "You are joking, aren't you? I haven't felt this... I haven't felt this *alive* in years. I can't remember the last time I awakened before the alarm clock. Now, I'm up at the crack of dawn."

"But it's dangerous," Paula persisted. "We could get caught. We could go to prison. We'd be the laughingstock of the nation. I can see the headlines in the *National Enquirer*: four women try to rob a fair using home-made pepper juice."

"You better not be trying to back out," Alice said merrily, pouring herself some more wine. "We need you."

"I'm not trying to back out," Paula said. "I'm just recognizing that you're all doing this because I asked you."

Jean shook her head vigorously. "You don't understand, Paula. This is the most fun any of us have had in years. It may be the most fun I've *ever* had. We've agreed to it, planned it and even rehearsed it. I'm planning on getting away with it. I'm certain we won't get caught. But even if I did get caught, I wouldn't have a single regret. To the contrary, you have my everlasting thanks for making life interesting again."

"Do you know what you're going to do with the money?" Paula asked Jean.

"Take a cruise, I think," Jean said. The quickness of her answer made it apparent she had been thinking about the subject. "One of those deluxe, month-long cruises that goes across the Atlantic and then into the Mediterranean. Something very luxurious where you dress for dinner every night and there are lots of ports of calls with interesting shops or exotic ruins. Just once I want to get away from everything that's familiar. A cruise sounds perfect to me. And, if there's any money left over, I'd like to put in a new shrub garden."

Paula nodded appreciatively. "What about you, Alice?

Alice didn't need a moment to think. "My first grandchild is going to be born in early October. I should like to be there when it happens."

"Unless you're chartering a jet, you're going to have some

money left over," Jean said.

"Maybe some new curtains," Alice said. "I sometimes think my apartment is rather drab." Then she added, "And get my foot fixed. I've had these terrible hammertoes for years. I want to get them straightened before they cripple me."

"What about you, Eleanor?" Paula asked.

Eleanor shrugged and gave a wan smile. "I can't really make any plans because of Phil. I don't know if he... well, it's all in a state of flux. And, his care is expensive. I want him to have what he needs for as long as he has left."

"What about you, Paula?" asked Jean.

Paula poured the last of the bottle of wine into her own glass. "My daughter needs some furniture for her apartment. I guess I was also thinking of doing some traveling. But, right now, I just can't wait for this to actually happen. Then, I've got to figure out how to get the money into a bank account. I never knew robbery was such a logistical nightmare." Paula then smiled at the others.

Eleanor, who had looked pensive through the discussion, added a new thought. "Maybe this is just a rationalization on my part, but I don't feel like I'm *stealing* from anyone. I'm sure the fair has insurance. Some insurance company will make good the loss."

Jean snapped her fingers. "Like the little old lady in *The Lavender Hill Mob* who has all the money after Alec Guinness is dead," she said. "She tries to give the money to the police. The police won't believe her and they tell her to keep the money. 'It's just a farthing on everyone's policy,' the sergeant in the police station says."

"Right idea, wrong movie," Eleanor said. "*The Ladykillers* is the one where Mrs. Wilberforce had all the money after Alec Guinness and Peter Sellers have killed one another."

"The Lavender Hill Mob," Alice said, dabbing at her mouth with her napkin. "We need a name like that. No self-respecting gang would attempt what we are about to do without having a name. Like the Jets and the Sharks in *West Side Story*."

"Or the Dalton Gang," Jean added.

"We could call ourselves the Hardington Mob," Eleanor suggested.

"The Brookfield Fair Heist Gang." Alice spoke the name, enunciating each syllable distinctly. "Assuming it's our only job," she added.

"The Garden Club Gang," Paula said.

There was a moment of quiet at the table while the other three women weighed the suggestion.

"The Garden Club Gang," Eleanor repeated. "And so alliterative, too. Perfect."

* * * * *

That evening, Paula's phone rang. It was Eleanor, who sounded near to tears.

"I just heard from the flower show people," she said. "The only two-to-six shifts they can give us are Saturday and Sunday. Their other openings are mornings and evenings."

Paula asked, "You mean the last two days of the fair? That's fine."

"No," Eleanor said. "Opening weekend. Five days from now."

Paula grimaced. *Can we be ready in five or six days? We need at least two more dry runs...*

"We'd need to do a dress rehearsal on Saturday," Eleanor said, interjecting her thoughts into the silence. "To make certain of the timing under real fair conditions. We'd have just the one day to observe. We'd have to pull the job on Sunday."

'Pull the job,' Paula thought. *How far we've come in a few weeks.*

"Are you there?" Eleanor asked.

"I was just thinking," Paula said. "We should meet

tomorrow, make certain we all understand what the change means, and see if everyone is still on board."

* * * * *

Tuesday morning, the four women met at Paula's home. Eleanor explained the problem.

"This whole plan depends on Paula and I being the flower show docents in the Flowers and Horticulture Building at the time of the robbery," she said. "Those two docents – unless they're completely blind or otherwise occupied – are going to have a bird's eye view of what happens out in front of the administration building. They're going to be among the first people questioned by the police and they're going to need to be able to tell the police a version of events that is sufficiently plausible that they're not immediately going to be the number one and two suspects."

"If anyone other than Paula and I are in those docent's chairs at five o'clock, it's a roll of the dice that we can't afford to take," Eleanor continued. "If someone else is on duty, it leaves too much to chance. Those two people may be wrapped up in their knitting and never see a thing. Or they may hear a commotion, turn, and witness everything. Worse, they may recognize us. That means we *have* to do this on Sunday. That's five days from now. We go to the fair on Saturday to make certain nothing has changed from previous years and to get down the timing of the armored car. Then, on Sunday, we either do it or we forget about it. What we can't do is choose some other day. Does everyone understand?"

Jean and Alice nodded their heads. The look on their faces was somber.

One by one, everyone said they understood. One by one, they agreed that it was Sunday or not at all.

* * * * *

After the other women left, Paula called Dr. Peterman's office. She was told the oncologist was with a patient.

"Tell her Paula Winters called. Tell her, if the surgeon she recommends can squeeze me in, we can do the surgery next week rather than the week after. Tell her Monday or Tuesday is fine with me."

* * * * *

Alice went back to her apartment after the meeting. The small, dark rooms with their small windows were depressing. She turned on all the lights in the apartment, pulled back curtains and opened Venetian blinds. She went to the wall air conditioner and turned it on, setting the unit to a comfortably cool temperature. She stood in front of the air conditioner with her eyes closed for several minutes, feeling the chilled air flow over her body.

She then went to the writing desk in her living room and, from the desk drawer, took out the Food Cupboard application. She ripped it into small pieces and dropped them slowly into a waste basket.

In five days, I shall either be financially solvent or else I will have been arrested, she thought. *Either way, I shall not need charity. Either way, the size of my electric bill will not matter.* Turning on her computer, she pulled up airline schedules for Boston to Denver for early October. She found a convenient, non-stop mid-afternoon flight and booked it, despite there being less expensive fares that required traveling in the evening or changing planes. *If this is successful, I will go. If it is not successful, it will not matter.*

* * * * *

Jean, too, returned home. She walked her perennial beds with a pad and pen, making notes on plants to be divided in the fall. Then she paused and traced a large oval with her foot in a sunny area of the lawn. After considering it for several minutes, she went back to her garage and filled a can with crushed limestone. She retraced the oval, this time with the white powder, giving it a more bona-fide existence and providing its first step toward realization.

There should be a bed here, she thought. *And it should be anchored by a tree. Not just any tree. This space needs a specimen. An oxydendrum, at least fifteen feet tall. It needs to be flanked by a dozen other shrubs and then surrounded with perennials. Done right, this bed could cost five thousand bucks. If we each get $35,000 from the robbery, that leaves $30,000 for a cruise. Maybe on that cruise I'll finally meet Mister Right. It will be forty years later than it should have happened, but better late than never.*

Jean scuffed out the original oval and tapped limestone out of the can to create a larger bed.

Al, you son of a bitch, I may have finally found out how to get from underneath your thumb. It will be my life's great achievement, finally saying that I don't give a damn what you want or what you've planned.

* * * * *

Eleanor did not go directly home from Paula's. Instead, she drove ten miles to the nursing home where her husband now lived. She found Phil in the television room, staring blankly at a game show. He had likely been led there sometime earlier in the day by a well-meaning attendant. She took him by the hand and led him to what the nursing home brochures called the 'families area'. It was a small, cool area arranged much like living room with sofas, comfortable chairs and soft, natural lighting. No one else was in this room.

Phil sat in one chair, glancing around the room, talking quietly to himself all the while. He showed no sign of recognizing his wife.

He is slipping away, Eleanor thought. *He will be 73 in December, and that may well be his last birthday.* Her husband would have once sat, ramrod straight in such a chair, commanding the room and everyone in it with his penetrating gaze and I'm-in-charge demeanor. Now, he sat meekly, hunched over, carrying on a conversation that only he could understand.

"Phil," she said quietly. "I need to tell you something. I

don't expect that you'll understand or remember it, but I need to say it anyway."

Phil turned his attention to his wife. He stopped talking to himself and seemed to respond with his eyes.

Eleanor spoke softly. "On Sunday, my life is going to change," she said. "Three friends and I are going to commit a robbery. We're going to steal money from an armored car at a fair. I think we're going to get away with it. And, if we do, my share will be about $35,000. It's not a fortune, but it means I can probably give you the dignity you deserve for a while longer. More importantly, it would mean I've done something that other people just daydream about."

Eleanor took her husband's hand. "Your being here has really shaken my faith in God, Phil. He took you away and put you in some awful limbo between life and death. It's the sort of thing that you said you never wanted but it was so gradual at first we didn't know it was happening. If this is meant to 'test' me, then I've failed. I don't know what to do about you, but I know this kind of existence is something you don't deserve."

Eleanor squeezed her husband's hand tightly. Now, their eyes met. She spoke even more softly than before. "Phil, I'm telling you this because there's an outside chance we may get caught. We may find ourselves surrounded by police two minutes after we grab those bags. Or there may be surveillance cameras we can't see and Sunday night they'll come knocking on my door. If they do, I've got no defense. Phil, if this doesn't work, I'm going to prison and you may never see me again."

"And, if I get caught, then this nursing home is going to boot you out and you're going to be placed in whatever Medicaid will pay for," she said. "But our money was going to run out anyway. Ten thousand dollars a month, Phil. That's what this costs. The insurance pays about three thousand, the rest comes out of our savings. Another two years – three at the most and that assumes I sold the house – and we'd be facing the same issue."

Eleanor cradled her husband's hand and placed it against her cheek. She felt the tears welling up inside her but forced them back. "Phil, I've got to do this. And I *want* to do this. Because for the past year, I've felt like there's been this giant crater in my life. I don't have you anymore and we're never going to do those things we dreamed about. Well, I never had 'join a gang and pull off a robbery' on my list of things to do in my life, but I've never looked forward to anything more than I do this."

As soon as Eleanor stopped speaking, her husband's attention began to stray to the surrounding room. His incoherent rambling monologue started up again.

Eleanor led Phil back to the television room and guided him to a chair. She kissed him on the cheek, then left to drive home. Only when she was in her car in the parking lot, away from the nursing home and out of the view of anyone, did she allow herself to cry.

* * * * *

Thursday morning, Paula drove into Boston to the Dana Farber Cancer Center for her pre-surgery consultation. She met with Dr. Peterman, her surgeon, an anesthesiologist, and a nurse. Each one explained risks and procedures. Consent forms were signed. Extensive medical histories were taken.

"Did you do that thing that made you feel you were truly alive?" Dr. Peterman asked when the last form had been signed.

"I'm about to," Paula said.

"Do I get to know what it is?" Dr. Peterman asked.

Paula smiled. "I'm afraid not. This one has to remain a secret."

"But you're ready to go through with the surgery?"

"I wouldn't have signed all those consent forms if I wasn't,"

Paula said.

* * * * *

On late Friday afternoon, the four women assembled for a final meeting, this time at Jean's home. The stroller was tested with eighty pounds of rocks and Jean, though just an inch over five feet and weighing less than 120 pounds, was made to push it up her driveway four times, simulating the probable distance she would travel from behind the Flowers and Horticulture Building to her car. The human-size infant, procured by Paula from a big-box toy store, was placed in the stroller and pronounced sufficiently life-like to pass a cursory inspection. Jean's arms ached by the time she had finished the fourth circuit.

Alice demonstrated her 'fainting' technique and graciously accepted criticism from the three other women that her swooning looked too 'staged'. On the fourth try, she was pronounced ready to faint from heat stroke in public.

Paula and Eleanor each sprinted across Jean's lawn twice, carrying thirty-five pounds of fireplace logs in cloth bags.

"If anyone could see us, they'd know we were crazy," Eleanor said, bent over with her hands on her knees, puffing from the exertion. "But I've learned something today: I'm going to wear slacks and tennis shoes on Sunday, even if I look terrible in slacks. And, when this is all over, I'm going to lose fifty pounds."

7.

On Saturday at noon, the four women drove together to the fairground for what they called the 'final dress rehearsal'.

They found one of the region's largest fairs on its opening day. Their first surprise was parking. Both the Main Gate and Midway parking areas were deemed full and a parking attendant pointed them up the road to the auxiliary parking lots half a mile distant at the Brookfield high school where a shuttle bus would take them back to the fair.

"Maybe you want to use that handicapped parking pass after all," Paula said to Jean. Jean extracted a handicapped parking tag from her purse and gave it to the attendant. They were waved through to an area less than a hundred feet from the Main Gate.

"A handicapped parking pass makes a car stand out," Eleanor said, clearly worried. "People are more likely to remember it and the driver. I'm not so sure it's a good idea for tomorrow."

"Unless the driver is an elderly woman," Jean said. "Then, she's invisible."

The four paid their admissions, noting that those in front of them in line offered cash for their tickets.

Eleanor nudged Paula and indicated the twenty dollar bills changing hands. "Lovely," she whispered.

Inside the Main Gate was a second, unwelcome surprise. Nearly two dozen teenagers loitered in the small, shady park adjacent to the administration building. They showed no sign of wanting to see the fair. Instead, they appeared content to spend the afternoon flirting with one another, practicing intricate skateboard routines and listening to music on iPods.

"For this they paid twelve dollars?" Eleanor said, watching the teenagers sit on benches or roll back and forth on skateboards, oblivious to the fair's enticements.

"Only a few dollars more than a movie," Paula said. "They get to spend a full day out of the house and hang out together doing something their parents consider wholesome. It's a bargain."

"How do we get rid of them?" Alice asked anxiously. "We've got to get them out of there tomorrow, or there's no way we can pull this off."

Paula shook her head. "I don't know."

Eleanor said, "I do." She turned to Jean and pointed at the administration building door. "Jean, you're the one person the police are never going to see tomorrow. If there's anyone in that area tomorrow, then at 4:30, you're going to walk indignantly through that door and tell the first person you see that there are boys and girls out in front of the building, they're smoking, and there's a distinct smell of marijuana in the air. Don't wait for them to ask your name or how you know the smell of marijuana. Just turn around and walk out in a huff. Whoever you talk to in the building is going to call security and security will disperse them regardless of what they smell. That will keep those kids away for at least half an hour."

Eleanor looked at her watch. "Paula and I are on duty at two o'clock and we can't be seen with you in the Flowers and Horticulture Building. We wait until we see the armored car pulling in before we do anything." To Alice, she said, "Use your whistle, but just so that we know we've got the timing down. Don't go falling down and calling attention to yourself."

Alice nodded her understanding.

At two o'clock, Paula and Eleanor entered the Flowers Building and immediately saw two more problems. The area was crowded with more than thirty people where they had expected perhaps ten or twelve. With this many people, it was inevitable that someone would be looking out in the direction of the armored car when the robbery took place. Also, the two docents on duty had positioned their chairs in front of the rear exit. The chairs commanded a better view of the room, but also looked out onto the parking apron where the van would be parked.

Paula and Eleanor relieved a pair of elderly women who had been there since the fair opened at ten that morning.

"Bunch of little rug rats with their hands all over everything," one of the departing women said by way of warning. "They liked to have tipped over a couple of the arrangements."

"Just awful," the second woman said.

"We'll have to move these chairs," Eleanor told the women, an authoritative note in her voice. "If the fire marshal comes in and sees us blocking this exit, we'll never hear the end of it." The elderly women nodded meekly.

"The nice thing about being in charge is that no one questions what you do," Eleanor said as soon as the two women were out of sight.

As they moved the chairs to a spot by the entry door, Eleanor inspected the displays. "Let's Go to France," she read from the display card. "How original. 'Can You Say Marseilles', 'An Evening in Paris', "A Nice Time in Nice', 'The Arch de Triomphe'. And to think someone spent time making up names for these categories."

By four o'clock., two watering cans had been placed outside the door and the walkway between the two buildings inspected to make certain it was clear.

"Now we wait," Eleanor said, settling into one of the chairs. "I just don't know how we can get people inside this building to not pay attention to what's going to be happening by the administration building."

"We'll think of something," Paula said.

At 5:12, there was the beeping of a horn outside the building as an armored car made its way up the access road. The horn was unnecessary as there were few people walking in through the main gate. Paula and Eleanor looked at one another and at their watches.

"Time," Eleanor said. She tapped on the face of her wristwatch. At the moment the armored car came to a stop, the two women left the building, walking slowly toward the parking apron. As they feared, a group of teenagers, now numbering more than two dozen, were lounging on the nearby benches. They seemed mildly interested in the sight of the armored car but soon went back to flirting and laughing. The two women drew scarcely a look, though, had a robbery ensued, Eleanor and Paula would certainly have been remembered and described to police.

"I've got an idea," Paula said. "To get rid of the kids." They had reached the other side of the parking apron and were a few feet from the teenagers' turf.

"What is it?" Eleanor whispered.

"Tell you later," Paula said. They paused a few moments until the two guards emerged from the administration building. They walked directly behind the guards and, as they did, they heard the sound of Alice's whistle. One guard momentarily looked up in the direction of the whistle but quickly went back to the task of stowing the five bags. Eleanor and Paula passed within a foot of the guards without attracting any notice from them.

Waiting the few seconds it would have taken to incapacitate the guards, they then walked briskly across the access road and into the walkway next to the Flowers and Horticulture Building. At the end of the building they turned left and found Jean with her stroller, ready to receive bags of money. They allowed thirty seconds for the transfer then watched Jean push the stroller toward the main gate.

Eleanor and Paula each picked up a watering can and opened the rear door to the floral displays. As soon as they were inside, they began watering arrangements, looking out of the corner of their eyes to see if their absence had been noticed. By their watches, they had been gone just two minutes.

Perhaps fifteen people were in the Flowers and Horticulture Building, a lull of sorts. Eleanor and Paula moved from arrangement to arrangement, discreetly whispering where they thought there was room for improvement in their plan. A couple, noticing Eleanor watering, approached her and asked her to explain the judging system, which Eleanor did.

At six o'clock, Paula and Eleanor were relieved by the next team of garden club ladies.

"Anything interesting happen?" one of their replacements asked.

"Dull as day-old donuts," Eleanor said. "We just watered the arrangements an hour ago, so they're fine. Just watch out for the little kiddies who want to pick the pretty flowers." Eleanor's comment earned a laugh from the two incoming docents.

They all met back at Jean's car, got in, and drove out of the parking lot.

"How did it go, Jean" Eleanor asked.

"No problems at all," Jean said. "No one looked twice at the stroller or at me. I could have been carrying all the gold in Fort Knox and they wouldn't have noticed."

"Alice?" Eleanor asked.

"When I blew the whistle, I had a perfect situation," Alice said. "A family of four was right there, two children about five and six. I could have taken either one down with me and it would have caused a pileup that would have taken fifteen minutes to untangle. I'm definitely all set."

"Paula, you said you had an idea about how to get those kids away from the area," Eleanor said. "Won't my idea work?"

"It's risky because, as soon as someone says 'marijuana', you may get a police presence or the fair managers may decide to post someone there for the rest of the afternoon as a precaution," Paula said. "I started thinking about deterrents and came up with what I think is a better idea."

"We're trying to keep people away from that little park," Paula continued. "I thought, 'how do I keep deer out of my garden?' The answer to both questions is, I think, the same: Liquid Fence. Until it dries, it smells like someone threw up. I say we just spray some in that little park about an hour before the armored car arrives, and replenish it if kids are still hanging around."

"Brilliant," Alice said. "But won't they see us spray it?"

"I'm not sure we need to spray it," Paula said. "Just pouring some from a cup ought to do the job. It's powerful stuff."

Eleanor nodded in agreement. "Well, that's a better solution than the one I came up with. I'm left with one question from what I saw today: there were five satchels instead of four and, from what I could see as they put the bags in the truck, none were coin bags. Which means either there's more money or, more likely, there's a lot of small bills. Either way, Paula and I have to carry five bags between us, which means one of us is carrying more than fifty pounds instead of thirty six."

"I don't think I'm up to carrying fifty pounds," Paula said. "Maybe we'll just have to leave a bag behind."

"Then you take two and I'll carry three," Eleanor said. "It's only a couple of hundred feet, and I don't want this extra bag being the difference between success and failure. We've got our timing down very well – two minutes from when we left the exhibit until we walk in that rear door. If we're gone that brief a period of time, and because we re-appear with watering cans and no bags of money, no one is going to look at us as suspects."

"Unless someone looking from inside the exhibit is looking out at the truck when the robbery happens," Jean said.

"I was looking where people's attention was focused this afternoon," Eleanor said. "When you're in with the flowers, you're looking at the floral displays. I'm reasonably confident on that point. Unless someone happens to be walking out of the exhibit just as we start our getaway, I think we're going to be fine."

"But what happens when the guards start screaming?" Jean pressed.

"By the time they know what happened, we'll be fifteen feet away. By the time they start screaming, we'll be down that walkway between the two buildings. And Alice will be causing such a commotion up the pathway, people will be looking there instead." She said this with such confidence that everyone nodded in agreement.

"If we're in such good shape, why don't we go out for dinner tonight?" Jean asked.

Eleanor shook her head. "No. Certainly not tonight. Only Paula and I were at the fair today. The two of you were at home all day. I don't want anyone saying they saw us together at some restaurant. Tomorrow is the day. We need to get a good night's sleep."

As they drove on, Paula listened to Eleanor's commanding voice and display of common sense and planning. *She's enjoying this*, Paula thought. *I've known her for ten years and I've never heard her so decisive and logical. It's as though she has some new purpose in life.*

And then she thought, *And damned if I'm not enjoying it too.*

* * * * *

Sunday at one o'clock, Paula prepared her robbery kit. She had a one-quart Mason jar containing a viscous, deep orange liquid. She had practiced screwing and unscrewing it multiple times such that she knew exactly how tight the lid should be to allow her to walk and simultaneously unscrew the lid, then throw its contents, all on one motion.

She now had a second bottle, this one also a Mason jar. In it was a light brown liquid, a commercial deer repellent called Liquid Fence. The product was normally applied with a sprayer after being heavily diluted. Paula had a less-diluted form of the repellent in the jar. She added a pair of rubber gloves to her arsenal. This was not a product you wanted to get on your hands. These items went into a flower-print canvas tote bag. A ball of yarn and two knitting needles went on top of the two jars.

Paula chose a pair of light-colored slacks and a tee, appropriate wear for a warm August afternoon and also clothing that attracted no attention and was unmemorable to anyone who might see her. She chose not to carry a purse, figuring that one would be in the way of carrying the satchels. Instead, she put a twenty-dollar bill in one pocket and her keys and license in the other. She would have ordinarily worn sandals on such a day. On this one, she wore sneakers and socks. She completed her ensemble with a pair of large sunglasses, which she pushed up into her hair.

Paula looked at herself in the mirror, adjusted the glasses, and pronounced herself satisfied.

Two miles away, Eleanor put her Mason jar full of Alice's concoction in her own, plastic-lined canvas tote bag. She, too, gave herself an inspection in the mirror. She would have preferred to have worn jeans. They would have allowed her to run faster. But Garden Club Ladies did not wear jeans to monitor exhibits. Further, jeans showed every ounce of the weight she had gained over the past few years. She settled for loose slacks and a blouse and figured it would help her blend better into the crowd if there were witnesses.

Garden Club Ladies were also supposed to wear appropriate

footwear, but Eleanor wanted her Keds for their speed and comfort. She, too, added sunglasses and belted on a fanny pack. She was ready.

In her apartment at Hardington Gardens, Alice carefully applied makeup and brushed her hair. Her role, she understood, was at once both the simplest of the four and the most critical. She must faint on the macadam convincingly and – her own addition to the plan – choose exactly the right child as a target in order to ensure the maximum amount of pandemonium. She must break her own fall but not injure the child she would take down with her.

She must look the part of the doddering, elderly lady. Her lipstick was too thick and too red, her rouge applied in a way that, to the casual observer, was being done by someone who was losing visual acuity and color vision. And her dress was one of her least-liked ones, a pink floral print that she had bought on sale several years earlier and worn only a few times because its color made her look old. She reasoned that such a woman would receive better care because she was quite possibly in her dotage and certainly frail. She added white sneakers and orange socks. The overall effect, she thought, was dreadful.

In other words, perfect.

Three miles away, Jean reinforced the stroller's stitching one last time with additional heavy, cotton thread. She had already opened the lining of the stroller to accommodate the possibility of a fifth money bag. She inspected the stroller's wheels and added a squirt of WD-40 to each. This infant-less baby carriage would make no noise as it exited the fairgrounds. She added Paula's life-size doll to the stroller, then closed the sun shade and mesh screen. No one would be looking inside this carriage to admire a baby.

For her costume, she donned what she thought of as her 'fair outfit'. Pink shorts and a tee that said, 'World's Best Grandma' across her chest. Her own daughter would never have given her such a tacky present. Jean had purchased it three days earlier at a Wal-Mart in a neighboring town.

Eleanor left her home at exactly one o'clock and drove the short distance to Paula's, and the two of them drove the twenty-two miles together to Brookfield. There was a surprisingly large backup on the two-lane feeder roads around the fair and the final two miles of the drive consumed more than twenty minutes.

The weather was ideal for fair-going. Clear skies, moderate humidity and temperatures in the mid-eighties. They were waved away from the main gate parking but, by pleading that they were minding the floral exhibits, an attendant allowed them to search for a vacant space which they found fairly quickly. They were at the Flowers and Horticulture Building a few minutes before two o'clock.

For two hours, Paula and Eleanor minded the exhibit, patiently explaining to visitors why there were only four entries for each grouping and who had done the judging. Small children were kept a respectful distance from displays. The docent chairs had not been moved by the ladies of the morning shift so there would be nothing to explain to the police in that regard. The watering cans were still in their place, full and ready as props.

At half past four o'clock, Paula excused herself and walked over to the small park by the administration building. As there had been a day earlier, groups of teenagers sat on the benches, talking and laughing. They paid no attention to the mother-aged woman who passed among them and did not see that she wore a rubber glove on her right hand and carried a jar.

Because they were preoccupied with their own world, neither did they notice that she splashed liquid from the jar on the leaves of the rhododendron that formed the foundation planting of the administration building, or into the mulch at the base of trees. Paula was there only a minute or two.

But within five minutes, the teenagers began to disperse, asking one another who had 'upchucked' in the bushes. They quickly found other places in the fairgrounds to congregate.

Paula returned at ten minutes before five and found the little park empty. She poured the remaining liquid on the benches where the teens had sat, ensuring that the park was uninhabitable for the duration.

* * * * *

Jean arrived at 4:40 and used her handicapped parking pass – one issued when her husband was still alive but with advancing emphysema – to park her minivan less than a hundred feet from the main gate entrance. It was, she considered, an ideal location.

She unloaded the stroller from her car slowly. She did not want anyone noticing that it was a doll that she placed in the seat. She carefully put the sun shade in place and zipped closed the mesh screen intended to keep out bugs. At 4:45, she paid her admission and made almost immediately for the rear of the Flowers and Horticulture Building. She did not want to be out of position in the event the armored car was early.

Alice had arrived at 4:30, but she had been shunted to the auxiliary parking with the bulk of other arriving fairgoers. The shuttle bus came quickly, however, and she passed through the Midway entry gate at 4:45.

Alice made her way down to the administration building, passing the fair's entertainment stage where, according to the marquee, Paul Revere and the Raiders were performing, loudly and badly. As she approached the administration building, she immediately smelled the deer repellent and saw that the park was empty. She smiled, knowing that Paula had done her part.

At a few minutes before 5 p.m., Alice positioned herself by the Fruits and Vegetables Building that adjoined the Flowers and Horticulture Building. She would wait here until she saw the armored truck arrive, then begin her walk up the densely packed walkway.

* * * * *

At 5:08, a Bay State Transport armored car pulled through the main gate of the Brookfield Fair.

'Armored car' was perhaps something of a misnomer for the vehicle. Unlike the vehicle used by Brinks and other national services, the owners of Bay State, which had won the fair's business the previous year, believed in smaller, more nimble vehicles that delivered reasonable fuel economy. The five-ton, soot-spewing diesel-powered vehicles were anachronisms. Bay State's owners also believed in minimizing labor costs. When an organization contracted with Brinks, they received a three-man crew, including a driver who stayed behind the wheel at all times. The driver was responsible for observing all surroundings and could, at the flip of a switch, lock all doors and secure all cargo.

By contrast, Bay State relied on speed and being inconspicuous. A crew of two could load one of the firm's beige vans in seconds and be away from the premises in two minutes or less. Their vans did not stand out as targets: only the dark brown 'BSTS' logo on the side even hinted that the van was laden with valuables. This strategy was at the heart of Bay State's success in winning contracts.

Bay State's rationale was not without merit. The preponderance of armored car robberies came by diverting vehicles in urban areas and pointing weapons at the drivers, who would readily exchange their cargoes for their lives. In thirty years of transporting currency, Bay State had never been robbed while loading or unloading satchels of money.

The driver, Eddie Caulfield, had called his contact in the Brookfield Fair's accounting department while the van was making its way through the fair traffic. As a result, he knew, the satchels would be waiting for them just inside the front door of the administration building, watched over by a clerk.

Eddie put the van in 'park'. There was no need to say, "Ready" or other such instructions to his partner, Mike Williams. This was their tenth pickup of the afternoon and mirrored a routine they had followed for years. They each opened their respective doors and Eddie automatically clicked the 'lock' button on his key ring.

Mike, who had been in the passenger seat, immediately noticed the smell. He smiled. "These kids can't hold their beer," he said. "Smells like some kind of a damned barf festival."

Eddie also smiled as he walked quickly to the door. He opened it, giving it an extra push to allow Mike to enter behind him. He neither noticed nor paid attention to the two women who were chatting with one another as they walked toward the two men from the left.

Just inside the door was a bored-looking twenty-something girl in blue jeans and a tank top. At her feet were five satchels, piled in a neat stack. She held a clipboard and Eddie scrawled a signature. As soon as she had her signature, she wordlessly turned and headed back into the comfort of her cubicle. She was already twenty feet back inside the air-conditioned building when the two men reached the van with their load. She would later say that she saw and heard nothing unusual.

As senior man, Eddie hoisted two of the bags. He waited just a moment while Mike picked up the other three satchels. Eddie then pushed the administration building door open with his back and allowed Mike to pass out to the van. When Mike was past, he fell in behind his partner, walked the few steps to the van and put down his bags to get at his key ring, which he would need to manually open the rear door of the van.

Later, Eddie vaguely remembered seeing something coming

from the left from the corner of his eye. Mike remembered seeing nothing at all. Amid the noise of the fair, neither remembered any shouts or screams until many seconds later, and then the screams they heard were their own.

* * * * *

As soon as the van pulled in, Alice began her walk up the main fair path. Six people could comfortably walk abreast on this strip of macadam, with people generally adhering to a policy of keeping to the right as they passed others. Because the Main Gate parking lot was full, there was little traffic moving northbound into the heart of the fair. Southbound traffic, consisting principally of people leaving the fair at the end of a long day, was much heavier.

As Alice walked, she began counting to thirty. *One thousand one, one thousand two...* When she got to twenty-five, she saw her marks, perhaps fifteen feet in front her. They were a family of four – mother, father and two children. She slowed when they were perhaps ten feet away and Alice began to veer into the oncoming crowd. Three teenagers looked annoyed at having to momentarily change their gait to step around her.

When the family was directly in front of her, Alice gasped, "Help me!" and clutched one hand to her chest. She simultaneously began sinking to her knees but, as she went down, she grabbed the five-year-old boy who, to that point, had seemed amused by the sight of an elderly women in distress.

"Mommy!" he screamed as Alice collapsed on top of him.

His mother screamed, as if on cue.

The family's father hesitated, uncertain of his role, which caused his wife to scream louder. This, in turn, had two effects: first, everyone stopped to look at where the screams were emanating. Second, the stopping of pedestrian traffic had an effect not unlike what happened when expressway traffic unexpectedly stopped. There were more collisions.

The husband was jolted to action by the sight of his son writhing under the elderly women who had collapsed in front of them. This old woman in a lurid pink print dress and orange socks was not moving. He reached down to lift up the woman but was uncertain of whether he would injure the woman in the process or perhaps somehow be accused of groping her. As a result, he stopped in mid-reach. This caused his wife to scream still louder.

Two women who had been behind Alice and had seen her suddenly veer into oncoming traffic also tried to assist. However, having seen many medical dramas on television, they feared that moving Alice might either kill or paralyze her. And so they began shouting for paramedics. Now, there was one woman screaming and two more yelling for help. This condition lasted for nearly thirty seconds, by which time a condition psychologists would recognize as mass hysteria took hold. At the end of those thirty seconds, fully two dozen people were screaming for one reason or another. No one moved away from the spectacle. To the contrary, those who had been headed toward the main gate turned around and came back to join the crowd, which now numbered nearly one hundred.

The boy, uneducated in the ways of *Grey's Anatomy* or *ER*, wriggled himself free of the woman on top of him. His mother promptly stopped screaming to the relief of his father, who had been frozen in a semi-crouched position.

Alice lay on the ground, face down, not moving. While she could not see what she had caused, there was a large crowd around her, all of them either offering advice or still shouting for paramedics. The crowd, in turn, completely blocked traffic attempting to get to other parts of the fair. No one dared touch her but neither did anyone feel they could leave as long as an elderly woman lay helplessly in the walkway. One woman annoyingly kept asking her, "Are you all right?" Alice wisely did not ask the woman to stop asking that inane question.

For more than two minutes, with a crowd stretching across the macadam to the booths on either side of the walkway, no one could move south toward the Main Gate. Those walking northbound who might have lingered at exhibits instead raced toward the screams. Vendors, who might have been sweeping the crowds with their eyes hoping for the contact that would lead to a sale, instead found their attention riveted on the mass of screaming and shouting people a few feet away. Except for two women beginning their walk toward the guards, the area in front of the administration building was deserted.

* * * * *

As soon as they heard the beep of the armored car signaling its arrival, Paula and Eleanor looked at one another and rose from their chairs. There were perhaps twenty-five people in the building. As soon as the van appeared, they began walking toward the parking apron, each carrying their bag containing a Mason jar. As the two men got out of the van, Paula and Eleanor passed within a few feet of them, chatting about nothing. Paula noted with satisfaction that neither guard took the least notice of them.

The smell from the small park was overpowering and it was deserted. People, in fact, appeared to be giving it a wide berth. As soon as the two guards disappeared inside the building, the two women stopped. They turned to one another once again and nodded.

Paula said, almost in a whisper, "This is it."

Reversing course, they now walked toward the back of the van as the two guards did the same. The first guard carried three satchels, the one behind him, two. The second guard put down his two bags. At that moment, Paula and Eleanor each reached down into their tote bags and unscrewed the lids to the Mason jars. When the two women were less than a foot from the men, they lifted the jars and threw them into the faces of the guards, Paula taking the one holding the three bags, Eleanor taking the one with the keys in his hand.

Both men wore sunglasses so Paula and Eleanor aimed for their foreheads. Both throws were perfectly on target.

The guard carrying the three bags immediately dropped the bags and said, "Jesus Christ," then pawed at his glasses attempting to get them off. The second guard threw down his keys and said, "Mike, what the hell happened?"

Paula picked up two of the bags the first guard had been holding. The guard she assumed was called Mike was attempting to wipe the liquid in his eyes away with his fingers. The liquid dish detergent in the mixture, however, made everything cling more fiercely to his skin and his eyes. He screamed obscenities.

Eleanor picked up the two bags dropped by the guard with the keys. They were the weight she expected and she was confident she could carry a third satchel as well. She scooped it up, avoiding the sightless flailing of the guard.

Wordlessly, the two women began walking briskly toward the gap between the Flowers and Horticulture and Fruits and Vegetables buildings.

Glancing to her right as they crossed the main fair walkway, Paula saw no one walking toward them from the main part of the fair, though she could see the large crowd a hundred feet up the path.

Eleanor glanced left inside the Flowers and Horticulture Building to see if anyone was paying attention from the entrance. She saw no one doing so. In fact, everyone was facing into the building and there seemed to be some excitement.

Though their loads were heavy, the pair made it quickly to the end of the buildings, turned left, and found Jean, the stroller empty, ready to load the satchels. The transfer was made, wordlessly, in less than thirty seconds. No one was in sight and no one was coming up the alleyway between the two buildings.

Jean stowed the last bag, positioned the doll in its proper place, zipped up the mesh and began pushing the stroller toward the exit.

Eleanor and Paula picked up their watering cans. Eleanor looked at her watch: less than two minutes had elapsed.

Paula opened the rear door and walked in to find pandemonium. Three displays had been upended by two children, neither over the age of four.

A woman, apparently the mother of one, was saying calmly, 'Now Ashley, stop doing that." She said it as though the child were playing with its food rather than running amok through someone's heartfelt artistic creation.

A second woman, equally oblivious to the destruction being caused by her son, said, "I'm going to count to three and if you don't stop it, you're not going to get to go on any rides."

Neither parent, of course, made any effort to restrain their offspring.

Four other women were attempting to right the displays with disastrous results. The competitive class, 'An Evening in Paris' was a shambles, with additional damage done as the good Samaritans attempted to re-set the displays.

"Oh, dear God," Eleanor said. She made a beeline for nearest child, perhaps it was Ashley, who was screaming and rocking an illuminated table display of a floral interpretation of the Arc de Triomphe. Eleanor grabbed her in mid-shake and turned the girl upside down.

One of the women who had previous addressed her child in a polite, non-confrontational tone, even as her daughter laid waste to other people's creative energies, now screamed at Eleanor to leave her precious Ashley alone.

Paula grabbed the boy, who was jumping up and down on the remains of the honorable mention entry in the 'An Evening in Paris' class.

The child's mother shook her head. "I told him to stop. Sorry." The woman smiled sincerely, as though her smile and use of the word, 'sorry' would heal the damage her son had wrought.

Paula looked at the woman incredulously and could think of nothing to say that she would not regret later.

"Everyone out of the building!" Eleanor shouted. "The exhibit is closed!"

The four women who had been attempting to help upright the displays looked at one another and shrugged.

"No," Paula put her hand on one of the women's shoulders. "Please, if you could, help us clean this up."

Five minutes later, they were still attempting to salvage any part of the displays when they heard the first wail of police sirens.

* * * * *

Jean had waited patiently behind the building, getting ready for her role to begin. After first making certain no one was in the vicinity, she unzipped the stroller's mesh screen, folded back the visor, and removed the doll from its seat. Seventy seconds after she heard the armored car squeak to a stop, Paula and Eleanor had come down the alleyway carrying five bags.

They quickly loaded the satchels into the carriage. As Paula and Eleanor straightened their clothing and picked up their watering cans, Jean efficiently turned the stroller back into an easily rolled getaway vehicle. The infant sat atop two satchels with three piled alongside it in the pram's other seat. The visor came back into place and the mesh was again zipped shut.

Jean turned left at the end of the Flowers and Horticulture Building and began pushing her way to the exit. There appeared to be a fair amount of consternation behind her but she did not look back. Two people coming into the fair glanced at her 'World Best Grandma' shirt and at the stroller. No one stopped and asked to see her 'grandchild'.

As she reached the exit, someone said, "Stamp your hand?"

Surprised, she looked around. An elderly man in a straw boater and a candy-cane-striped jacket had an ink pad and stamp in his hands.

"Do you want to come back in?" he asked.

"No," Jean said. "I'm quite tired and I've had enough."

"But didn't I just see you come..." the man started to say. "No, I guess not."

Jean continued out to her car, and waited until no one was in sight. She then carefully loaded each of the heavy satchels into the side of the minivan, pausing each time to catch her breath and to ensure no one was in sight. The adrenaline rush from the robbery allowed her to complete the task in just a few minutes.

When the last bag was stowed, she folded the stroller and put it in the back seat. She then got in the car, adjusted her mirror, and backed out of the handicapped space.

As she was driving out the dusty parking lot, the first three police cars came in, screaming with full lights and sirens.

8.

Detective Martin Hoffman of the Brookfield Police Department surveyed the crime scene, recording that first impressions he found were so often the clue to solving the crime.

The first thing he noticed was the horrific, pervasive stench. Part of the source of the smell was at his feet. The two armored car guards had lost everything in their stomachs as they lay on the ground, incapacitated by whatever had been thrown in their faces. But the smell was more widespread. Walking the small park, the 'rotten egg' smell seemed to come from the bushes, the benches and even the asphalt itself.

"What the hell happened," he asked the fair manager. "Did someone forget to change the grease in the fried dough machine?"

The fair manager, a man who identified himself as Tony Erskine and was still visibly upset, shook his head. "It's just here as far as I know. A lot of kids hang out here after they get tired of the rides."

Hoffman walked over to the benches and examined them. "No sign of vomiting. Do you hose down the area regularly?"

"We wash everything down first thing every morning," Erskine said. "Whatever happened here happened in the last few hours. It smelled fine at three o'clock."

Hoffman nodded. He looked at areas that would have had a ringside seat for the robbery. The ticket-takers at the main gate, were they looking in instead of out, could have seen something. There was a building with a wooden sign over the entrance marked 'Flowers and Horticulture' that opened in the direction of the parking apron. Next to it was one marked 'Fruits and Vegetables', but that building's entrance was at its far northern end and afforded no good view.

"What's that over there?" Hoffman asked, pointing at a building on the other side of the little park.

"The Grange Building," Erskine said.

Hoffman shook his head. Unfortunately, its only entrance faced away from the crime scene. Someone coming out of the building might have seen the robbery, but anyone inside the structure would have been oblivious to it. Beyond the Fruits and Vegetables building on the left was an amphitheatre. On the right was a picnic area. The converging of what was now five police cars – the entire Brookfield force – all with lights still flashing, had attracted a crowd of onlookers, most of whom congregated near the picnic area, craned their necks to see the source of the new excitement, and talked among themselves of what it all meant.

The offices along the front of the administration building were uniquely situated to see anything going on in the parking apron, but Erskine said the offices in the front were used for materials storage because they lacked air conditioning. Only those offices at the back of the building had window units.

Complicating all this, Hoffman had been told, was a near-simultaneous medical emergency. An old lady had collapsed in the middle of the main pedestrian thoroughfare, tying up the volunteer first-aid corps that aided patrons. There had, in fact, been twin 911 calls to the Brookfield Police Department, ninety seconds apart, neither of them from the fair administration. The first had asked for assistance with the old woman, who had reportedly collapsed on top of a child. The second, nearly incoherent, message said a pair of armed security guards were writhing on the ground having been maced with something that had their faces swollen into grotesque forms. At first, no one seemed to notice that five satchels of money were gone.

Which brought up the first basic question in Hoffman's mind:

was this a professional job? The guards were still in the back of the EMTs unit getting eye lavage. They would be in no position to talk for at least another half an hour, he was told. He would have to wait to find out what they had seen.

His guess was that it was professional. Mace in the face was quick-acting though non-lethal. If the guards didn't turn and see their attackers in the split second before they were hit, they would have seen nothing.

Four members of the Brookfield Police Department had canvassed everyone in the vicinity and had found six people who claimed knowledge of what had happened. While he waited for the guards to regain coherence, he would talk with the witnesses. The police, in the meantime, had taken up stations at the three exit gates to ask if anyone had seen anything and to look for persons with bulky packages.

The first witness was the woman who had called 911 from her cell phone. She had been coming into the fair with her boyfriend at ten minutes after five. As they walked by the armored car, they heard, then saw, the two guards on the ground, covered in their own vomit, clawing at their faces.

"It was horrible," the woman said. "And it smelled worse."

"Did you see anyone running away from the scene – toward the gate or into the fair?" Hoffman asked.

She shook her head. "No. And a few seconds later, once people looked and realized that something had happened, everyone started running toward the van."

Which was logical, Hoffman thought.

The second 'eyewitness' was a teenager who had been leaving the fair at the time of the robbery, but had come back in when he heard screams. He was inarticulate as only a seventeen-year-old could be. "It was like, awesome," the boy said. "Everybody was running in circles. Totally flipped out."

"Did you see anyone running away from the guards," Hoffman asked.

"Nuh-uh," the boy responded.

The third person was a woman in her 40's. She was to meet her sons at the administration building but had been repelled by the smell. The armored car had not yet arrived.

"You're sure it hadn't arrived?" Hoffman asked.

The woman gave him a look of disdain. "I would remember if it was here."

"But the smell was already here?"

"Like I just said. The stench was already in place, yes."

"Where did you go to wait?" Hoffman asked.

The woman pointed to the Flowers and Horticulture Building. "I decided to look at the flower show entries. I'm not much for that kind of thing, but I thought it would occupy me for a couple of minutes. I was inside for just a minute when some idiot parents let their children run wild. A boy and girl ran into the flower arrangements and started pushing on them. Their parents, of course, did nothing."

"Did you see what was happening here? At the armored car?" Hoffman asked.

The woman shook her head. "The two women who I guess were in charge of the exhibit came in and ordered everyone out. I decided to walk over here and wait for my sons. That's when I saw the two men – the guards – on the ground."

"Did you see anyone running away?" Hoffman asked. "Anyone with satchels or bags?"

"No."

Hoffman nodded. The only new piece of information was that the stench preceded the robbery, whatever that might mean.

The last witness was an elderly man who had been leaving the Grange Building and was preparing to exit the fair. He was thin-haired and stooped and wore thick, frameless spectacles.

"My eyesight's not so good," he said. "But I saw what happened."

Hoffman tensed. A smoking-gun-grade witness, in the flesh.

"I usually walk right through that little park, but the smell was awful, so I went the long way around. The van had pulled in and they had just gone into that building." The man pointed a gaunt, shaking finger toward the administration building. "They weren't in there but a second. They come back out and are at the back of the van. Two people come walking up behind them, the guards started waving their arms. The two people took off behind the van."

"Could you describe the two people?"

The old man scratched his chin. "Just two blurs. Could have been kids, could have been anyone. I said I can't see so well except what's in front of me. I don't drive, you know."

Hoffman asked the elderly man to show him where he had stood. They moved to a point near the Grange Building, perhaps a hundred feet from the site of the robbery.

"Where were the two people?" Hoffman asked.

"Just standing there as far as I could tell. Maybe they were moving."

"Then they walked toward the guards?"

"That's what I said."

"And they ran away behind the van?" Hoffman asked.

"You heard me right."

From the vantage point of where they now stood, the van obscured a swatch of terrain more than sixty degrees wide. The perps could have gone anywhere from directly out the main gate — their most likely path — to the Fruits and Vegetables Building. They could also, he noted, have run up the narrow alley between that building and the adjacent Flowers and Horticulture structure.

Hoffman decided to run a test. "Stay right here," he asked the man.

Hoffman asked one of the policemen standing by to take up a position by the van. He then walked back to the elderly man. "Can you describe what you see by the van?"

"One person," the man said.

"How old? Man? Woman? Clothing color?"

The man shook his head. One person. It's a blob. I told you: I don't see distances so well."

"But you're sure you saw two people by the guards when it happened?"

"That much I'm sure of."

Hoffman got the old man's name and telephone number. So much for the eyewitness.

I'm looking for two robbers, Hoffman thought. *Which isn't really hot news given that one person would have had a hell of a time hefting those bags alone and then running away.*

He then went to the Flowers and Horticulture Building. What was it the one woman had said? Children had knocked over flower arrangements?

A handful of people were in the building. Two women were seated in chairs. These were the exhibit minders. They were, of course, facing into the exhibit, not out toward the parking apron where the robbery had taken place.

"Good afternoon, ladies," Hoffman said. "I'm with the Brookfield Police. I'm investigating the armored car robbery across the way."

The women rose from their chairs.

"I'm Eleanor Strong," one of the women said. She was in her mid-sixties and carried probably fifty extra pounds on a five-foot-six frame. The blonde hair was not becoming on someone her age.

"And I'm Paula Winters," the second woman said. She was

about fifty, a few inches taller than her partner, very attractive with brown hair and slender to the point of being thin.   A real Mutt and Jeff team.

"You were here this afternoon," Hoffman said.

"Since two," the older woman said. "We'll be relieved at six."

"I heard you had a commotion here," Hoffman said.

The younger woman rolled her eyes. "Two children got out of control and decided to 'act out' on a couple of the displays." The woman gestured at an empty space at the back of the building. "There was 'An Evening in Paris'. Four very nice floral displays that people put a lot of time and effort into. Only one survived."

"Isn't your job to stop them before they destroy the flowers?" Hoffman asked.

"It is their *parents'* job to stop them," the older woman said. "Something parents no longer seem to understand. But we would have, except that we also have an obligation to keep the arrangements watered. We went outside for about thirty seconds to get watering cans. The little urchins got to four arrangements before we could pull them off. And then I was screamed at by one of the parents for touching their precious child."

Hoffman laughed at the thought of coming back to such a scene. "You went outside? Out the front?"

The older woman pointed at the door at the back of the building. "No, we keep the watering cans outside the back of the building.   The fair management is very clear that we're not supposed to leave anything in front that clutters up the area or makes it unsightly."

"When did you become aware there had been a robbery?"

"We had such a mess to clean up we ordered everyone out of the building except for two or three people who seemed to know what they were doing," the younger woman said. Hoffman noticed she was not wearing a wedding ring. "We may have over-reacted.

Anyway, we didn't know there was a robbery until we heard the sirens." The woman smiled at Hoffman.

"You're with the garden club here in Brookfield?"

He had asked the younger woman but it was the older one who answered. "The flower show at the Brookfield Fair is a district-wide project. Judges come from all over the state, the 'docents' – that's us – come from all over the district. We're from Hardington."

"Hardington," Hoffman repeated. "Are you going to get in trouble for what happened?" He was still looking at the younger woman. Pauline? Paula. Paula Winters.

"I doubt we'll be asked back after what happened today," the younger woman said with a bit of a laugh. "Eleanor has done this for years. This was my first year. Probably my last."

"I'll need your name and contact information in case I have any other questions," Hoffman said. *Jesus Christ, I'm asking her for her telephone number*, he thought.

When he had done his initial assessment of the crime scene, Hoffman went into the administration building to hear fair manager Erskine's side of the story. Tony Erskine was a short, dark-complexioned man in his forties whose face still bore decades-old acne scars. A moustache and goatee had probably been grown with the intention of giving him a more dignified appearance. Instead, the effect was sinister. With Erskine was a woman, Brenda Chadwick, who was the fair's financial officer. Chadwick looked to be in her late forties, medium height with a pale face and once-blonde hair that was being allowed to go gray.

"You didn't see anyone loitering in the area or casing the building yesterday or today?" Hoffman asked Erskine.

Erskine shook his head. "I start walking the fair three hours before it opens," he said. "I've got a security patrol that keeps an eye out for trouble. I didn't see this coming."

"Where were you when the thieves hit the armored car?"

"Back in the Midway," Erskine said. "We had a couple of reports of kids with beer. I was checking it out with the security detail. Then, just before the robbery, I started getting calls about some old lady who collapsed from the heat. I was on my way to check that out when I got the alarm about the robbery."

"How much did they get?" Hoffman asked.

Erskine didn't need to consult any paperwork or Brenda Chadwick. "They got $127,640," he said, promptly.

"That's the day's gate?"

Erskine nodded. "We take in two-thirds of the gate before five o'clock. That means maybe $40,000 sits in the safe overnight and there's someone with it all night."

"But you never thought of having your guards posted at the door when the money was transferred?"

"Never had a problem," Erskine said. "And the armored car guards carry weapons. The only thing my security guys have is a uniform. I'm not even allowed to give them a nightstick. State regulations."

Hoffman nodded. It all made sense.

"Somebody said there's usually a crowd of kids out in front."

"The 'pick-up patio'," Erskine said. "The fair opens at ten and by noon, there's usually two, three dozen of them out there." He shrugged. "They paid their admission. They're free to go where they want."

"But there was a smell out there like a dozen kids got sick all over the place," Hoffman said. "Is that normal?"

Chadwick, who had been silent until now, spoke up. "I don't think that was vomit," she said. "I'd say it was a deer repellent."

Hoffman looked surprised. "Deer repellent?"

"You know, to keep deer out of your yard?" Chadwick said.

"Deer don't like the smell?" Hoffman said, trying to grasp the idea that Bambi in the yard was something people in Brookfield tried to avoid.

"You don't live around here," Chadwick said.

"Does a condo in Framingham count?" Hoffman asked.

She shook her head. "There are probably a million white-tail deer in Massachusetts. In a place like Brookfield, the deer easily outnumber the people two-to-one. They're a constant nuisance if you have a garden or any kind of exotic plants in your yard. Some people put up fences, but one of the best ways to keep the deer out of your yard is to spray it with stuff that makes the foliage taste bad to the deer. One bite and they move on." Chadwick shrugged. "Or at least that's what the bottle says."

"And it smells like someone vomited?" Hoffman asked.

"Until it dries, which takes a couple of hours," Chadwick said.

"I'll be damned," Hoffman said. "Where do you buy the stuff?"

"Any garden center. It isn't cheap though. The stuff is at least fifty bucks a bottle."

"Fifty bucks?"

"You've never seen what a half dozen deer in your yard can do to a couple of thousand dollars worth of plants in a night," Chadwick said. The sound in her voice told Hoffman she had experience in the subject.

"I'll be damned," Hoffman said, again. But he was thinking. *You're going to rob the armored car, but there are twenty or thirty witnesses just a few feet away. How do you get rid of them? You splash some of this stuff around the area. The kids all go somewhere else. Ingenious.*

"How long does it take for this stuff to become potent?" Hoffman asked.

"You spray it on and you smell it immediately," Chadwick said.

"So, if someone came out at, say, four o'clock, the kids would clear out before five?"

"If it were me, I'd be gone in less than a minute," she said.

So the perps plan the robbery and use this deer juice to get rid of the witnesses, Hoffman thought. *Smart, very smart. Non-lethal. These are intelligent guys.*

"Last questions," Hoffman said. "First, did the armored car come at the same time every day?"

"We asked for a pickup between five and five-thirty," Erskine said. "Yesterday and today they got here right at 5:15."

"Is that just this year or have you had the same schedule in the past?"

Erskine shrugged. "I've been here three years and it's always been the same."

"Is the amount of money being deposited pretty much the same every day?"

"There's more on weekends and more on opening weekend," Erskine said.

"But a gang would know they were getting roughly $125,000?"

"Yes," Erskine said.

But in that answer, Hoffman saw something. An involuntary flinch. He heard a hint of a quaver in the voice. He pressed.

"There might have been more or less depending on circumstances?"

"No, no," Erskine said. "We announce attendance. People know what it costs to get in. They can guess what the split is between cash and charges. They'd figure it was about $125,000."

Erskine had tried to smooth out the quaver. He hadn't succeeded. Hoffman looked at Chadwick. "Is there someone on staff who could have planned this? Did everyone know how much money was in those bags?"

Chadwick's pale face reddened. "Of course, everyone knew.

But no one would have stolen it."

Jesus Christ. What are they lying about?

"Look, if there's something I need to know to help catch these crooks, now's the time to tell me," Hoffman said. "Don't surprise me tomorrow or in a week."

Hoffman had another thought. "When did you go out to see about those reports of kids drinking beer?" he asked Erskine.

"About a quarter to five," Erskine said.

"And you didn't smell this deer repellent?"

"There's a back exit next to my office," Erskine said and indicated an area on the other side of his office wall. "It saves walking around the building."

"So the money was bagged and counted before you left?"

"It was the last thing we did," Erskine said. "The money went into the bags about four thirty."

Hoffman glanced at Chadwick, who looked very uncomfortable with the answer.

"You agree with that, Ms. Chadwick?" Hoffman asked.

"We finished the count at half past four," she said, tersely.

"We've told you everything," Erskine said. The quaver was gone.

There was a knock on the door. One of the Brookfield Police officers poked his head in. "Beg pardon, detective, but we've got some more people for you to talk to."

Hoffman knew he had taken the conversation with Erskine as far as it could go until he had more facts.

"I'm coming," Hoffman said to the policeman. To Erskine and Chadwick, he said, "I want to solve this robbery. I'm going to need your help doing that. I'm on your side on this thing."

Hoffman had no way of knowing if he was getting through to either of the two. He left his card and then went with the policeman.

The canvass had turned up five people with information to offer. All but one had been brought to the parking apron where the van was still parked. The first was a girl of perhaps fourteen who said she saw three men carrying bags through the Midway. "They looked like, really heavy bags," the girl said.

"What did the men look like?" Hoffman asked. "Were they young or old? Tall or short?"

The girl shrugged. "I didn't get that good a look at them. I just saw them carrying bags."

Hoffman didn't like the direction this was taking.

"Well, then, what did the bags look like? Were they white or colored? Cloth or plastic?"

She shrugged again. "Just bags."

"Were you with anyone when you saw these three men?"

"My two friends."

"Did they see the three men?"

"I don't know."

"Did you say anything to them about it at the time?"

"No."

Hoffman shot the policeman a look. *I hope the rest of your witnesses aren't like her.*

"Well, thank you for coming forward," Hoffman said.

The next person was an elderly woman who said she had been by the van when it first pulled in. "I was headed for the show ring," she said. "My granddaughter has a sheep in the 4-H competition. I was right there when that woman fell down in the middle of the sidewalk."

"You looked back and saw something happening at the van?" Hoffman asked.

"No," the woman said. "It was the woman in front of me. The way she fell down. She did it deliberately to block traffic."

"Why do you think that?"

"She had been walking perfectly fine up to that point. Then she just veered into a crowd and took down that little boy with her. She fell deliberately."

"Thank you," Hoffman said. "I'll look further into it." He gave the policeman a second look. *Two down three to go. It had better get more informative from here.*

The third person was a sixty-something-year-old man who identified the stench coming from the little park as a deer repellent. "I use the stuff. I know what it smells like."

Hoffman thanked the man and asked where someone might buy it locally. The man mentioned two garden centers in Brookfield, but added it could be bought over the internet for a little less.

The fourth person was a woman in her mid-thirties who said she had been one of the first to arrive at the van after the robbery. She said she had called 911 but had been told the incident was already reported.

"I was trying to help one of the guards," the woman said. "I had a handkerchief with me and was trying to wipe away whatever had been thrown in his face. The man was truly in agony. But the reason I talked to the policeman was because I noticed something about the liquid." She opened her purse and took out her handkerchief, now stained red.

"I took it to the washroom and rinsed it numerous times. It kept foaming, which is when it hit me that it was soap." She held up the handkerchief for Hoffman. He sniffed it. Some kind of chemical scent underneath the overwhelming pepper smell. He handed it back to her and shook his head.

"Liquid detergent," the woman said. "When I tried to rinse it out of the handkerchief, it just kept making more lather."

Hoffman took out his notebook. "Liquid detergent? Like dish or laundry detergent?" *Deer repellent that smells like vomit and a dish detergent to make the pepper spray or whatever they used stick to the guards. This is one resourceful set of thieves.*

He thanked the woman and asked the policeman where the fifth witness was. "He's at the ticket booth," the policeman said. They walked the hundred feet to the main gate where a gaunt, silver-haired man with a red-and-white striped vest and a straw boater greeted them. He introduced himself as Pete Baumeister.

"I was telling your policeman here that everything was pretty quiet at this gate," Baumeister said. "I waved through the armored car just about ten minutes after the hour. Everything was normal and inbound foot traffic here was fairly light because the lot is full and they're parking people down by the high school and shuttling them back to a different gate. The only people using the entrance are people who park out on the highway and walk half a mile, and people who have handicapped stickers."

Baumister continued. "Now, I was getting a handful of people leaving the fair through this gate, and about three minutes after the armored car pulled in, a woman pushing a stroller left. I asked her if she wanted her hand stamped so she could come back in. I ask everyone, but I was surprised when she said 'no' because I was pretty sure I recognized her. She – or some woman who looked just like her and also pushing a twin stroller – came through the gate about a quarter of five. Less than half an hour later, she's leaving and she doesn't want to get her hand stamped to get back in. Struck me as kind of odd."

"What's so odd?" Hoffman asked. "Maybe she didn't like the noise or the crowd. Maybe the baby got upset and started crying."

Baumeister shook his head. "It would be a first. I've been taking tickets here for fifteen years. You fight your way through all this traffic. You put up with the dust in the parking lot. You pay your admission charge. You get in here and you stay a while. Even if you start feeling ill and think you're going to leave, you still get your hand stamped. It doesn't cost anything."

"What did the woman look like?" Hoffman asked.

"Little pixie of a woman – silver hair, probably mid-sixties," Baumeister said, holding his hand to the middle of his chest. "But a small woman. Had on a white tee shirt that said 'world's best grandma' or something like that."

"How about the stroller?"

"One for twins. She had up the sun canopy with a netting over it so I couldn't get a good look inside, though I saw what I'm pretty sure was a baby sitting up in there. I didn't think anything about it until the police cars started swarming in here and I realized there had been a robbery. It got me thinking: either that money is still somewhere in the fairgrounds waiting to be taken out tonight, or else someone had to figure out a way to get it over the fence."

"How do you figure that?" Hoffman asked. He liked this elderly guy who, despite the barbershop quartet costume, was thinking like a cop.

"This fair has four gates – all manned – and a big fence to keep people from coming in without paying," Baumeister said. "Two of the gates are up by the Midway and I suspect anyone running through the fair carrying bags of money would stand out. Nobody went through this gate carrying any big bags and the only other entrance on this end of the fairgrounds is the one for exhibitors. The thieves could have run out that exit but then they'd have to walk pretty near a quarter mile to get to their car because it's all vans and campers over there."

Unless the thieves were exhibitors, Hoffman thought. *Unless the money was put in some lemonade cart and is being stashed under a pile of hay as we speak.* He began making notes on search possibilities as Baumeister continued to speak. Now, Hoffman was only half-listening to the old man.

"So, the way I figure it, either the money is still inside, hidden, or else it came out this gate," Baumeister said. "It's funny, but that stroller could have had a bag or three of money in it."

"Was the woman having any trouble pushing the stroller?" Hoffman asked.

Baumeister scratched his head. "Not so I could tell. Come to think about it, she just pushed it like it was, well, a stroller. No strain."

Hoffman nodded. A slight, elderly woman pushing a baby carriage filled with bags of money. It was not a promising image. But it left open the question of how the thieves had gotten the money out of the fairgrounds. The fence to which Marsh had referred was a standard, eight-foot cyclone fence topped with a single strand of barbed wire. It was suitable for keeping out casual gatecrashers, but a man with reasonably strong arms could have thrown the satchels over the fence and walked through the exits with both pockets turned out. Or, could still be in the fairgrounds eating hot dogs and watching sheep dog trials. Hoffman thanked the gate attendant and said he would probably be back in touch.

Hoffman followed the fence a few hundred feet looking for evidence of tampering or perhaps for a lucky footprint. He found areas dug under the fence by animals and some suspiciously trampled grass at one point. On the other side of the fence was a double row of large pines beyond which was parking. The thieves could have parked by the pines when the fair opened and chosen a spot on the most direct route to the parking apron where the van would be. He noted two empty parking spaces abutting the fence.

The two buildings behind him were the Flowers and Horticulture and Fruits and Vegetables buildings, and they were just ten feet from the fence. Between them was an alley just a few feet wide. Now, looking back up the alley from the fence, Hoffman could see the van. The sprint from the point of the robbery to the fence would be about a hundred and fifty feet. If the thieves threw their pepper-spray-laced detergent and grabbed the bags, they could be at the fence in under thirty seconds, which would explain why no one saw thieves running through the fairgrounds with satchels of money. A confederate, or confederates, would have been on the other side of the fence, stowing the bags as quickly as they were heaved over. The thieves would have then casually walked out, maybe even had their hands stamped to return later. A neat, three-man robbery team.

Hoffman radioed for two policemen. When they arrived, he explained his theory and instructed them to inspect either side of the fence looking for footprints or the kind of detritus that lazy crooks leave behind – cigarette butts or candy wrappers with fingerprints.

He then thought about the two women who had left the flower show exhibit to retrieve watering cans. And, indeed, there were watering cans by the rear entry to the Flowers Building. The timing of the two women's retrieval of those cans make it possible they might have seen the thieves as they were transferring the money. Surely, they would have noticed something as odd as men heaving bags over a fence with someone else waiting to catch them on the other side. But what if that task was already done and the men were just making their casual getaway?

He took out his notebook. He had both names.

He knew which one he would ask first.

But when Hoffman went back into the Flowers and Horticulture Building, he was told the two women from Hardington had been relieved, by prearrangement, at six.

"Three shifts, each just four hours long," said a heavyset, elderly woman with a beak-like nose and something of a sniff to her speech. "You would think that, being asked to work such a short time, volunteers would not find it necessary to leave their posts for extended periods." The woman indicated the missing exhibits in the back of the building. "In the ten years I've been working the fair, this has happened only once before. It certainly wasn't while I was on duty."

"The women who were here said they were out of the building for less than a minute," Hoffman said.

"Less than a minute is all it takes," the woman said, her voice taking an imperious manner. "That's why we request that our docents never both leave the exhibit at the same time. One may leave for a few minutes, but the other is always here."

"They said they just went to get watering cans," Hoffman said. He felt he was defending the two women, and especially the younger one, Paula.

"That's what they told me, too," she sniffed. "I reminded them of the rules. One of them could have retrieved watering cans, one at a time, if that's what they felt compelled to do."

"What do you mean, 'compelled'?"

"The arrangements are thoroughly watered first thing every morning," the woman said. "The exhibits were fresh on Saturday morning. Oasis should hold enough water for a day, even in a warm building. Miriam and I would have watered the exhibits on our shift. I'm saying there was no pressing need to water them at 5 p.m."

"So, they were just being conscientious."

"Perhaps. But they both left the exhibit. And I'm the one who is going to have to call the women who put dozens of hours into creating these arrangements and tell them they've been ruined by those two women's carelessness."

"One of the women said she had worked these exhibits for several years," Hoffman said.

"Eleanor Strong," the woman said with disdain. "They're both from Hardington, which is not an especially floral-design-centered club. I don't know the other one."

"And you're from...?" Hoffman asked

"Concord," the woman said.

A tap on the shoulder saved him from further conversation. One of the Brookfield policemen said, "Detective, there's a lady from the insurance company who wants to talk to you."

* * * * *

Her handshake was firm, and she looked Hoffman directly in his eyes. She said her name was Samantha Ayers and she represented Massachusetts Casualty. She was a tall, light-skinned African-American woman with a round face, long black hair and light brown eyes. She wore a blue, skirted suit, an oddity at a fair and even more of an oddity on a Sunday late afternoon. Perhaps it was the sprinkling of freckles on her face, Hoffman thought, but she also looked to be about twenty-five.

"Are you representing the fair or the armored car company?" Hoffman asked.

"Bay State Transport Services," she said, handing him her card. "They're on the hook for this if we don't recover the money."

Hoffman noted the use of the word 'we' and looked at his watch. "The paramedics should have had time to clean up the two guards. We can talk to them together if you like."

En route, Hoffman told her what he had concluded so far. "It was well thought out and probably planned far in advance," he said. "There should have been a gaggle of kids out in front of the administration building which would have deterred any theft. Instead, the place was empty because the thieves sprayed some kind of noxious-smelling liquid, probably sold as a deer repellent, an hour or less before the robbery. Then, with no witnesses around, two thieves threw a concoction of pepper spray and liquid detergent into the eyes of the two guards – and, by the way, there were two guards rather than three, in case you want to make a recommendation back to your underwriter review board."

Hoffman pointed to the spot between the two buildings where uniformed officers were still looking for clues. "There's an outside chance that it could have been a vendor or exhibitor and they could have put the money inside a cart and wheeled it into the fair, but my guess is that the two guys made a beeline for the fence around the fairgrounds and heaved five satchels over the top to an accomplice waiting on the other side. With two guys throwing bags, from the time they hit the guards to the time the money was over the fence was less than ninety seconds. The robbers probably walked out one of the gates immediately thereafter. Of course, with the money safely out of the fairgrounds, they could also be in the Midway riding the Tilt-a-Whirl right now and we'd have no way of ID-ing them. The closest thing I have to an eyewitness is a guy with 20/400 eyesight who saw two blobs running away from the crime scene."

"That's the bad news," Hoffman continued. "The good news is that the fair manager and the financial officer know more than they're saying. I don't know yet if I'm looking at an inside job – always a possibility with something like this – or if something else was going on. What I know is that Erskine, the fair manager, was lying about something and Chadwick, the accounting manager, was dancing around the truth when I spoke to them a little while ago. I've also got one other slim lead: two women in charge of the flower show in the building opposite the robbery site would have been out in back of the building right around the time the robbers were heaving bags over the fence. I spoke with them briefly but hadn't figured out the getaway sequence. I'll close the loop with them tonight or tomorrow morning."

Hoffman and Ayers arrived at the paramedics truck. The two guards were sitting up, their eyes still bandaged. Hoffman introduced himself and the insurance investigator and asked if they were ready for questions.

"We don't know anything," Eddie Caulfield said.

"Happened so fast we didn't know what hit us," Mike Williams offered.

"Just tell us what you remember," Ayers said.

The two guards gave their brief accounts, which offered nothing different than what other witnesses had provided.

"Was there anything out of the corner of your eye, something you're not certain of what it may have been?" Ayers asked.

They remembered seeing nothing.

"Think back to yesterday," Hoffman said. "Whoever did this must have had a dry run of some kind. Was there anything different about today that wasn't there yesterday?"

Caulfield responded first. "The smell wasn't there yesterday."

Williams added, "And the place was stiff with kids. They were noisy as hell."

"But did anyone approach you? Or stand around by your van?"

They could offer nothing that was significant.

After twenty minutes of fruitless questioning, Hoffman knew there was nothing more to learn from them. He asked the paramedics if they had gotten samples of the liquid that had been thrown in the faces of the guards.

"Policeman took them," one said. "Some kind of home-made mace."

"Why do you say home made?" Ayers asked.

The paramedic shrugged. "I've seen people hit by mace. This was the same active ingredient – Capsaicin. It had the same effect on the eyes and face. The stuff that hit them wasn't as concentrated, but it had a better wetting agent." He reached into a stack of clipboards and handed Hoffman his notes on the treatment of the two guards.

"Wetting agent?" Ayers asked. "I'm not familiar with that term."

The paramedic nodded. "A wetting agent is a surfactant – sorry, that's a surface acting agent – that reduces surface tension. In other words, something that makes it stick better. If it had been just Capsaicin suspended in water or oil, the guards could have wiped it out of their eyes. It would have stung like crazy, but they would have seen who hit them. The wetting agent made it both cling and be absorbed." The paramedic then added, "I had a semester of chemistry in college."

"How about liquid detergent as a wetting agent?" Hoffman asked the paramedic. "One of the people who were first on the scene said it was liquid detergent, like dish or laundry detergent."

The paramedic nodded. "That would do it."

"So we're dealing with thieves who are also chemists," Ayers said. "They spray the area with deer repellent to get rid of the kids, then they throw homemade mace laced with detergent to blind, but not kill, the guards."

"This is not your average gang heist," Hoffman said to Ayers. "It sounds more like something a group of college kids would pull."

"Why college kids?" Ayers asked.

"They wanted the money but they didn't want to hurt anyone," Hoffman said. "Your average pros either would have used ski masks and guns, or else clubbed the guards with something guaranteed to put them out cold for a couple of hours. They wouldn't give a damn if one of the guards had a cracked skull or worse. It would have taken the same amount of time as what these people did and required a lot less thought."

Hoffman ticked off points on his fingers, tapping against the clipboard the paramedic had given him. "Also, the fact that no one noticed them before or after the holdup says they weren't wearing disguises, masks, or anything else that would have made them stand out. They did it in street clothes. They trotted the hundred and fifty feet to the fence, tossed the bags over, and then walked out of the fair like nothing had happened. They're smart and they're organized, but they seem to have made a point of being non-lethal."

"What I can't figure is how they managed to get in among the kids who were here earlier today without being noticed, and how they got right up to the guards. It means they were someone so ordinary they were invisible."

Ayers had an idea. "Maybe they were high school kids. They could walk in among the other kids without being noticed."

Hoffman shook his head. "Two problems: first every other kid would notice them because they were interlopers. That or else they'd be checking out their clothes, hair styles and music. Second, I've never seen any three or four high school kids be this well organized."

"So, what do we do?" Ayers asked.

There's that 'we' again, Hoffman thought. "I go quiz the patrolmen and find out if they saw something they didn't recognize as a clue. I look for similar heists over the past few years. I suggest you use your resources to do the same. But I'm going to make you a bet that the group that did this has no priors. Someone dreamed this up as a one-off."

Hoffman thanked the paramedics and started to leave the medical van.

"Hey," the paramedic said. "My chart. I need that for my report."

Hoffman handed back the chart. "Sorry."

The paramedic looked at the chart. "Huh, gave you the wrong one, anyway."

"Wrong one?"

"This one is for the heat stroke lady we treated. Never had someone who was in such bad shape when we got her put up such a fight to say she was all right. I have a feeling she was afraid we'd take her to the emergency room and she'd get charged. And I thought all those Hardington people were rich."

"Hardington?" Hoffman asked.

"Yeah." The paramedic consulted the chart. "She didn't even want to give her name, but her Medicare card said she lives in Hardington. Said she was feeling fine as soon as we gave her something to drink. My guess is she's poor."

"Huh," Hoffman said.

"Which leaves us with your other hunch," Ayers said, interrupting his train of thought. "The folks who work for the fair know more than they're telling. I'm going to work on my sources to run that one down, too."

When they had left the paramedics van, Ayers stopped and looked at Hoffman. "We're partners on this thing as far as I'm concerned," she said. "If I uncover something, I'm going to call you immediately and share it. I expect you to do the same. I don't think that's too much to ask."

"This isn't about turf," Hoffman said. "If I find something, I'll let you know."

"That's all I ask," Ayers said.

And with that they went their separate ways.

9.

Jean drove home carefully, never once exceeding the speed limit or failing to come to a complete stop at stop signs. She parked in her garage, something she almost never did during the summer months. With the door closed, she removed the heavy bags, using a Radio Flyer wagon to shuttle the satchels from the car to her dining room table.

Then, after meticulously pulling closed all the first-floor drapes in the house, she began sorting the bills into same-denomination stacks. The first surprise was that there were an abnormal number of hundred-dollar bills in the first satchel she opened. The second surprise came when one satchel was filled entirely with hundreds. The third surprise was that there were no ones or fives.

There's a lot more than $135,000 here, she thought. *And far too many hundred dollar bills.*

She began the count just before 6:15 p.m. At 8:50 p.m. she had done two counts and was satisfied with the result, albeit astonished by it.

The five bags had contained $477,640. The amount tied to the deposit slip she found in a manila envelope in the third bag she opened.

The agreed-upon plan was that the four women were to meet at 9 p.m. It had been further agreed that each person would, between 8 and 9 p.m., be somewhere public and make a purchase that would demonstrate they had not immediately met after leaving the fairgrounds.

In being mesmerized by all the hundred-dollar bills, Jean had completely forgotten about the plan. When her doorbell rang, she had just started a third count, not that she expected three hundred and fifty thousand excess dollars to disappear between counts. Perhaps irrationally, she also chided herself that she had failed to put on a pot of coffee. Now, she would be thought a poor hostess.

Paula was the first to arrive. Paula saw the look of concern on Jean's face.

"Something's the matter," Paula said. It was a statement rather than a question.

"There's too much money," Jean said. "There's nearly half a million dollars here."

The two women were in the dining room, looking at the piles of hundred dollar bills, when the doorbell rang a second time. It was Eleanor. When told of the problem, she, too, went into the dining room to stare at the money.

Alice was only a minute behind Eleanor. She gasped when told the amount.

"There are two logical explanations," Eleanor said when they were assembled in the living room, everyone having thumbed through the bills to assure themselves that there was no fundamental error in the count. "The one that I'd like to believe is that the fair's front office was handling receipts from everyone – vendors, Midway rides and ticket sales. The problem is that there's only one deposit slip. Also, if I had the Aunt Fanny Fudge stand, I wouldn't want my income washed through that of the central office. There's a reason those places don't take credit cards, and it has everything to do with keeping income out of sight of the IRS."

"The second explanation is the one I suspect is what we're really seeing." She paused, trying to find the right words.

"Someone is using the fair to launder money," Jean offered.

"The Brookfield Fair is a front," Eleanor said. "Which amounts to the same thing."

Alice, who had washed the excess makeup from her face and

changed out of her 'ditzy lady' dress and was now more casually attired, raised her hand. "A front for what?"

"It could be many things but, whatever it is, it's illegal," Eleanor said. "Let's say you're taking bets on football or baseball games – which is against the law in Massachusetts. It's a cash business. You take bets in cash and you pay out in cash. You can't just deposit that money in a bank account."

"A bank has to report all cash transactions over $2500," Alice said.

Eleanor nodded her thanks. "So someone running this illegal betting parlor needs to find someone who does a lot of cash business and who makes regular deposits. Someone who won't be noticed because they do it all the time. The problem is that, in an age of credit and debit cards, there are fewer businesses all the time that do much business in cash. And very, very few that aren't part of a corporation. If a supermarket starts depositing twice the usual amount of cash, alarms go off at the parent company."

"So this could be illegal gambling profits we stole," Paula said.

"Paula, that's the most benign explanation I can come up with," Eleanor said, her voice trembling slightly. "It could also be drugs. If we've robbed someone's laundered drug money, someone is going to come looking for that cash. And when they do, they're not going to be nice about it."

"But no one saw you," Alice said.

There was silence in the room.

"Did we commit the perfect crime?" Paula asked.

"It depends," Eleanor said. "Good enough to fool the police, or good enough to fool a drug cartel?"

"I can't see the Medellin drug cartel laundering its profits through the Brookfield Fair at the rate of $350,000 a day for nine days," Paula said. "That doesn't make any sense."

More silence.

"She's right," Eleanor said, sounding more confident. "The fair can only send so much cash a day and it runs nine days. Even if someone has gotten every fair in the Northeast to launder its money, that's only good from July to the start of October and, as conspiracies go, that's a bit hard to handle."

"So it isn't drug money," Jean said, relieved.

"But it's someone's money," Paula said, "and they're going to come looking for it."

10.

Hoffman stretched his back muscles and rocked his head from side to side, listening to the snap of cartilage in his neck. The clock in the corner of the computer screen read 10:50 p.m. The preliminary notes on the Brookfield Fair robbery were nearly completed.

In point of fact those notes had been effectively finished for an hour. He was a fast typist and well organized, and the transfer of notes from his pad to the screen had gone smoothly. During that past hour he had checked his spelling and punctuation and re-written paragraphs to emphasize levels of certainty or doubt.

In short, he had been killing time.

In a different world and a different time, he would have been home now. On the same day of an earlier year – say, six years ago – he would be curled up on the couch right now, his feet propped up on the coffee table, an open bottle of wine and a take-out pizza box on the floor. There'd be some stupid Sunday-night chick-flick movie on one of the cable channels and he would be in a state of bliss.

His arm would be wrapped around Kelly, who might or might not still be awake. She could never hold her wine. If she were awake, they'd be talking about schedules for the coming week. Her classroom plans would be perfectly organized and her homework graded. She'd be telling him about some kid named Tino or Li and how they were coming alive because of the summer session enrichment program. And he would be genuinely interested and could imagine some gap-toothed, nine-year-old budding math prodigy, diligently absorbing Kelly's lessons.

He would talk about his own work – his own case load – only if asked. He didn't care to frighten Kelly with the reality of crime gangs around Central Square or the tracking of low-lifes driving in for a night of crime from Chelsea or Everett, looking for easy pickings from the well-appointed homes of Harvard and MIT faculty.

There had been so many Sunday summer nights like that. Peaceful evenings with wine and pizza or Chinese take-out. Wonderful days when he could look in Kelly's animated face and see that education was the most important thing in the world to her – well, next to him, and maybe it was a close second. She had a gift. She had the passion. She couldn't wait for the school day to start.

Now, there was only the reality of a one-bedroom condominium in a thousand-unit complex in Framingham. It was furnished with what he found at Ikea, checking off three rooms of furniture and furnishings like ordering from some Danish restaurant. The Frijden sofa with the Kalpaa end tables and a Hallbeeji entertainment center. It had all been packed into a U-Haul and set up, just like in the model rooms. It still looked showroom new.

The real furniture – the belongings of his home in Cambridge – had gone to the kids. He didn't want to sit on that wonderful, lumpy sofa because he couldn't bear to be reminded of Kelly every time he did. He didn't want to sleep in that bed or pull his clothes from that dresser. It was better to start fresh with bland, birch veneer over particleboard of some unpronounceable style from an acres-large store. The intolerable alternative was to wake up each morning and encounter furniture on which he could lovingly recount the origin of every nick and stain.

So, on a Sunday night at 10:50, Hoffman changed a word or two and found a reason to add a clarifying sentence. In the Brookfield Police Department he was the guy who regularly signed up for the weekend shift and then waved off the days promised in trade. He was the highly competent guy who was last out the door and whose case files were immaculate. In court his testimony was perfect and his observations unshakeable.

He was also the guy, everyone knew without having been told, who just didn't want to go home.

He was presumed to be one of those legions of fifty-ish divorced men with grown kids and no means of starting life over again at such a late date. His fellow officers looked at him and saw a cipher, a reasonably good looking guy without the usual pudginess that came from decades on the job. His desk held none of the usual clues about a past personal life. There were no photos of family, no souvenirs of trips to Disney World or Cozumel.

It was presumed by everyone in the department that adultery was at the root of the absence of a Mrs. Hoffman. It usually was. Policemen, and especially detectives, came into contact with scores of women whose lives were in upheaval. Some of those women threw themselves out of gratitude at the man they perceived as their rescuer. Others considered sex a legitimate form of currency for payment of present or future favors. A detective with a desire for extramarital sex would find it with little effort.

Because Hoffman had previously been with the Cambridge Police, there was also the satisfying possibility that the other woman or other women had been students. Hoffman didn't use dyes to hide the gray but he had a full head of hair and it showed no signs of thinning. His face had the creases that could just as easily pass for wisdom as for age. Perhaps he had been a father-figure-fixation to a Harvard co-ed with languid, sex-infused afternoons in a luxury apartment overlooking the Charles.

The truth was none of these. The truth was as crushingly prosaic as it was painful. Kelly had set off one morning to the supermarket to stock the Hoffman family home with groceries. At 11:32 a.m. on a Saturday morning in May, four years earlier, her beloved Toyota Tercel, which had a curb weight of 2,322 pounds, had been broadsided by a car full of teenagers in a 4,000-pound SUV. The driver, in possession of a license for less than two months, had thought that by speeding up he could get through a traffic light while it was still yellow.

Instead, he had slammed into the driver's side of a vehicle half the SUV's size. Kelly's car had been pushed thirty feet sideways through the intersection into the engine compartment of a truck waiting to make a left-hand turn.

Kelly was dead before the first policeman arrived at the scene.

Hoffman knew none of this for more than an hour. Instead, he passed the time replacing pieces of split siding on their home, and his last memory before the phone call was a mild annoyance that Kelly had promised to be home before noon, and it was now half past twelve.

He had no time to frame a proper goodbye. The transition from happily married man to grieving widower was instantaneous. In the space of a few seconds the book of his life turned to a new, unwanted chapter. He was forty-five, alone, with two children grown and on their own.

The worst part – and what kept Hoffman awake at night for months afterwards – was that Kelly's death had been meaningless. There was no disease to be conquered and no terrorists to be vanquished. The kid who was driving wasn't on a cell phone and wasn't drunk. The driver possessed a valid license and was fully insured. He simply lacked the experience and had thought he could get through the light with a little extra acceleration.

He was wrong and Kelly was dead.

A year after Kelly's death, Hoffman completed his twenty-five years on the Cambridge force. He sold the house, gave its belongings to his kids, and sought a new start. Armed with his two-thirds-pay pension plus generous benefits, he had sought out a small department in the vast ring of commuter towns around Boston and had found a willing employer in Brookfield.

Like most such towns, Brookfield enjoyed a symbiotic relationship with these retired police officers. The pay was horrible but the work was not demanding. The town knew the preponderance of its policemen's income was coming from pensions funded elsewhere and, because few would stay longer than a decade, the town's pension liability for these officers was inconsequential. The towns got experienced law enforcement personnel on the cheap. The suburban policemen and detectives got a de facto handsome bump in salary. Except for the staggering pension load carried by cities like Boston and Cambridge – a result of having failed to take into account human behavior in granting such generous pension terms – it was an equation in which all sides won.

Hoffman did not think of these things as he re-read his report. He only thought of the emptiness of the condo.

He also thought about Paula Winters. He had spoken with her for only a few minutes but he was a quick judge of people. There was a vulnerability in her eyes, as well as a profound sadness born, he suspected of loneliness. She was attractive. There was nothing in her appearance, voice, or mannerisms that reminded him of Kelly, yet the overall effect on him was to make him feel... alive.

In four years Hoffman had found no woman who attracted him. He had spent much of the first year grieving but, by the end of that first year when he retired from the Cambridge force, he had been willing to at least entertain the idea of a female friend. But there had been no one who interested him, much less aroused feelings of passion or romance.

He did not know and could not say that Paula Winters was some soul mate or whatever it was the dating service ads promoted. What he had felt was an attraction and, for the first time in those empty years, he felt compelled to act on that attraction. He intended to do so tomorrow.

On the third page of the report he found a paragraph that seemed to give too little weight to the elusive statements by the fair financial officer.

He erased that paragraph and started over.

* * * * *

Twenty-two miles away in a grand colonial set on five acres, two of which were exquisitely landscaped perennial gardens, Paula Winters sipped a Scotch.

She lay in her bedroom — a preposterous twenty-five-foot-square space with a stone fireplace and coffered ceiling — on a king-sized bed. Behind that king-sized bedroom was an equally fanciful master bathroom with a large Jacuzzi, walk-in bath with half a dozen shower heads, and a steam sauna that, to the best of her knowledge, had never been used.

Paula felt at once exhilarated and apprehensive. *She had done it.* Five hours earlier, she and three women recruited by her had pulled off the perfect robbery of an armored car. They had done so in broad daylight at a fairground filled with thousands of people. It had been done with split-second accuracy and had happened so quickly that no one had noticed.

She, Paula Winters, had masterminded a heist. She had done the most incomprehensible thing she could imagine and pulled it off, from conception to execution, in a month.

If her goal had been to prove to herself that she was alive, she had succeeded beyond her wildest dreams.

It was more than just the robbery, of course. It was the daring nature of it. So many moving parts to keep track of and so many things that could have gone wrong. Alice, Eleanor or Jean could have backed out in which case the scheme would have been abandoned without a further thought. The ingeniousness of clearing the area with Liquid Fence. That had been her idea.

But what if the fair's maintenance staff had noticed immediately and sent out a crew with a hose and scrub brushes? The heist never would have happened. What if a crowd of people had walked through the main gate just as they were preparing to throw their pepper juice? She and Eleanor would have kept walking, nodded at the guards, and gone back to the exhibit, empty-handed except for unopened Mason jars. What if Alice had staged her fall fifteen seconds too late – or too early? Dozens of fairgoers would have been in the area by the van, or else the guards would have heard the screaming on their way into the building and been vigilant instead of complacent.

Even the pandemonium inside the Flowers and Horticulture Building had worked to their advantage. No one left the area. Everyone either tried to help or stood, transfixed, by the destruction taking place. Paula had said to the other women that she would think of a way to keep people inside the building, but she had instead left it entirely to chance.

What if someone had come out of the building's door just as she and Eleanor began their run across the parking apron down the narrow alley between the two buildings? There had always been a few seconds when they were vulnerable – when they had grabbed the satchels but were in the open for everyone to see, clearly having committed the robbery but not yet into the safety of the alley between the two structures.

Had she wanted to be caught?

No, she thought. The *goal was always to commit the robbery and leave no trace.*

But she had been questioned. The detective. Hoffman, he had said. Morton? Martin? He was a good looking man. Not too tall, not too short. He was probably a few years either side of fifty and not trying to hide his age.

Not like Dan.   Dan, who worked out at a gym every afternoon, except that he had undoubtedly spent a lot of those afternoons getting a different kind of workout with Patty Courtney, now Mrs. Patricia Winters.

She had been dumb not to see it coming. She had missed every warning sign, and they had been plentiful. Dan's 'work day' stretched to twelve and then to fourteen hours – and Paula fretted that he might have a heart attack at his desk, alone. Then, there were the last-minute business trips and the weekend 'retreats'. Paula was oblivious to it all. She had trusted Dan, right up until the evening he returned from a 'business trip' to New York and announced he needed to 'change the direction of his life'.

Even then she harbored the illusion that the marriage could be saved. It wasn't until the week after the divorce was final and Paula was told by a friend that Dan was inviting a few close friends to his upcoming wedding that she realized it had all been part of a grand plan.

What an idiot I was, she thought.

She found that Dan's guilt had translated into a multi-million-dollar settlement plus an annual payout from the proceeds of his business. She was forty-eight and in possession of a modest fortune, more than sufficient to her needs. Certainly ample to take round-the-world cruises that would take her across the path of an eligible bachelor of a certain age.

What would Jane Austen have said? *It is a truth universally acknowledged that a divorced, forty-eight-year-old woman in possession of a fortune, must be in want of a husband...*

Instead, in two years she had grown accustomed to being alone.

She had been 'set up' with half a dozen men. Their ages ranged from their early forties to their early sixties. They were

divorced – it was never *their* fault, the marriage had just grown stale
and ended on amicable terms (or so they said) – or they had never
found the time to marry. On one such date with the oldest of the
men, she felt uncannily as though she was being interviewed as a
future nurse/companion.

The internet brought dozens of names of men looking for a
'mature woman' and a 'social, fun-filled relationship'. The men
were handsome in the photos they supplied to the dating sites and
the essays sounded so sincere it was as though they had been
ghost-written by counselors. She canceled her subscription after a
month without ever replying to any of the men who had clicked on
her profile.

Then came the day of her annual mammogram and the phone
call almost immediately thereafter from her physician. The
technician hadn't waited for the images to be uploaded to India or
wherever such things were read. She had taken one look at them
and summoned Paula's internist. The internist had taken one look
at the first image of her right breast and walked it over to the head
of radiology. The lumpectomy had been performed a week later.

Now, two years after the divorce and nineteen months after
her first cancer surgery, she had done the thing she had promised
herself. She had taken a true risk. And, in return, on Tuesday
afternoon she would check herself into the hospital to prepare for
a mastectomy the following day.

She poured another ounce of Scotch and added seltzer.

But suddenly, it isn't over, she thought. *Whose extra money is it?
And how far will they go to get it back from us?*

At midnight, she was still pondering that question.

11.

It was just after 9 a.m. and Detective Martin Hoffman saw the trouble coming from the other side of the room. One state trooper in full regalia and one unfamiliar man in a grey suit, both accompanied by Sam Ashton, Brookfield's chief of police.

Twenty-eight years of police work, twenty of them as a detective, told him both men approaching Hoffman were 'staties' – state troopers – and to judge from their age, lifers. He considered such men dangerous because of the Massachusetts State Police's reputation for patronage and corruption. In Hoffman's view, someone who stayed with the State Police for an entire career was either an idealist, incompetent, or on the take.

"This is Captain Moynihan and Detective Sergeant Woolsey," his chief said. "This is Detective Hoffman, who ran the preliminary investigation at the fair yesterday. I'll leave you three to talk."

The key to the conversation was the use of the past tense: '...Detective Hoffman, who *ran*...' The Commonwealth of Massachusetts was announcing its intention to take over the investigation.

"Have a seat, gentlemen." Hoffman indicated vacant chairs at other desks scattered around the small bullpen that served the department.

Hoffman sipped coffee from a departmental cup. He made no offer to point the two interlopers in the direction of the coffeemaker in the kitchen. They could stop at Dunkin' Donuts and get their own damned coffee if they were going to swipe his case.

In front of Hoffman was the reason why the two staties were

now before him. Summer was the slowest news season and Sunday was the slowest news day. The lead article, splashed across the front page of the Metro section of the *Boston Globe* this Monday morning was 'NO CLUES, WITNESSES IN DARING BROOKFIELD FAIR ROBBERY'. With no other competing news, the story had jumped to an inside page where readers could see more of the story and three related photos. Hoffman had been quoted extensively. No doubt, the article had been the principal topic of discussion this morning when state police officials met to decide in which local investigations they would interfere. The two officers pointedly ignored the copy of the *Globe* article laying open on Hoffman's desk. If asked, they would probably deny having even seen it.

"The state takes a special interest in armored car robberies," said Captain Moynihan, the man in the suit. "We have an extensive database of incidents and believe we can spot patterns that aren't available to local law enforcement agencies."

It was all a crock, of course, though Hoffman knew protesting would be pointless. When the state police elected to intervene in a case, towns cooperated. So, Hoffman nodded politely and continued to sip his coffee.

"We'll need your files and notes, of course," Moynihan continued. Hoffman looked at Detective Sergeant Woolsey, who sat, rigid-faced through the meeting. Hoffman judged him to be mid-fifties, which meant that the Detective Sergeant, who was still in uniform, had thirty-plus years with the state. *What kind of pitiful record did this guy amass to still be in his bear suit?* Hoffman thought. *And he's not even allowed to talk.*

"We will, of course, provide you with progress reports on the investigation…" The droning went on. "…but we expect that all liaisons with the press will be handled by the state and that any further queries will be directed to us and there will be no 'anonymous source' back-channel communications with the media…"

Ah, there was the crux of it all. All future headlines and on-camera interviews are the exclusive property of the Massachusetts State Police, Hoffman thought. He allowed himself a smile for the first time.

"Is that all clear, Detective Hoffman?"

"Perfectly," Hoffman said.

"Then, if you'll provide us the materials we discussed, we'll leave you to your other duties."

Solving this robbery is my duty, Hoffman thought.

As though reading his mind, Moynihan said, "If we find you're conducting an independent investigation, we'll drop the hammer so fast you won't see it coming. From here on in, anything you do with regard to this investigation will be deemed by the state police as 'interference' and your chief and town administrator will have the riot act read to them. Is that clear?"

"It was clear even when you couched it in pretty-please language," Hoffman said. "I am to stay the hell out of it."

"Just so we understand one another," Moynihan said.

Hoffman turned over a file folder containing the ten pages of notes he had laboriously typed up Sunday evening.

"Here's everything you need to get started," Hoffman said.

"We'll keep you posted."

Like hell.

When they were safely out the door Sam Ashton came by. Ashton, silver-haired, was in his early sixties. He had been police chief in Brookfield for more than a decade and had hired Hoffman after a single, 45-minute interview over coffee. The two had an excellent rapport made all the healthier by the wide latitude Ashton gave Hoffman in pursuing and investigating cases.

"Grabbing for headlines?" Ashton asked, taking a seat on the edge of Hoffman's desk and picking up the newspaper.

"More or less," Hoffman replied. "Plus, I was told it's now their investigation and that if they catch me in the act of doing police work, they'll use their infinite power to squash me like a bug."

"You got any leads?"

"You have the report. Anything I have is better than what they've got."

"You going to keep on investigating?"

"Of course," Hoffman said. "That is, if it's OK by you and the town selectmen can stand having a guy in a bear suit tell them at an emergency Board of Selectmen meeting that they're contributing to a return to the law of the jungle by having me on the payroll."

"I'd be honked off if you didn't solve the crime before them," Ashton said, grinning. "Just let me know if any of your leads are starting to pan out and leave the politics to me."

* * * * *

Back when the estimated take was $135,000, the four women had planned an equal, four-way split. Unbeknownst to the other three, Paula had intended to forego her share so that the other three women would each get about $45,000.

Now, on Monday morning, they sat in Jean's darkened dining room, the drapes still drawn, with four piles heaped up on the dining room table, each containing $119,000. The money took up most of the surface of the table.

"What do we do with it all?" Alice asked, touching the tops of the stacks, straightening them as she went along.

"Well," Eleanor said, "the first thing we do is get it out of sight. Anyone who comes to the front door is going to get a real eyeful. As to where it goes from here, it's a matter of when and if we think anyone is going to come looking for it."

Eleanor looked at Jean. "You're the only person who wasn't

known to be at the fair yesterday," Eleanor said. "Paula and I were interviewed by a detective; Alice was treated by the paramedics. If there are any follow-up visits, it will be to us, not you. So, I vote that the money stays here, but somewhere a little less conspicuous than your dining room."

"I'm not sure I'll feel comfortable with all this money in the house," Jean said. "In fact, I hardly slept last night worrying about it. Can't we just start depositing it?"

"No way," Alice said quickly. "Banks are required to report all cash deposits over $2500. And, any string of cash deposits is going to get noticed. I know that, at the bank, after any robbery within a fifty mile radius, we were always asked to make note of any unusual cash deposits, even ones well under that limit. You can be certain that the police have blanketed the region with notices. So no, it's going to be quite a while before we can make any deposits."

"Then, can we spend it?" Jean asked.

Alice picked up a hundred dollar bill from the top of a pile and examined it as she spoke. "A little at a time, sure. No one at a grocery store blinks at a hundred dollar bill any more. But don't go paying your taxes in cash or try to buy a car. Any transaction like that will be flagged."

"After we put the money somewhere else, we've got a more serious problem to ponder," Eleanor said. She spread the morning's Boston *Globe* on the table with the money. "According to the fair people, we stole $127,640. The deposit slip showed $477,640. There's $350,000 more than the police think is missing, or that the people at the fair are acknowledging is missing."

"That raises two interesting questions," Eleanor continued. "First, why did this Erskine man lie to the police about how much money was taken? And, do the police accept at face value that $127,640 is the right amount?"

"To me, it's fairly obvious that $350,000 is the amount of money being laundered," Paula offered. "And it also seems obvious that the fair manager is in on the laundering scheme."

"One person or more than just the one person?" Jean asked. "You can't have that much money sitting around without everyone noticing."

"You'd be surprised about that," Alice said. "When you're handling a lot of money, it stops being money and becomes paper with green drawings on it. And, if the money being laundered was kept separate from the fair gate receipts, it's possible that only one or two people were involved. If this Erskine person bagged the money himself, he may have been the only one who knew."

"But, Jean, we're going to have to leave the money here for the time being," Eleanor said. "When the police don't have any clues right away, they're certain to start re-interviewing everyone who might have seen something. You're the only person who has no connection of any kind to the fair from yesterday."

Reluctantly, Jean agreed.

They decided on Jean's attic as the least likely place that someone would look. Each person's share was placed in a doubled paper grocery bag, labeled with their name, and carried to the second floor. From there, a ladder was the only access to the attic. As the strongest of the four, Eleanor volunteered to take the money the final leg of its journey.

"It's behind some trunks," Eleanor said when she returned from the last trip up the ladder. She also held out eight, crisp hundred dollar bills. "It's not much, but if anyone feels like celebrating, here's some mad money."

"Is there any chance it's marked?" Jean asked.

Everyone looked at Alice.

"No," Alice answered. "The fair wouldn't keep track of serial numbers. Only the bank might do that. The money is safe."

"So we go home and wait," Eleanor said. "We may have to wait a while."

"I'll be out of touch for a few days," Paula said, quietly. "I'm going into the hospital tomorrow."

The other three women looked at her with alarm.

"I've had a recurrence of my breast cancer," Paula said, keeping her voice calm and even. "My doctor says it's Stage III, not Stage IV. It's in my right breast and I'm going to have a modified radical mastectomy and reconstruction the day after tomorrow. I should be home on Friday or Saturday."

"You never said anything," Eleanor said, uncertain of what else to say.

"I didn't know until a few days ago," Paula said. It was a lie, but it would avoid a lot of awkward questions she did not want to answer right now.

"Will you need help when you come home?" Alice asked.

Paula shook her head. "My daughter is coming up from Virginia." Which was another lie. Paula had declined her daughter's offer to spend a week with her, opting instead for a private home health aide to come in. But she saw the look of concern on the others' faces. "It's two nights in the hospital and a week of bed rest at home. I'll be back on my feet before Labor Day." She forced a smile.

"And besides, I've got the memory of this to keep me active," Paula added. "And I've got to figure out what to do with my share of the money."

The others sat motionless. This was new and disquieting information.

"May we come see you?" Jean asked, breaking the silence. "I mean, in the hospital or as soon as you're home?"

Paula considered her answer. "Ordinarily, I'd say yes. And I'd love to see you. But for the first day after surgery I understand

I'll be on fairly heavy meds. I'm also worried about us being seen together – as a group – before this dies down. I don't want any smart policeman putting two and two together." Paula saw that her answer wasn't satisfactory. "I'll call you as soon as I'm home, I promise."

The other women glanced at one another, then back at Paula. Paula was their ringleader. Paula had planned this. Now, Paula was, if not abandoning them, leaving them to their own devices for a week.

The looks on their faces said they did not like what they had heard.

"Oh, all right," Paula said, smiling. "We're all part of the Hardington Garden Club and this is the Garden Club Gang. I check into Dana Farber at 2 p.m. tomorrow. The surgery is supposed to be at 9 a.m. Wednesday. Come see me Wednesday night or Thursday morning. And bring chocolate."

The other three women's faces brightened measurably.

12.

The office exuded prestige. A large blue marlin was mounted on one wall, below it was a framed, 8x10 color photo of the fish being exhibited at dockside by the man who now spoke in hushed tones on the small, cheap phone. Another wall was taken up by a massive bookcase but, instead of books, it was plaques and framed certificates that filled the shelves. Each of these items attested to the charitable good works, laudable public service, low handicap and business acumen of the office's occupant, one Gordon McLeod.

A third wall, covered with a richly textured wall paper selected by Mrs. Gordon McLeod, held a dozen family photos, each one in a custom frame of a rich, dark wood. Two angelic children were at the center of most photos, with Mr. and Mrs. McLeod flanking them. The backdrop to these photos was as diverse as the Great Wall of China and an exclusive Hawaiian beach.

The fourth wall was of glass. It, unfortunately, overlooked a parking lot though, at this early hour, there were only a handful of vehicles present. Beyond the parking lot was a modest shopping center. As a result, the cream-colored drapes were usually kept drawn.

McLeod, age 38, attired in an expensive, light blue suit suitable for a warm August day, checked the heavy oak door to his office. He pushed it open just far enough to ensure that the outer reception area was empty. He then pulled the door to his office closed and locked it before continuing the conversation.

"Tell me everything you know," he said, simply.

A man's voice was on the other end of the line. The voice had a decided Latino accent, full of clipped-off 'T's' and 'I's' that came out as 'E's'. "We don't know squat yet," the man said. "No eyewitnesses." It came out as "We don' know squa yeh. No eye-weetnesses."

The man continued. "Whoever did it cleared out the area by smelling it up with some kind of stuff that smells like puke. One old guy saw two people…"

"I read the paper this morning," McLeod said angrily, cutting off his caller. "What do you know that isn't in the paper?"

There was an uncomfortable silence on the other end of the phone.

"I'm waiting," McLeod said.

"It may take a day or two," the voice said. "But I'll find out who did it, and I'll get the money back. All of it."

"What about Erskine?" McLeod asked.

"He wasn't in on it, if that's what you mean," the man with the Latino accent said.

"What makes you so goddamn certain?"

"Because one of my boys put a gun under Erskine's chin last night and said he had ten seconds to tell my boy where the money was. All Erskine did was crap in his pants and cry. He doesn't know."

"And what makes you so certain you'll know something in a day or two?"

"Because I've got somebody on the inside," said the man on the other end of the phone. "That's all you got to know. I got this thing wired."

13.

At the Massachusetts State Police Criminal Investigations Unit in Framingham, Detective Sergeant Alvin Woolsey re-read the crisp, typewritten notes provided by the Brookfield detective.

It's utterly bizarre, Woolsey thought. *Deer repellent. Homemade pepper spray suspended in a liquid detergent. What the hell kind of criminals pull off a heist like that, leave no trace, yet use such rank amateur tools? They're either the smartest crooks in the Commonwealth or else they're the luckiest sons of bitches ever to pull off a job.*

The M.O. database – the lovingly created, computerized file of every crime committed in the state in the previous twenty years, had turned up exactly nothing. A group out of Revere had targeted armored cars three years earlier. They had been apprehended and were now in various prisons serving lengthy sentences. They left behind no disciples and their *modus operandi* had been a display of automatic weapons that scared the bejesus out of the ten-dollar-an-hour security guards. There had been a few one-off armored car heists: a Springfield bank delivery had been hit the previous year but the perp had left behind fingerprints, palm prints and size 12 footprints. He had been apprehended three hours after the heist.

There was only one unsolved incident involving an armored car. Two security guards were distracted by a co-ed at Boston University sunbathing topless on the balcony of her campus apartment. While they watched her wiggle back into her top, someone reached down and picked up a bag of money. The checks and bag were found in a university dumpster, $30,000 was never recovered.

The history of fair robberies was even less illuminating. Because they came and went in a week, criminals never had time to formulate a plan to rob them and so the fair circuit had led something of a charmed existence. There had been three instances of smash-and-grab intrusions into fair offices over a ten-year period. In one case, thieves made off with a little over three hundred dollars in coins but immediately abandoned part of the haul because of its weight. The pair had been apprehended trying to exchange handfuls of quarters for bills at the fair's Midway. In another, a security guard had alertly clubbed an intruder with a desk lamp as the would-be robber stuffed bills into a paper bag. Police arrived while the would-be robber was still unconscious. In the third, the thief had grabbed a few thousand dollars, fled the building, and made it no further than the perimeter security fence before being apprehended in front of a hundred witnesses. In all three cases the perp or perps apparently acted without a plan, and with predictable results.

To rob a fair, Woolsey concluded, is a crime for fools.

Except that the people who planned and executed the Brookfield Fair heist were too clever to be fools. They had hit the armored car on the second day, before the cash pickup routine was well known to observers. According to Detective Hoffman's notes, a minimum of three people had been involved; four if the thieves wanted to quickly load the satchels into their getaway vehicle.

Woolsey drummed his finger on his desk.

College kids? he thought. The suggestion appeared in the notes. It could have been three or four kids who hadn't figured out that a theft gone bad would end their chances of working on Wall Street or getting into law school. College kids would be employed by the fair to pick up garbage or do the sweaty stuff that any fair needed. A college-aged kid pushing a broom or wielding a picking stick would be invisible to the multitude of teenagers milling around the park next to the parking area.

Fair employees, he wondered. The fair manager would have a payroll list with social security numbers. These could be checked not only against the state database of criminals, but against those criminal's dependents, in the event that someone had planted their offspring on the fair's employment rolls with the specific intent of robbing the fair.

Woolsey started making his own notes.

His captain, Terry Moynihan, tapped at the door frame of Woolsey's office.

"Getting anywhere?" Moynihan asked.

Woolsey glanced at his watch. "I've got a few ideas," he said. "I'm going to check the system and see if we've got an out-of-state group that decided to branch out. I'm also going to listen to the tip line the local guys in Brookfield set up."

"Keep me posted," Moynihan said. "There are a lot of people upstairs who want to see a quick arrest on this one."

* * * * *

Samantha Ayers stood where the armored van had been, seventeen hours earlier. The fair would not open for another half hour so, for the moment, there were only vendors and fair employees around her. Though the smell from the deer repellent had dissipated after a few hours, two teenagers washed down and scrubbed the little park, eliminating any vestige of the previous day's odor.

The boy hosing down the area kept glancing in her direction. He was, she estimated, eighteen or nineteen. He would be wondering why she was there, standing in the middle of the parking apron with notebook in hand, periodically taking a small camera from her purse to photograph something. He might be building up his courage to come over and say something.

Samantha felt she was cursed. She was tall, she looked considerably younger than her twenty-seven years and guys of all races considered her 'cute', whatever that meant. As a result, getting taken seriously was a constant challenge.

She was the daughter and the granddaughter of policemen and the combination of family pressure and two years at MassBay had convinced her that police work was a good career choice. Her grandfather had been one of the first half-dozen token blacks who had 'integrated' the Worcester Police Department in the 1950's. While he patrolled only African-American neighborhoods and had been verbally forbidden from ever arresting a white citizen of the city, he was nonetheless proud of his career. His son – her father – had followed him into the department, reached the rank of lieutenant, and had been awarded numerous citations for bravery. At twenty, fueled by family stories of heroism, she was ready for a career of crime-fighting and eager to break down the glass ceiling of women in law enforcement. She had joined up.

Five years with the Worcester Police Department demonstrated that while race had ceased to be a hindrance to advancement, gender was still very much at play. As a woman, she was deemed suitable for filing and secretarial duties. When she complained, it marked her as a 'non-team player'. When she won street assignments, it was invariably undercover duties either at high schools or on 'john' patrol. Two years ago, she had quit, convinced that law enforcement was still a decade or two away from being an equal opportunity employer of women.

The investigation position with Mass Casualty had been a tip from her father. There, she found that results were what mattered and she had distinguished herself in ferreting out fraudulent claims. That she had been called minutes after Mass Casualty learned of the robbery of one of its vehicles was strong evidence that she was appreciated by the company.

Her lone concession to her age and appearance had been to eschew the jeans and tops of her age peers in favor of dressing 'older'.   Sometimes, it kept away the sub-drinking-age crowd. Today, it did not.   From the corner of her eye, she saw the boy turn off the hose and make his approach.

"Hey," the boy said.

She turned to him, her face impassive.   She said only, "What?"

The kid shrugged.   "Just wondering what you're doing here. You know, the fair not open yet.   And I was wondering..." He shrugged again and his face contorted into some kind of a visual version of 'yada, yada, yada'.   Was he inviting her into the shrubbery for a quickie?

"Where were you yesterday afternoon between two and four o'clock?"   Samantha opened her notebook, her pen poised to take down the response.

"Whoa, lady," the boy blinked.   "I didn't know you were the cops."

"The question stands," she said.   "Where were you in the two hours before the robbery?"

The boy's mouth was open.   He was processing the question but no answer came out.

Had I ever been like this, she wondered.   *Incapable of responding to a change in environment?*

He squinted.   "Picking up trash back in the Midway, I guess," he said finally.

"Where were you when you heard the sirens?"

His mind was moving more quickly now.   He silently repeated her question, his lips moving.   He pointed toward the grandstand. "Litter patrol, over there.   Listening to the geezer acts." He smiled at his own wicked humor.

"I'm sure you spoke with the rest of the crew afterwards," Samantha said.   "Were any of them in this area when the robbery happened?"

The boy shook his head. The answers were coming more quickly. "A couple of them were trying to help the old lady who collapsed. They came here as soon as they heard the sirens. They thought it was the paramedics. It was, but it was also the cops. You guys."

Samantha didn't correct him.

"What are their names?"

The boy jerked his thumb over his shoulder at the second boy, who lackadaisically scrubbed at the park benches. "Carl was one of them."

"Carl!" Samantha shouted. "Come on over here." To the other boy, she said, "You better get back to work."

The first boy left, all romantic thoughts smashed.

The second boy, Carl, looked to be still in high school. He had an ingratiating, mischievous smile and blonde hair that hung down well into his eyes.

"I was just talking to your buddy," she said, indicating the other boy with her chin. "He says you were one of the ones trying to help the old lady who fell."

"Uh, huh," Carl said.

"Which direction did you come from when you heard those shouts?"

Carl looked around. He pointed toward the Grange Building. "I was on litter patrol over there."

"You saw the armored car pull in?"

Carl squinted through his hair. "Yeah, I guess so. I think I heard it beep and I looked up and saw it pull in. Then I went back to picking up stuff."

"Did you see anyone waiting in this area?"

Carl scrunched his nose. "Nah. In fact, it was kind of weird because there's usually a crowd hanging out."

"How long after you saw the armored car pull in did you start hearing the screams about the old lady?"

"Maybe twenty, thirty seconds."

"When you heard the screams, which way did you run?"

Carl pointed to the back of the administration building. "That seemed like the shortest way."

Damn, she thought.

"Carl," Samantha said, now peering directly into the shag of hair in front of the boy's eyes, "I want you to think very hard. Did you recognize anyone that came to help the old lady who ran from this direction?"

Carl closed his eyes, apparently trying to visualize the scene.

"Maybe Don," he said after about thirty seconds. "I think Don ran up from the admin building."

"Who is Don and where do I find him?"

"He's, like, a dude in my class at school. I guess he's at home."

Samantha bit her lip. It was no time to get angry with anyone. "Could you call someone who might know his full name and number?"

A light went on somewhere in Carl's head. "Yeah," he said. He pulled a phone from his pocket. Three calls later, Samantha had the name and address of Don Zimmerman, the closest thing she had yet to an eyewitness.

* * * * *

Detective Martin Hoffman knew how to stay out of sight of the state police. He also had a very good idea, based on previous dealings with that agency, which avenues of investigation they would pursue first. The staties would initially put their faith in their computer resources and look for similar crimes and similar situations. Infatuated by their data, the state police would pursue those avenues regardless of how tentative the links. Hoffman had long ago concluded the state police played investigative odds rather than intuition or even common sense. Only after all database-generated leads had been exhausted would they consider new ideas.

Even though Hoffman had typed up his notes just eleven hours earlier, his mind had subconsciously worked on the case overnight, creating new links and discarding others. By the time the state police came in, he had already relegated the information in those notes to the status of 'starting points' though he had made no offer to provide the state police with his updated thinking.

This morning, he had awakened with a realization that the group that had committed this robbery knew the routine of the fair sufficiently well that they had been able to time their actions to the second after just one day. This, in turn, implied the thieves might have worked at the fair for several years. That they were not noticed by the guards indicated the two men who overpowered those guards, as well as their accomplice or accomplices, had lain in wait nearby while managing not to attract any attention.

He had initially considered that the thieves could be vendors and they might have used a cart of some kind to hide the money and transport it deeper into the fair where the satchels could be hidden. A cart, however, would have required the use of the main walkway into the heart of the fair exhibits. For more than ten minutes after the robbery, however, the route between the administration building and the rest of the fair was choked off by the crowd that gathered around the elderly woman who fell. No witness made any mention of a cart attempting to push its way through the crowd.

Nor had the robbers fled back through the little park and into the fair through the Grange Building or kiddie rides. The old man with the 20/400 vision said the criminals had fled behind the van, meaning toward the fence or the Main Gate. The money, Hoffman concluded, had been taken out of the fair. It wasn't being hidden among bags of potatoes or horse chow.

His subconscious mind had also kept coming back to the use of the deer repellent and the pepper spray imbedded in liquid detergent. Each incident by itself was ingenious and displayed an uncommon intelligence. The two actions taken together displayed something more: an attention to detail that was beyond the grasp of the kinds of criminal groups that dealt in smash-and-grab robberies. Over the course of the past three decades he had worked on – and cracked – cases involving well-financed and well-rehearsed heists. But those criminals had been after much larger amounts of money or jewels. One, involving a Cambridge jeweler, had gotten away with several million dollars of gemstones.

Considering the risk, the average group of intelligent criminals would set a threshold considerably higher than the $127,000 this group had stolen. And, for run-of-the-mill robbers, planning was not part of their tradecraft. The display of a gun was the answer to all obstacles and brute force was the alternative if guns were unavailable. By contrast, these robbers had planned and executed the heist with the explicit intent of avoiding the use of force. Everything about this case was contradictory. Nothing was clear.

He had not ruled out college students as the culprits. Childhood friends now in college and getting together for the summer could have taken it into their heads to embark on a crime spree, either for the money or as a lark. The size of the heist meant a three-way split of roughly $40,000, serious money to a college student. Hoffman made a note to get a list of college-age fair employees who had attended the same high school.

Finally, there was the hesitation on the part of Erskine, the fair general manager. He knew more than he was telling and he needed to be questioned under controlled circumstances. However, for him to be an insider in the heist was illogical. Robberies received far too much police attention. If the general manager of a fair wanted its gate receipts to disappear, there were far better ways than involving thieves. And, if the general manager had been coerced into cooperation with thieves, there would have been other, telltale clues. Everything about Erskine's manner indicated that the robbery had come as a shock to him. He was lying about something, but it wasn't about having been a party to the robbery.

Hoffman was left with few leads that could result in a quick solution to the case. If they did not pan out, he would need to rely on one of the thieves making a large, cash bank deposit. Given the care that had been shown in the planning of the heist, he was not counting on such a slipup.

Before he went back to confront Erskine and the fair's financial manager, he first wanted to close the loop on a couple of other hunches.

Inside his car, Hoffman got out his street atlas of eastern Massachusetts. He turned to the tab for Hardington.

14.

At their meeting that morning, Paula had volunteered to get rid of the distinctive satchels used by the armored car service. They were canvas, so they would burn nicely as part of a pile of brush, but it was August and a fire would attract attention. Her fallback plan, which she had just completed, was to reduce the bags to unrecognizable pieces that could be disposed of at the town's refuse transfer station on Tuesday.

It was a few minutes before eleven in the morning. She had ripped the stitching out of the bags and cut the resulting pieces into four-inch squares. Her hand ached from cutting the heavy canvas, but now there was only a pile of scraps, together with buckles and zippers, which she had just dispersed among multiple bags of household trash and double-bagged. She was in her garage, about to put them into her garbage can, when a car pulled into her driveway.

The car was an unfamiliar sedan and Paula stood, frozen in place for the moment, with the black garbage bag at her feet. From the car emerged the police detective she and Eleanor had spoken with Sunday afternoon. Seeing who it was, she regained her composure and placed the last trash bag inside the garbage can and walked out of the garage to meet the unexpected visitor.

She saw the detective walking toward her. He wore a tan suit and a summery tie. She was in shorts and a sleeveless blouse. Seeing him, she felt both underdressed and exposed, as though he had deliberately come when she was least expecting him.

"Detective Huffman, isn't it?" She forced a smile but was aware of the perspiration building on her forehead.

The man smiled. "Hoffman with a 'O', but you came close

enough." He looked around at the façade of the house, a massive colonial with its attached, three-car garage. "Nice place. Very nice place."

"Thank you," Paula said. And waited. She liked this man's easy-going manner and loose body language. Also, he was as handsome this morning as he had been yesterday evening. True, the face was weather-beaten, befitting someone whose work kept them out of doors, but there was something that she called 'eternal youth' about him, something she hadn't noticed yesterday. He was probably about fifty yet his eyes had not dulled and his skin did not sag. Part of it was probably taking care of himself but most of it was a matter of spirit.

Hoffman had hoped for something more from her than those two words; an opening for a conversation. He looked around again and took in the extensive gardens and shrubs. "The gardens are beautiful, too."

"I'm pleased you like them," Paula said, smiling.

"A lot of upkeep, I would imagine." Hoffman noticed the beads of perspiration on her face. The day was neither hot nor especially humid.

"I like growing things," Paula said, now wondering where the conversation was headed. *Why is he here?* she thought. *Does he know something? No. If he did, he wouldn't be making idle conversation.*

Hoffman could see that she was ill at ease. There would be no idle banter. He should have called and conducted the interview by phone. No getting to know her this way. Not that there should be. Paula Winters was an attractive woman, but there was obviously no interest on her part. He noted there was no still no wedding band on her left hand today. In fact, no jewelry of any kind on her hands nor tan lines indicating any had been worn and taken off. It didn't go along with this huge house unless she was widowed or divorced. He forced himself to get mentally back on topic.

"I'm sorry to barge in on you, Mrs. Winters, but I'm pursuing a couple of leads from the robbery and I was hoping for a few minutes of your time..."

The tone of his voice confirmed that he knew nothing or suspected nothing and Paula began to relax.

"You, and anyone in that building with you, had a ringside seat to what took place..."

"But I was looking into the building, minding the flower exhibits," Paula said. "I wasn't looking outside. I didn't even notice the armored car pulling up." As she spoke, Paula noted something else about Hoffman's appearance that she wasn't able to immediately identify. A sense of loneliness, perhaps, or of loss. It was nothing specific, nothing in his face or his eyes. But she had a feeling that this man was trying to resurrect something that had left his life. Of course, she thought, it could also be a projection of her own loss.

Hoffman nodded. It was the answer he expected. "But someone had to be standing around waiting for that van to arrive. The robbers could know approximately when it was coming but they had no way to time its arrival perfectly. Therefore, they had to be in the vicinity of the administration building for at least fifteen and perhaps even twenty minutes. Did you notice anyone linger in the flower show exhibit?"

Paula thought for the moment and then shook her head. "We had a stream of people, almost all women – that's who mostly is interested in flower shows – a handful of men with their wives, and some younger women with children..."

"Including the ones who ran amok through the exhibit," Hoffman said and smiled.

"Especially them." Hoffman noted that, for the first time, Paula Winters smiled.

"So did anyone seem to linger?"

Paula paused before answering. "Some people took a few minutes in front of the fans, but that was to cool off. And, frankly, none of them looked like someone waiting around to commit a robbery. Plus, the average age was over sixty-five."

Hoffman laughed. "How did you decide it was time to get the watering cans?"

This was an answer Paula and Eleanor had agreed upon. "Our shift ended at six and we had decided we should water in the last hour. There was something of a lull in traffic at five o'clock and so we just said to one another, 'how about now?'"

Hoffman was surprised by the answer, which sounded like something that had been rehearsed a couple of times. "One of you couldn't stay and watch out for the kiddies? The ladies who came on after you were kind of huffy on that point."

"Everything had been quiet up to then."

Another rehearsed answer, Hoffman noted. *Why?* he thought, and filed away the responses to ponder at a later time.

"You walked out of the back of the building and got your watering cans," Hoffman asked.

"Right."

"How long were you back there?"

Paula shrugged. "Thirty seconds, forty-five seconds."

"This is the important question, Mrs. Winters: was anyone else back there? Anyone walking toward you or away from you? Anyone who seemed to be waiting on the other side of the fence out in the parking area? Anything at all unusual?"

Paula understood the question. It was their opportunity to throw suspicion elsewhere. She and Eleanor had debated inventing a couple of Hispanic males or twenty-somethings. Eleanor had strongly argued for creating such a diversion. Paula had said she would have nothing to do with it. The police would pursue the leads and, when the leads turned up no one, suspicion would fall on them.

"I've racked my brain, detective," Paula said. "I don't remember anything unusual going on back there. No noises, no footsteps. No one talking. If there was someone on the other side of that fence, it didn't register. I'm sorry."

Damn, Hoffman thought. And, her answer sounded sincere.

"My problem, Mrs. Winters, is that you and Mrs. Strong are apparently the only two people who were in exactly the right position to see whoever committed this robbery."

"Unless they came running down the path between the two buildings right after we went back inside," Paula said.

"How did you know…"

"I read the article this morning, detective. I read your quote about the robbers fleeing between the two buildings and throwing the satchels over the fence. It's why I realized you were so interested in what we might have seen. If I had remembered anything, I wouldn't have waited for you to get back in touch with me. Eleanor and I didn't know we were supposed to be paying attention."

Hoffman noted she smiled again.

"Did you recognize anyone you knew at the exhibit just before you and Mrs. Strong left to get the watering cans?"

Paula thought for a moment, then shook her head. "No, a few people from earlier in the afternoon, but no one after about four o'clock. I'm sorry."

Another dead end, Hoffman thought. "Then I've taken up too much of your time," he said. He turned to leave.

Now or never, he thought. He turned back to face her.

"By the way, Mrs. Winters. When this investigation is over, could I buy you lunch one day?"

Paula was stunned by the question. She realized her mouth

was open. *Oh, my god*, she thought.

"I'm sorry," he said. "I realize that was way out from left field…"

"No," Paula said. And then corrected herself. "I mean, yes. Sure, give me a call. I meant, no, please don't be sorry…"

What on earth am I saying? she thought.

"Then I'll leave it at that," he said. "I'll keep you posted if there's anything to report on the robbery."

Paula stood in the driveway long after Hoffman's car had backed out.

I just got asked out on a date, she thought. *I just got asked out to lunch by an age-appropriate man. And I'm going in for surgery tomorrow…*

* * * * *

Samantha Ayers stared at Tony Erskine. There were half a dozen ways of staring information out of people. She did not cock her head nor did she rest her chin on her hand. Those would have been the 'be a buddy and tell me' ways of extracting information. Nor did she use a cold, icy stare that meant, 'I already know the truth so spill it and I'll go easier on you'.

She had prefaced the stare with a simple statement. "Unless you stop bullshitting me, I'm going to leave this office and mark the file, 'do not pay under any circumstances'. Do you understand?" She had then sat back in the chair and waited.

They were in Erskine's office at the Brookfield Fair. It was a dismal place with a single, frosted window that admitted little outside light. A noisy wall air conditioner rumbled inefficiently. Overhead, water-stained ceiling panels were interrupted by a pair of fluorescent lights that hummed even as they cast a ghoulish yellow light. Erskine's desk was piled high with papers. If there was a filing system for all this, it was not in evidence.

Erskine's eyes darted to all parts of the room. To the dented, brown filing cabinets with drawers not quite closed. To the narrow closet door. Samantha saw that he was perspiring heavily now. She had struck a nerve.

"We had scheduled a five o'clock pickup," Erskine said. "We had twenty-four-hour receipts of $127,640. Two tellers and I made two counts of the money. The money went into the satchels..."

"Who put the money in the satchels?" Samantha asked.

"I did."

"Where did you do that?"

"Here, in this office," Erskine replied, and several drips of perspiration fell from his chin onto papers on the desk.

"With no one watching."

"We had already done two counts of the money. Why the hell did I need someone to watch me put it in bags?"

"You carried the money in this office." Samantha leaned forward. "You picked up those piles of money and brought them back into this office in order to put them in the bags. You didn't bag it out in the bullpen which your staff says was the usual way of doing things. Instead, for the first time in anyone's memory, you brought the gate receipts in here and filled the bags yourself, and that just happened to be the one day that someone decided to steal those bags. "

"I was more comfortable doing it in here, alone."

Samantha slammed her hand on the desk. "I said no more bullshit!" The sound of her hand hitting the desk seemed to reverberate around the tiny office and she knew that her words had carried to the cubicles beyond, where the members of the finance staff were doubtlessly listening; straining to pick up every word.

"I don't trust the girls," Erskine whispered.

"You were afraid that one of them was going to slip a fifty out of a pack?" Samantha sneered.

"I was suspicious," he said, a little louder. "I did it for security."

"And you filled out the deposit slip yourself."

"Yes."

"Which everyone agrees you've *never* done. Yesterday was the first time anyone ever remembers you filling out the deposit slip."

"I said I was suspicious of them."

"And there's no chance that maybe one of those bundles of money never made it into the satchels?"

Samantha saw color creep into Erskine's face. It was a reaction, but not the one she expected.

"I did not take a penny from that deposit, Miss Ayers," Erskine said, speaking slowly and deliberately. "The deposit slip tied exactly to the amount in the satchels: $127,640."

She drummed her fingers on the desk and contemplated his answer.

"You better hope to hell that the police get lucky on this one, Mister Erskine. And you better hope to hell that, when the police recover those satchels, they contain exactly $127,640. Because right now, my report is going to say that this was an inside job and that you were party to it. Either those bags were stuffed with newspapers and that money went out in the trunk of your car last night, or else you did something else that – when we find out – will ensure you never work in this business again. I told you not to lie to me. But you've been lying through your teeth all afternoon."

She saw that Erskine was again sweating heavily. His mind was racing, but with thoughts unrelated to this conversation.

There's something else going on that I don't get, she thought. *At least not yet. Someone has scared this guy more than I ever could. Now, all I have to do is figure out what he's hiding.*

* * * * *

Detective Sergeant Alvin Woolsey read the computer printout for a third time.

The definition of insanity is doing the same thing over and over again and expecting a different result, he thought.

The words did not change. The conclusions did not change.

No one had ever committed this kind of a crime before. Not in Massachusetts. Not anywhere in the United States where records were computerized, which was now everywhere.

This was what they called a 'virgin M.O.'

Which means I get to do some real detective work, he thought. He found his hat and headed for the door.

"Got something?" It was his boss, Terry Moynihan.

"Not yet, but then I've just started digging. I'm headed over to Brookfield now."

"We're looking for a quick solution," Moynihan said. "Stay on it. Let me know if you need other resources. But you've got to keep me posted on anything you learn – any kind of progress. The guys upstairs are all over me for something to give to the press. Keep me in the loop. That's an order."

"I'll do that," Woolsey said.

* * * * *

Alice Beauchamp arched her back as she took a break from pulling weeds. Bending over for extended periods was painful and, even with a kneeling pad, she had at most an hour's stamina before her aching joints took their toll.

The carrots and green beans were weeded as were the tomatoes. It was August now and she was no longer worried about tiny weed seeds robbing her crops of moisture. But she cared about the appearance of the rows of vegetables. Weeds were a symbol of disorganization and sloth. She could see the weeds protruding from the butternut squash and the melon vines, areas she had not yet attacked. And as long as there were weeds, she could not leave this garden.

But neither could she hide the exhilaration she felt. There was now a grocery bag in Jean Sullivan's attic with her name on it.

In that bag was more than $100,000. For the first time in a decade, Alice did not fear the future. She did not fear opening bills or letters from unknown points of origin.

I am free, she thought. *I don't even need to weed this garden. I can go to the supermarket and buy whatever I want.*

But she continued weeding. Weeding was part of her nature. It was like tidying up her teller's station at the bank several times each day, emptying the waste basket and spot-checking her tray to ensure that she had not mistakenly placed a twenty-dollar-bill in the drawer meant for tens.

She saw the unfamiliar sedan pull up and park along the side of the road with the other vehicles owned by those who had plots in the community garden. She knew all the weekday regulars – the retirees and stay-at-home moms with children in school – and she even knew a few of the gardeners who tended their plots only on weekends. She was certain this car did not belong, and she tried to discern the license plate in the event that it was someone who decided to help themselves to flowers or vegetables from one of the plots closest to the road.

That the man had on a jacket and tie confirmed her suspicion. He probably had a plastic grocery bag in his pocket. He would pretend to admire the gardens, then choose one well away from where people were working. When the man thought everyone had lost interest in him he would go in and help himself to tomatoes, green beans or lettuce. If the man did, Alice would copy down his license plate number and call the police when she got back to her apartment.

But the man stopped at the first garden plot being worked – some string bean girl named Rhonda who never pulled the weeds at the base of the fence around her garden – and she saw Rhonda point in Alice's direction. The man nodded and began walking briskly toward her.

Alice took a drink of water from her bottle and stood up.

"Are you Mrs. Beauchamp?" the man asked. He pronounced her name 'Bo-champ'.

"It's pronounced 'Beech-im'," Alice said. "And you would be?" She let the question trail off.

"Detective Martin Hoffman of the Brookfield Police," he said. He took out his wallet and showed her a gold badge. Just like on *Dragnet* all those years ago. Sergeant Joe Friday, Badge 714. "You weren't at your apartment and some of your neighbors said you were likely down here."

Alice was surprised any of her neighbors had any inkling that she kept a garden here.

"Brookfield, you say?"

Hoffman nodded. "I hear you had an accident at the fair yesterday. I wanted to make certain you were all right."

Alice nodded. *Don't trust him*, she thought. *Don't trust him any further than you can throw him. Policemen don't come around inquiring about your health.* "I'm all right now," she said.

Hoffman shielded his eyes from the bright sun. "Can you tell me what happened?"

Alice indicated the pine trees along the edge of the road. "We can find some shade over there." The walk allowed her to assemble her story and regain her composure.

Be very careful when you talk to this man, she thought. *Don't say anything that helps him in any way.*

"You drove all the way over here to check on me?" she asked when they were in the shade.

"Well, they said you were out cold there on the walkway for a while."

"I just fainted in the heat," Alice said. "I didn't take my blood pressure medication yesterday. Just forgot. I got to the fair and was enjoying it so much I just stopped thinking. Round about five o'clock, my pressure must have started falling. Too much sun and too stubborn to sit down and wait it out." She tried to say these words casually so as to make it sound like something that had happened to her before.

Hoffman nodded. "You had been outside all afternoon?"

"Except when I was indoors. And even then it was unpleasant because none of those buildings were air-conditioned. It was hot for an old lady like me."

"And you fainted."

"That's what they tell me."

"Somebody said you sort of veered into the oncoming traffic and took down a little boy with you."

"I have no recollection," Alice said. "I just remember thinking how hot it was and feeling dizzy. The next thing I was inside that ambulance and they were giving me fluids, asking me all kinds of questions. Trying to take me to the emergency room…"

Stop saying so much, she thought to herself angrily. *You're helping him!*

"People also say you fell right across the walkway."

"I really have no recollection."

"You were walking up from the main gate up toward the Midway," Hoffman said. "Where had you been?"

"Oh, all around." *Be vague! Volunteer nothing!*

"There's not much down at that end of the fair," Hoffman said. "Just the Flowers and Horticulture stuff, the Fruits and Vegetables exhibits, and the administration building."

Alice was perplexed that the man would not just accept her dizziness story and let it be. "One can also walk for the exercise," she said. "Or just for the enjoyment of being alive. I am not a wealthy woman, detective. When I go out for a day and I pay twelve dollars to get into some place – not to mention the gas to get there – I want to get my money's worth. I want to take in everything."

"The paramedics said it took them a…"

At that point Alice determined it was time to put an end to this questioning.

"Detective… you said your name is Hoffman? Is the town of Brookfield going to send me a bill for having had the poor luck to faint in the middle of its fairground?"

"No ma'am."

"Then why are you asking me where I was walking and what place I might have seen?"

Hoffman let out an involuntary 'huh.' "You know there was a robbery just a hundred feet away from where you fainted."

Alice nodded. "I shared the paramedics' van with those poor, unfortunate guards. They were in rather a great deal of discomfort. And it excuses — up to a point — the unimaginative language they were using."

Hoffman smiled. "You would have been walking from the direction of the main gate just about the time the armored car pulled in."

"I suppose so," Alice said, wary again. "It made no impression on me." She hoped her answer sounded sufficiently vague.

"Did you see anyone loitering in front of the administration building?"

Alice gave him a blank look. "What building is that?"

"The one that would have had the rather bad smell."

Alice nodded and also remembered her fall-back story. The one she would use in case she was questioned by the paramedics in the van. She had created it after consulting a map of the fairgrounds.

"Oh, *that* one," she said. "I gave it a wide berth because of that smell. I had been at the Grange Museum. There were still

Granges when I was a little girl. I would have walked through that area but the smell was horrible. But I don't remember the armored car." Alice paused for a moment and put her finger to her lips. "Do you suppose that might have been why I fainted? I have rather a sensitive sense of smell."

Hoffman smiled again. "Perhaps that was it."

It had been a one-in-a-thousand shot that she would have seen something before fainting, Hoffman thought. She had been in the right area – near the parking apron – at the right time. But her blood pressure had been low, so she would not have been especially observant.

The timing and location of her fainting, though, couldn't have been better from the point of view of the robbers. What a great diversion: someone faints just seconds before the heist, directing attention away from the main event. As everyone stops to look or to help, they jam up the walkway so no one can get through. The crowd grows, preventing would-be witnesses from stumbling onto the crime scene. It would have been a perfect feint. But this was your basic little old lady, tending her garden...

Her garden?

He looked around, as if seeing the spot for the first time. This was a community garden. Alice Beauchamp was a gardener.

Is there a link? he thought. *Tiptoe up to the question.*

"One last question, Mrs. Beauchamp. Did you get to the flower show exhibit in the time before you fainted?"

"I suppose I did. I'm not much interested in those big expensive arrangements, though. I like getting my hands dirty. There was a whole building next to it filled with garden exhibits. Perfect zucchini. Beautiful tomatoes, and a number of them were heirloom varieties. I should have entered mine..."

"But you were in the flower show building?"

"I guess so." *Be evasive,* she thought. *This man wants to put you in jail.*

"Do you know Mrs. Winters or Mrs. Strong? They were monitoring the exhibit."

"Why yes, we're all members of the Hardington Garden Club."

As soon as she spoke the words, Alice began to feel a sense of dread coming over her. Why had she so quickly acknowledged knowing Eleanor and Paula? For the first time in the conversation, she feared she had said too much; given away more than she should. Even though she had not expected to be interrogated she had carefully thought through likely lines of questions. But not this one. Alice could not imagine being asked if she knew her friends.

"Did you see them?" Hoffman asked. "Say hello to them?"

"I'm not sure… perhaps I did…"

"Were you there just before you fainted?"

"No," Alice said, carefully, trying to remember to go back to her story. "I had been in the Grange Museum."

For the first time, Hoffman concluded this elderly woman was evading his questions. But why? What earthly reason did a seventy-something-year-old woman have for lying about where she had been in the minutes before the robbery?

Unless she was, somehow, part of the robbery.

Hoffman caught his breath. *Slow down. Don't scare her. You've got one chance to glean a nugget of information.*

"Mrs. Beauchamp, this is a difficult question to ask, but I have to ask it. Did someone ask you to fall down and pretend to faint? Did they give you money?"

The look of revulsion – or maybe it was fright – that crossed her face told him he had asked the wrong question.

"That's a horrible thing to ask an old woman. I don't want to talk to you anymore."

My god, he thought. *I'm getting too old for this. What the hell am I doing, accusing an old lady of being part of a criminal conspiracy?*

But all the way back to Brookfield, Hoffman could not shake the feeling that he had missed something or had asked the wrong question. The whole fainting business was just too convenient...

* * * * *

Detective Sergeant Alvin Woolsey scanned through the tip line recordings, listening to a few seconds of each one before determining whether it merited further consideration. He was in Chief Sam Ashton's office at the Brookfield Police Department. Ashton's office, in turn, was the only office that afforded any privacy for his effort.

The tip line had been established in the hours after the robbery and the number printed in the *Globe* article that morning. Of course, the investigation had been under the jurisdiction of the Brookfield Police at that time and, to Woolsey's annoyance, the town police had declined to make a copy of the recording and send it to Framingham. Moreover, the town's chief of police insisted on being present while Woolsey listened to the messages.

There were 73 of them. Most were obviously junk: people saying they had been at the fair that day and had seen the armored car – long after the robbery occurred. One caller placed the armored car at the fairgrounds at 11 a.m. Another recounted teenagers with skateboards smoking cigarettes in the vicinity. Woolsey made notes on a few calls but found none worth replaying until the 47th:

"Uh, hi, this is Dick Oster, 43 Page Hill Road in Acton. I don't know if this makes any sense to you, but my family and I were leaving the fair right after five on Sunday. We didn't know the robbery had taken place until we read about it this morning. Anyway, we were parked in the main parking lot – way out at the east end. Ummm, we were walking in a couple of rows of cars but there was this woman – a short elderly woman – who was taking stuff out of a baby stroller. One of those twin strollers. At first I thought it was

diapers but if they were, they were the heaviest diaper bags I've ever seen because she was having a lot of trouble lifting them. Anyway, I saw her put two of these bags into a minivan. She was parked in one of the handicapped spots. It's kind of weird, but after I read about the robbery, I wondered if they might be the transit bags that were in the photo."

Woolsey replayed the message and jotted down the caller's information.

The rest of the calls were about suspicious people at the fair including several possible terrorists. A few singled out cars and vans parked in the area Hoffman had identified in his written report as the likely transfer point for the bags. One man said he had been parked against the fence and that there were shoe prints on the roof and hood of his SUV. Woolsey made note of that caller as well.

"Slim pickings," Chief Ashton said, commiserating.

"You never know what you're going to get from a tip line," Woolsey said. "For the most part, people only see what they expect to see. But sometimes you get lucky."

As Woolsey drove toward Acton, he ran his finger down the page of Detective Hoffman's notes:

Gate attendant Pete Baumeister reported an elderly woman leaving the fair through the Main Gate just after the robbery and less than half an hour after entering the fair. Woman declined to have hand stamped to return to fair. Woman was pushing a twin stroller with sun visor down and screen mesh in place. Woman described as gray haired, five feet or less, 100 lbs. and wearing white tee shirt with 'world's greatest grandma' or similar message.

The timing of the two reports made it likely the two witnesses had observed the same woman. What would be in a twin stroller that was the size and shape of diaper bags, but have sufficient weight that it would give a hundred-pound woman difficulty lifting? As ridiculous as it appeared on the face of it, money fit the description.

Valerie Oster, a pretty woman in her mid-thirties, answered the door and said her husband was at work. She remembered a woman putting something in a minivan but said they were at least a hundred feet from the woman and never stopped to take a closer look.

"Neither Dick nor I mentioned it to one another at the time and I had forgotten about it until we read the article," the woman said. "We didn't even know there was a robbery until we saw the paper at breakfast. Then Dick got all excited about seeing that woman."

"Did you also see her?" Woolsey asked.

"Just for a second," the woman said. "I was trying to keep the kids together. That doesn't leave a lot of time to enjoy the scenery or take in the sights."

"Does your husband ever see other things like this? Things that look as though they're part of something mysterious?"

She shook her head and laughed. "Dick's an engineering manager. He always says he doesn't believe anything until he can take it apart and see how it works."

"But it didn't strike you that way."

"I had two kids to ride herd on. But do I think that little old lady robbed the armored car? No way. She was *tiny*."

Valerie Oster got her husband on the phone at the company where he was employed. The Osters had a speaker phone in their kitchen.

"Walk me through the sequence of events," Woolsey said. "You're leaving the fair. You're headed for your car. What do you see?"

"We were angling toward our car, maybe two rows deep from the main gate," Dick Oster said. "I noticed a woman unloading a stroller right up against the fence along the south side of the fairgrounds and I remember thinking that I wish I had been able to get a spot like that. Then, I realized those were reserved for people with handicapped plates. As we pulled even with her car..."

"How far away were you from it?" Woolsey asked.

"Hundred feet. Maybe a little less."

"And what kind of car was it?"

"Minivan. I don't know the make. They all look alike to me."

"Color?"

"Light blue or gray."

Woolsey turned to Valerie Oster. "Does that sound right to you?"

"I agree about the color. More likely a light blue. And I'd say it was a Chrysler or Plymouth. It definitely wasn't a Honda. Those are more distinctive."

Woolsey nodded. "Go on, Mr. Oster."

"It was an elderly woman – at least in her sixties – and she was short. Probably five feet tall because she wasn't all that much taller than the carriage. She was fairly slender as older people go. I mean she wasn't fat."

"What was she wearing?"

"I have no idea," Dick Oster said.

"Pink shorts and a white tee shirt," Valerie Oster said. "That's the one thing that stuck in my mind."

"And what was she doing?"

"She had just lifted a bag or something out of the stroller – it was one of those side-by-side twin strollers," Dick Oster said. "I figured it was a diaper bag at first but she had a devil of a time getting it into the minivan. Then she took another bag, the same size, and apparently just as heavy."

"Just the two bags?"

"I have no way of knowing. We were headed away from her by that time."

"What color was the bag?"

"White or buff-colored."

What color was the stroller?"

"Dark blue," Dick Oster said.

"Does that sound right to you, Mrs. Oster?"

"Like I said, I was taking care of two kids, making certain they didn't run out into traffic. Dick saw the bags, not me. But the stroller was definitely dark blue."

"You wouldn't happen to have a stroller in the house, would you?"

"Down in the basement with all the other baby stuff."

Woolsey inspected the Oster's stroller, which was for a single infant rather than for two. He tested the seat of the stroller and determined that the seams would likely rip if the seat was loaded with satchels of money. But, if someone reinforced the bottom sufficiently, it might work. In addition to reinforcing the seat, the wheels might need to be replaced with something able to carry more weight. Properly refitted, the one stroller could have held three bags. A twin stroller could hold five satchels easily... and a hundred pounds of money inside them.

Woolsey thanked Valerie Oster and walked back to his cruiser, pondering what he had just heard and seen.

Inside the cruiser, Woolsey tapped the steering wheel. *It was crazy,* he thought. *The idea of using someone's mother as the bag man and getaway driver for a heist. But it was also perfect: the old lady pushes her stroller through the main gate and the only attention she attracts is not asking to have her hand stamped for re-admission.*

Woolsey picked up his microphone and got his captain on the line.

"Terry, how many towns are there in a twenty-mile circle of Brookfield?"

Forty towns, give or take, he was told.

"How many of those have town dumps or transfer stations

open on Monday?"

Virtually none, he was told.

"How about Tuesday?"

Maybe ten. More would be open on Wednesday.

"There's a slim chance someone may throw away a twin stroller tomorrow or Wednesday," Woolsey said. "It will be dark blue and have a heavily reinforced bottom. It may even have special wheels. I've got a strong hunch that it was used to transport that armored car heist money from the fairgrounds to the getaway car. If that stroller shows up, I want to intercept the person who throws it away."

"Jesus Christ," Captain Moynihan said. "Tell me everything."

* * * * *

Samantha Ayers knew that The Stare would not work on Don Zimmerman. Don Zimmerman, a chunky, seventeen-year-old boy with curly brown hair, appeared to have only a tenuous grasp on his own physical existence. He was probably a whiz at computers and video games, but only because they moved at a speed he could control and existed in a world of microprocessors. Here, in the world of reality, things happened at a painfully slow speed. As a result, Don Zimmerman was falling asleep.

"Think," Samantha said, slapping his hand.

Zimmerman blinked and tried to place this woman in a world he could understand. His hand stung. His Wii never did that to him.

"Sunday afternoon, 5 p.m.," Samantha repeated. "You're at the fair. You went to the park by the administration building. It smells rotten there and none of your friends are hanging around. You start walking back into the main part of the fair. You see the van pull in. What happens next?"

Zimmerman nodded slowly. It was like backing up a DVD and pushing the 'frame advance' button for the cool stop-motion effects.

"It's like, not really an armored car," he said. "It's just a big white van with writing on the side."

"How far away were you from the van?"

"Couple of feet. It didn't hit me or nothing."

"You looked around," Samantha prompted. "What did you see?"

Zimmerman advanced the frame in his mind. It was cool that he could step into this mental game and look around as though he were a live-action figure inside a static display. That he had always possessed such abilities, and that it came standard equipment as something called *imagination,* did not occur to him.

He closed his eyes and pressed his fingers to his temples. "The van comes to a stop. The doors open. Couple of guys in uniforms get out."

"Now look at anything else in your field of vision. What's there?"

Zimmerman nodded. "Couple of old ladies coming out of the building on the left."

The Flowers and Horticulture Building, Samantha thought. "What else?" she said.

Zimmerman, his eyes still closed and his fingers still on his temples, swiveled his head several times. "Nothing else," he said.

"Then describe the two old ladies."

"One's, like, my grandmother's age. Blonde hair and fat. The other one is my mom's age or a little older. Brown hair and kind of thin."

Two more potential witnesses, Samantha thought. *All I have to do is find them.*

"How were they dressed?"

"The old lady has on slacks and a blouse. The one my mom's age has on slacks and a tee shirt."

"Long hair? Short? Curly?"

Zimmerman shook his head. "The fat lady has short hair. The skinny one's hair comes down to her shoulders."

Two needles in a haystack, she thought. "What happens next?"

Zimmerman advanced a frame. "The two guards walk into the building. The two old ladies walk toward the van. The guys go into the building. That's when I hear the scream from up the walkway. I, like, break into a run because I figure someone fell off one of the rides and there'd be all these body parts." Zimmerman opened his eyes and shrugged. "Instead, it was just this really old lady sprawled out on the sidewalk."

"Did you see anyone walking toward the van as you're running to the screams?"

Zimmerman closed his eyes and bit his lip. "Couple of people were headed toward me, but as soon as they heard the screaming, they all turned around and started back. That lady, like, really caused a panic."

She asked Zimmerman a few more questions but got no further useful information.

But she had a description of two potential witnesses. And they hadn't shown up in any of the canvasses of fairgoers by the policemen who fanned out in the first fifteen minutes asking anyone who might have seen the robbery. The two women would likely have seen the two men who the half-blind guy had seen walking up behind the guards as they put the money in the van.

Then again, Zimmerman was a dubious witness. He, too, had not come forward and there was the possibility he was inventing details to please his interrogator. Samantha sighed and called the fair office.

"Tell me who ran that exhibit in the flower show building at the time of the robbery," she said. It took two more calls to get the names of Eleanor Strong and Paula Winters, both of whom lived in Hardington.

* * * * *

Forty-five minutes later, Samantha was at the home of Eleanor Strong. As soon as the woman answered the door, Samantha was startled by how closely this woman tied to the description of one of the women provided by Don Zimmerman. Overweight, blonde hair and somewhere in her sixties, which would seem ancient to a teenager.

Samantha showed the women her insurance credentials and asked if she might have a few minutes. "We've got very few leads on this thing and I need every bit of help I can find," she said.

The woman invited her in and led her to a kitchen sitting area. Samantha looked around and saw the trappings of a woman who lived alone. A single plate and coffee cup were drying on the kitchen counter. Cookbooks lined two shelves of a bookcase. On the kitchen counter were several photos of a somewhat younger Strong with a man eight or ten years older than her. There were no photos of children anywhere to be seen. Iced tea was offered and accepted. They sat at a small table in a nook just outside the kitchen. To all appearances, this was where the woman ate all her meals.

"I've already told the police everything I know," the woman said, pouring the iced tea.

"You and Mrs. Winters were the people watching over the flower displays?"

"We were the docents for the flower show," the woman said, correcting Samantha gently. "We were there from two to six."

"Around five o'clock, you and Mrs. Winters left the building?"

The woman nodded. "We went to get watering cans. The exhibits needed to be watered every afternoon because of the heat."

"You went outside the front of the building and were walking toward the administration building when the armored car arrived?"

The woman shifted in her chair perceptibly and sipped at her tea before answering. "No," she said. "We went out the back of the building. The watering cans were by a back door. We filled them when we first came on duty and were allowing the water in the cans to warm up to air temperature. It's important not to shock the flowers with cold water."

The answer confused Samantha. She also noted the shift in body language. "There's no chance that you went out the front entrance."

"None at all," the woman said, taking another sip of her iced tea.

Samantha paused to catch her breath. "I spoke this morning with a boy who was in the vicinity of the building when the armored car arrived. He said he saw two women – one whose description sounded much like you – walk out of the flower exhibit and toward the armored car as it arrived."

The woman gave a slow shake of her head and sipped some more tea. "He was mistaken or he saw someone else," she said, then added, "There were a number of people going in and out of the flower show. Most of them were women and more than a few were my age. I don't doubt but that your witness saw two women, but it wasn't Paula or me."

Samantha leaned in. "If you saw something and are afraid to tell the police, I understand. But I'm not the police. I work for the insurance company and just want to recover the money from whomever stole it. If you were threatened…"

The woman put down her glass with a thud. "The boy with whom you spoke saw someone else," the woman said, her words clear and strong. "Paula and I left by the rear door. There were perhaps twenty people in the exhibit, any one of which will attest that we went out by the rear exit and came back in the same way."

"I'm sorry, Mrs. Strong," Samantha said. "I wasn't trying to accuse you of withholding information."

"Then it's amazing what you can do without trying," the woman said. "Any one or two of those twenty people *could* have left, and any visitor *would* have left by the front entrance. The rear exit was not for use by the general public. Only docents could use that door. We were gone less than a minute – more like thirty seconds – and when we came back, two children were pushing over floral displays and their parents were doing absolutely nothing."

That's part of the explanation, Samantha thought. *She's been reprimanded by the flower show people for leaving her post.*

"I'm sorry all that had to happen while you were on duty," Samantha said. "Did you know anyone in the exhibit at the time you left?

The woman shook her head. "No. I saw some familiar faces earlier in the day, but none around five o'clock."

"There were two women," Samantha prompted. "One about your age, blonde hair worn short, dressed in slacks and a blouse. The other was probably about fifty, brown hair and apparently on the thin side. She was in slacks and a tee shirt."

The woman gave a surprised look for an instant, then said, "You just described half the peoples inside that building."

Dead end, Samantha thought. *Unless...*

"I'll try Mrs. Winters, just in case," Samantha said, rising from her chair. "I know she's also in Hardington. Is her home far from here?"

The woman shook her head with a grim look on her face. "I suspect Paula isn't very keen on visitors right now. She's going into the hospital tomorrow for surgery. Cancer surgery."

The last two words caught Samantha completely by surprise.

"I guess I'll wait before I talk to her," she said quietly.

The woman offered a refill on the iced tea but Samantha, now standing and having collected her purse, declined. She was shown to the door.

Samantha left quickly but pulled into the first driveway out of sight of Eleanor Strong's home to think through what she had just learned. On the surface it had all been exactly by the book. The woman had answered all questions forthrightly. But everything else about the interview had been wrong. Most critically, Samantha would have given long odds that the two women seen by Don Zimmerman were Eleanor Strong and Paula Winters and that, were she to go to Winters' home, she would be greeted by a slender, fifty-ish woman with brown hair.

There had to be a reason for the lie and the most probable reason was that these two women had seen the robbers. They, alone among all the fairgoers, could identify the two men who pulled off the robbery. To avoid acknowledging that fact, they had agreed upon a story that they had gone out the back door of the building and never glanced out the front, much less been in the vicinity of the armored car. They were afraid to tell the truth out of fear for their safety.

Samantha didn't blame them. Years of watching television and films sent the clear – and largely accurate – message that witnesses weren't safe from someone determined to silence those who had seen them commit a crime. The simplest expedient was for a witness to say nothing to the police. If questioned by the police, two witnesses could agree on a story that placed them somewhere else – such as at the back of the building instead of at the front.

But the thieves who had stolen the gate receipts from the fair were not violent men. They had, in fact, distinguished themselves by the absence of guns and the use of clever ruses to clear the area and disable the guards. These men would not kill a witness. Eleanor Strong and Paula Winters needed to be made to see that they had nothing to fear.

Samantha turned her car around and drove back to Eleanor Strong's house. She knocked on the front door and the woman appeared, holding a telephone in one hand.

Get it all out, Samantha thought. *Get through to her before she closes the door.*

"Mrs. Strong, I just want you to know that nothing bad is going to happen to you and Mrs. Winters if you give me a description of the men you saw in the park outside of the administration building. Those men aren't violent. They used their heads to steal that money, not weapons. And all I want is to get back the money so my company doesn't have to pay the insurance claim. I can track them down. I can even make certain the police are never involved. I know how to do that. I was a policeman, my father has been a policeman for more than thirty years. I swear to you, you have nothing to fear."

The woman looked impassively through Samantha's plea. Finally, the woman said, "Give me your card and, if I remember anything I saw, I'll call you."

Yes, thought Samantha.

* * * * *

"That was that insurance investigator again," Eleanor said after she closed and locked the door. "Did you hear any of it?"

"Enough," Paula said. "She's convinced you and I saw the robbery and are fearful for our lives."

"So, why don't we give her a description?" Eleanor said. "Two swarthy Hispanic men in ski masks."

"Because no one wears a ski mask in August," Paula said. "And because if they had on ski masks, how could you tell they were Hispanic? Or 'swarthy', whatever that means. Also, the men don't exist. So after she's run out of swarthy, Hispanic men with ski masks in their back pockets, she's going to come back to us and ask for a better description. We don't want that. Whoever the 'boy' was that she spoke to, he saw us, but he's probably not a reliable witness. So, we stay with our story because no one can shake it as long as we agree on what we did."

"You remember the police detective we spoke with yesterday?" Paula continued. "Well, he was here a little while ago. And he didn't suspect a thing. He wanted to know if I remembered anything more from when we were in back of the building. In fact – and I'm still trying to wrap my mind around this one – I think he asked me out on a date. I mean, it was for lunch, but it was, 'may I call you when this is all over'."

"It's never going to be over," Eleanor said. "I mean, I'm thrilled for you. But we've got nearly half a million dollars sitting in paper bags in Jean's attic and police running all around looking for who did it. I don't know if our lives can ever go back to the way it was before."

"You're sorry we did it?" Paula asked.

"Good lord, no!" Eleanor said. "I wouldn't change it for the world. But I don't like policemen or insurance investigators knocking at my door. It bothers me no end that the fair says we got one amount but there's far more in those bags. It's the uncertainty. I never thought it would be like this. It was supposed to be simpler."

15.

The call came in on a cell phone, one of the kind where the minutes were purchased with cash and the identity of the telephone's owner was untraceable.   It was the same phone Gordon McLeod had used that morning in speaking to his contact. McLeod recognized its distinctive chirp and reached into his coat pocket.

"You'll have to excuse me for a minute, ladies and gentlemen," he said. "This is probably my daughter. I promise I won't be but a minute."

The people around the table smiled and nodded, pleased that a man as important as Gordon McLeod would consider a call from his daughter worth interrupting a meeting.

McLeod went into his office and closed the door.

"What?" he said.

"We got a problem," said the Latino voice on the other end of the line. "Erskine says he can't make the second deposit. Some insurance investigator went into his office this morning and scared the shit out of him because he bagged the money on his own. She thinks he skimmed the receipts and covered it up with the robbery."

"By the way, that's what I still think, too," McLeod said. "But as to the rest of the deposits, the fair runs for nine days. He's used up three of them…"

"He says he'll give you the rest of the money in cash today."

"Dammit, I don't want cash," McLeod said through gritted teeth. He wanted to scream but knowing there was a room full of people on the other side of the wall. "I can't use cash. He's got six days to get the rest of the money into the bank.   There's no alternative for him. You tell him in exactly those words."

"That's what I'm going to do. And this time, it will be in person."

"What about finding the first tranche?"

"The first what?"

"The first $350,000. You said you have people on the inside."

"I'm still waiting for a call. You'll know as soon as I do."

McLeod clicked the 'off' button on the phone. He resisted the urge to hurl the phone to the ground and grind it under his shoe into the carpeted floor. He needed to regain his composure before rejoining the meeting. Clients would lose faith in him if they saw him visibly upset by a phone call, even if it was ostensibly from his nine-year-old daughter.

Who in hell had known about the transfer? Who could have pulled off the robbery while first so conveniently clearing the area of people? It had to be Erskine. There was no other rational explanation. The notion that some gang had serendipitously picked the day he was arranging for the deposit of the first of the money was ludicrous. They knew the timing of the armored car too well.

If it turned out to be Erskine, he was going to have him killed.

McLeod took a deep breath. The phone went back into his pocket. He opened the door of the conference room and walked in, smiling.

"My daughter tells me she taught our dog to roll over," McLeod said. "I've been trying for five years without luck. She apparently has a gift."

There were more appreciative smiles all around the table. McLeod sat back down and resumed the meeting.

16.

Detective Sergeant Woolsey watched the printer spew out pages. There were fifty names per page and he had stopped counting at thirty pages. On these pages were the names and addresses of every registered vehicle with either a handicapped plate or assigned a handicapped placard within a twenty mile radius of Brookfield. The search had further been refined to minivans more than three years old and omitted colors such as red and black that the Osters would have readily remembered and volunteered.

The printer stopped. Woolsey picked up the last sheet.

Total records found: 2247.

This is not my lucky day, he thought, thumbing through the stack of sheets. He picked up a pen, intent upon culling the list to a more manageable number. Then, he had an inspiration. *In this business, you have to create your own luck.*

He set the pen down, picked up his phone and called the Brookfield Fair manager's office.

Half an hour later, Woolsey was taking in the disheveled appearance of Tony Erskine's office. A fair needed to be run efficiently if it was to make money. This office was chaotic with mounds of papers in every corner. This disorganization was offensive to Woolsey. Within the state police, neatness was a mandate. Each detective's annual evaluation included a section about the orderliness of files. Bonus points were awarded to those who consistently showed tidiness, and sloth meant demerits and a slower ascendancy up the pay scale.

"I've already told the police everything I know," Erskine said, his face showing exasperation. Woolsey noted the beginnings of perspiration beads on the man's forehead, a telltale sign that Erskine had been lying then and was lying now.

"You spoke with the local police," Woolsey said. "Now you get to tell me. It's our investigation now." The detective lifted a pile of papers from a chair and placed them on the floor. He sat down and stared, impassively, at Erskine.

"We had cash gate receipts of $127,640," Erskine said, the sweat now pouring down his face. "We turned them over to the two guards. They were robbed in the driveway. What more can I say?"

"You can start with how many people knew the armored car's routine," Woolsey said. "How many people knew what time it arrived? How many knew there were only two guards? How long it took to make the transfer?"

Erskine shook his head. "Everyone in this office knew the schedule. It was no secret."

Woolsey smiled, his point made. "So, you're telling me that after just one day, some thieves who had absolutely no connection to this fair managed to guess the armored car's routine. Then, those guys or their accomplices sprayed the front of this building with deer repellent without anyone inside the building noticing the smell or being told of the smell. And, finally, a couple of guys were able to hang around the building, unobserved until the van arrived, then overpowered the guards with home-made pepper spray."

Erskine spoke in a resigned tone, his arms limp at his side. "The people who work inside this building tend to stay here all day. No one wanders around the fairgrounds for the heck of it. They all have assigned duties in here. The people who work outside have no reason to come into this building. If I find them inside this building, I tell them to get back to work..."

"Do you have a mother?" Woolsey asked, cutting off Erskine's explanation.

"What the hell do you mean, do I have a mother?"

"That's my question: is your mother alive?"

"Yes."

"Where does she live? How old is she?"

"In New Jersey. She's eighty-something."

"I'd like for you to pull together the people in this office," Woolsey said. "I want to know if any of them have a parent with a minivan that has a handicapped plate or permit."

"You want them to drop everything they're doing?" Erskine asked, incredulous.

"Here's my problem," Woolsey said, slamming his fist on Erskine's desk. "This crime is too convenient. It reeks of being an inside job. And the best explanation I have on how the money was taken out here is that a sixty-year-old woman pushed it out in a baby carriage. I'm also going to need to talk to the ticket-taker who saw the woman and put him together with a sketch technician. And I want to talk to your staff – now."

Twenty minutes later, Woolsey had the information that four staff members had parents or grandparents with handicapped-license-bearing minivans. Two of them, however, were presently in Florida, one of them hadn't driven in over a year, and one was a widowed male.

Either the 'world's greatest grandma' with the money-filled carriage was a chimera, or else it wasn't an inside job. But every sense of intuition in Woolsey's body told him he had the first real lead in the case, and that the perpetrators were people who knew the route and schedule of the armored car.

It was time to turn up the heat.

* * * * *

Tony Erskine washed his face again in the tiny sink in the men's bathroom of the administration building. He could blot away the sweat that was pouring down his face but as fast as he did there was more to take its place. No matter how long he ran the water he couldn't make it cold enough to stop the sweating.

It was all going wrong. It was all going disastrously wrong and, in the end, he was going to be the fall guy.

If he wasn't dead.

The town detective had seen he was lying. Brenda Chadwick, who had no idea of what was going on, had tried to cover for him and the detective had picked up on her discomfort. Then, last night, McLeod or Boz had sent around some goon with a gun. The goon had put his gun up under Erskine's chin and demanded to know where the money was. Erskine thought he was going to die then and there. He had been honest: *he didn't know.*

And he still didn't know. Somehow, someone had figured out the armored car's routine. That someone almost certainly knew that yesterday was the first deposit of McLeod's cash. So, that someone probably worked for McLeod and was double-crossing his boss. But he didn't dare say that to the goon with the gun because he didn't have a name, much less any proof.

How do you tell a man like McLeod he's being ripped off by his own people?

He knew it was going to end badly because of the insurance girl. She had waltzed in this morning and, in half an hour, learned that he had taken the fair receipts into his office and stuffed the bags himself. He had filled out the deposit slip, something he had never done before – giving Brenda Chadwick a deposit slip for the amount they had together counted and putting the actual amount of the deposit on the ticket that went into the envelope that was shipped with the satchels. The insurance investigator was smart: she understood that it was the little breaks in office routines that pointed to fraud.

Except that she had concluded that his goal was to send the bank *less* money than the fair took in. Not *more.*

Skimming. Skimming was for small-time crooks. Whatever McLeod had done made skimming a few thousand off the top of some gate receipts look like a game of Monopoly. If anyone had asked Erskine to open the safe in his office, they would have gotten an eye full.

And now Boz said McLeod was demanding that he deposit the next installment. Right! Like he could put another $350,000 on top the fair receipts and fill out another dummy deposit ticket and have no one notice.

Jesus Christ, didn't they *understand*? It was over. There was no way in hell everyone wouldn't be watching his every move for the next week. He was going to have to make a big show of doing everything by the book. And, even then, his staff was going to think he was the inside man.

Except, of course, unless it was someone on his staff who had masterminded the theft, as unlikely as it seemed. That was a thought at least as chilling as the culprit being one of McLeod's own men.

And now, there was a state policeman on the case. Who not only didn't believe him, but who had some mad idea about using someone's mother to wheel the money out of the fair in a stroller. And it was clear the trooper had something up those gray sleeves of his. He was going to pull some kind of a stunt.

The worst part was that Erskine never had a choice in it. When McLeod approached him two weeks earlier he had resisted. Then, McLeod offered him the alternative: the loss of everything he, Erskine, had built up in the past few years. The whole new identity and the respectability he had achieved. Dammit, he was *good* at this job. The fair was making money. The fairgrounds, once unused most of the year, were rented for more than thirty weeks a year and they were covered in snow much of the rest of the time.

And the state trooper had asked the question about his mother. It had come out of the blue. Before he could think, he had told the trooper the truth. What if the trooper had demanded he call his mother? That would have been a riot: *"Hello, Mrs. Erskine, do you have a son named Tony? Oh, your name isn't Erskine, it's Marsh and you have a son but his name is Bill..."*

What an idiot I am.

It was all going to come undone. And there was not one damn thing he could do about it except watch it happen.

* * * * *

Hoffman went over his notes, seeking to refresh his memory. His encounter with Alice Beauchamp still bothered him in a way he could not put his finger on. Chief Ashton cleared his throat and Hoffman looked up.

"Your buddy Woolsey was here this morning," Ashton said. "Listening to civic-minded citizens who thought they saw something yesterday afternoon."

"Apart from the fact that he isn't my buddy, what did he go away with?" Hoffman asked.

Ashton took out a note pad. "Guy from Fitchburg named Schuster was parked next to the fence near the robbery scene. He said there were shoe prints all over the top of his SUV. And a guy in Acton named Oster who saw a little old lady putting what could have been moneybags into her minivan, which was parked in a handicapped spot."

"Shoe prints on top of an SUV next to the fence means kids were jumping into the fair, not out of it," Hoffman said. "I'd like to hear the tape of the guy talking about the little old lady. There was one pushing a baby stroller out of the fair at just the right time."

Ashton went back to his notes. "The guy in Acton said she was taking whatever it was out of a stroller. Said it was heavy."

Hoffman stood up. "You got a number for the guy?"

"Right here," Ashton said, tearing off the top page of his notes.

* * * * *

Jean Sullivan poured out another cup of coffee for Alice Beauchamp. Alice's hand shook visibly as she grasped the cup, sloshing coffee into the saucer. Alice was in the third re-telling of her encounter with the detective. Each time, the detective became more unfriendly, his questions more pointed, his countenance more menacing.

"He knows, Jean," Alice said. "He doesn't just suspect. He *knows*. He sees right through that falling down business. I'm going to be the undoing of this entire plan. He was in my garden! He was looking right at the pepper plants, putting two and two together. I'll bet he'll have policemen going through my garden tonight with flashlights, pulling up pepper plants. They've got some machine that will compare my hot peppers with the ones on the guards and they'll see they're the same."

"I threw away the dish detergent," Alice continued. "When I got home I poured better than half a bottle of it down the drain and threw the empty bottle into the recycling bin out in back of the complex. I hope no one saw me. I hope that wasn't a stupid thing to have done."

"I think you're being overly sensitive," Jean said, trying to calm her friend. "You grow hot peppers. So do thousands of people. And, weren't those last year's peppers you used for the spray? They were already dried. So, no one can say they were the same peppers. And I sincerely doubt that anyone would care for one instant that you took a bottle out to the recycling bin. That's what you're supposed to do."

Alice thought that it was easy for Jean to offer such reassurances. Jean had been spared any visits from policemen. She was the one member of the Garden Club Gang who had completely escaped the notice of anyone. No one knocked at her door or called her on the telephone. Jean's words sounded soothing, though. Perhaps she worried too much.

But Jean was also concerned. Alice was given to exaggeration, but the story she told was one that Paula and Eleanor should hear. Also, it caused Jean to fret about the money in her attic and the stroller in her garage.

"That detective asked me if I had fallen down and *pretended* to faint," Alice said for the third time. "He wanted to know if someone had given me money. He was horrible."

"But you told him you had been in the Grange Museum, like we agreed, didn't you?" Jean asked.

Alice nodded. "But I could tell he didn't believe me."

"Did he ask you anything about what you saw in the museum?"

"No, and I'm glad he didn't," Alice said. "Because I've never stepped foot inside the place. I don't even know why there's a Grange Museum at the fair. I know what a Grange is but why a Grange Museum? Do you suppose it might be named for someone called Grange?"

Jean was silent for a moment while she thought.

"We need to go back to the fair," Jean said. "We need to get your alibi straight. The next time someone questions you, you're going to know all about that place, chapter and verse."

They drove to the fair in Alice's car, which lacked a handicapped sticker. Though it was Monday, the main parking was full and they were directed to the Midway lot at the north end of the fairgrounds. Jean pulled a hundred dollar bill from her purse, one of the eight that Eleanor had passed around that morning. 'Mad Money' Eleanor had called it. Well, Jean thought, this money was going to be used to ensure that Alice's alibi held up under any cross-examination.

It was nearly 5 p.m. and the Midway was choked with people. The rides all played noisy rock and roll songs and children – and especially teenaged girls – screamed inappropriately, Alice thought. The two women made their way south past the Ferris wheel and the ride that tipped people at dangerous angles. People screamed inside a 'fun house' that seemed like anything but amusing. Didn't these children have parents? And did their parents mind that their daughters dressed in tight-fitting, midriff-baring tank tops and shorts that were, well, too short?

Then they were down to the horses and the noise was less obtrusive. The crowds were better behaved. Now there were families looking at barns containing goats and pigs and sheep. An entire building was devoted to raising bees for making honey and pollinating fields.

The 'Grange Museum' turned out to be the Grange Building, which also housed an exhibit chronicling the history of the Brookfield Fair, thus giving the building – at least for purposes of fair maps – the name 'Grange/Museum'. They learned that granges were alive and well in the twenty-first century. There were exhibits of quilts made by granges around the state as well as old farm implements. In twenty minutes, Alice memorized enough of the exhibit to be able to answer any questions from any police officer. For the first time since the detective's car had pulled up to the community garden, she felt supremely confident.

Coming out of the building, they had the option of passing by the administration building or cutting across a picnic area. But something odd was going on in front of the administration building. The armored car was there, as were several television news trucks. A crowd had gathered around a state trooper in full gray uniform.

Hesitantly, Alice and Jean made their way to the back of the crowd, which included both reporters and curious fairgoers. The state trooper directed his words to the reporters and television cameras closest to him, but his words were clearly audible to everyone in the vicinity.

"....Happened yesterday afternoon just after five o'clock. The thieves overpowered the two guards using a home-made pepper spray. They then fled the scene and escaped without detection. We're looking for the help of anyone who may have been in this vicinity at the time the armored car arrived yesterday. We're especially looking for one woman who may have information that would be helpful to our investigation."

The state trooper held up a drawing, one of those composite sketches police artists were always drawing in the crime shows on television. Jean and Alice were too far back in the crowd to make out details on the sheet of paper the trooper was holding up. "This woman was leaving the fair just at the time of the robbery. She left through the main gate and was pushing a blue, twin stroller baby carriage. Her car, a pale-colored minivan with either handicapped plates or a handicapped access placard, was parked less than a hundred feet from the gate. She was wearing pink shorts and a tee shirt that said 'World's Greatest Grandma'. She is believed to be in her mid-sixties. She is about five feet tall and weighs about a hundred pounds and has gray hair. She is not a suspect, but she is believed to have information that could be of value in solving this case. If anyone knows this woman, please contact the number at the bottom of this sketch..."

Alice and Jean did not wait for the rest of the trooper's statement or the questions from the reporters. They especially did not wait for a copy of the composite drawing that was being handed out by a young woman trooper. Instead, they walked as fast as they could through the crowds, back out the Midway gate to Alice's car.

Alice beeped impatiently at the exiting traffic in front of her. Jean, in the passenger seat, began formulating her own action plan.

"Getting rid of the tee shirt is easy," Jean said. "I hate that thing, anyway. As soon as I get home, I'm going to cut it into a hundred pieces. And I don't need the handicapped pass. I never use it. Thank goodness it isn't a license plate. No one can prove I didn't throw it away after Al died. And, I've still got some of Al's metal tools down in the basement. I can turn that stroller into a pile of metal scrap in about twenty minutes…"

"And what happens when five hundred people call the state police and say that it's you in the drawing?" Alice said, leaning on her horn again.

"I don't know five hundred people," Jean replied. "And only the three of you know I was at the fair on Sunday. If anyone asks me, I was home pulling weeds. And I dare them to prove otherwise."

"You're not frightened?"

"Frightened? No!" Jean said. "On my guard? Absolutely. And I think we all need to get together this evening and make certain we understand what we have to do from here. I know Paula says we shouldn't meet, but this is a change in circumstances."

"How can you be so calm about it?" Alice asked and gunned her engine to be the last car to make the turn out of the parking lot and onto North Street.

"I put up with Al for thirty years," Jean said softly. "When you have to cope with someone like that, you find all kinds of ways to be calm while you work your way out of situations."

Alice looked over at her friend with surprise. In all the years she had known Jean, she had never spoken things like that; never said an unkind word about her husband.

Without question, committing this robbery has changed us all, Alice thought. *If nothing else, life from now on is going to be a lot more interesting.*

* * * * *

Samantha Ayers sat on the sofa in her apartment, catching up on paperwork she had brought home from her office while her television droned in the background. It was a few minutes after six. She had microwaved a frozen pizza and thrown together a green salad. Those items, comprising her dinner, sat on a tray off to her side. In one hand was a can of Diet Coke, in the other, a pen to fill out forms.

At twenty-seven, Samantha had not given up on finding the right man, but she was beginning to believe that he did not exist. Her height excluded that sizeable percentage of men who could not bear to be seen with someone who was five-foot-ten in flats. Her five years as a police officer scared off many men who demanded a docile, ultra-feminine companion. Her present occupation as an insurance investigator with its requirement for an aggressive personality and take-charge attitude scared off still others or else attracted the kind of man who wanted to be dominated. Added to that was the indisputable fact that she had never learned to cook and had no interest in learning.

Her good looks, on the other hand, drew considerable interest. Though her father and grandfather would have apoplexy at the thought, she did not believe that skin color was a barrier to romance. First dates were seldom a problem; it was the second dates that were rare. Once she began talking about herself and her work, most men seemed to lose interest.

It was also a matter of finding someone whom *she* found interesting. That she was dining alone tonight, in front of the television while doing office work, was eloquent testimony that her social life was severely lacking and unlikely to improve any time soon.

As she worked through the forms in front of her, Samantha's mind was never very far from the Brookfield Fair heist. She had reached the tentative conclusion that Tony Erskine had engineered the whole thing as a means of hiding an embezzlement of funds.

The fact that he had filled the bags in the privacy of his office set off alarm bells in her mind. There was a very real chance that the guards had taken away satchels stuffed with cut-up newspapers from the lobby, then been relieved of those bags by cohorts of Erskine, and that Erskine had driven home that evening with $127,000 in his trunk.

Adding credence to her theory was her discovery this afternoon following a thorough records search that Tony Erskine apparently did not exist until a few years ago. The social security number he used to gain employment had been issued in 1965 to an infant named Anthony Erskine in California, but there had been no activity associated with it up until just a few months before he was hired as manager of the Brookfield Fair. While she had no access to the resume he would have presented to the hiring committee, she suspected that the references and prior employment history contained in it were forgeries.

Who was he? Her plan for tomorrow was to take her findings to Mass Casualty's Claims Committee. They would recommend a 'no payment' finding unless the Town of Brookfield, which owned the fairgrounds and was Erskine's employer, produced convincing evidence that the town had not violated its contract with Bay State Transport by placing someone with an assumed identity – and who therefore might be a felon – in the chain of custody for the cash that was being given to those guards. That action would unmask Erskine and get Mass Casualty off the hook for the robbery proceeds.

It would also, Samantha noted, get her yet another letter of commendation from the company's headquarters office and earn her a bonus of about $3,000. Not bad for two days' work.

Samantha heard the phrase 'fair robbery' and glanced up at the television. She had just taken a drink of her soda and nearly choked as the Channel 5 reporter held up a drawing of a little old lady.

"*State police are looking for this woman, whom authorities say is in her sixties, is about five feet, and weighs about a hundred pounds. The state police will say only that she may have information of use to their investigation of yesterday's fair robbery. They refuse to say if they believe she was involved. Instead, state police stress that she was leaving the fair just after the robbery and was pushing a blue twin stroller and wearing pink shorts and a white tee shirt that said 'world's greatest grandma'. She is believed to have been driving a pale-colored minivan with either handicapped plates or a handicapped access windshield placard. Anyone who believes they know this woman is urged to contact the state police at the toll-free hotline at the bottom of the screen...*"

Samantha put down her paperwork and grabbed for a pad of paper. She knew from her law enforcement career that the state police would not be interested in the woman if she was merely a witness who 'might have seen something'. The state police would not assign a dozen troopers to listen to a thousand rambling telephone conversations this evening in hopes of hearing the one that said, 'that's my neighbor' or 'that's Aunt Mary' if the sole purpose was to find out what this woman might have witnessed on a Sunday afternoon at a fair.

The woman was a suspect. And, if she was pushing a baby carriage, she was more than just a suspect. She was likely the bag man for the job, and the state police were after her because someone saw her put something in that minivan.

This is what the world has come to, Samantha thought. *Now grandmas are pulling armored car heists.*

As quickly as she had thought it, Samantha tried to put it out of her mind. *No, it's so far off the scale of demographic possibilities that it isn't even worth considering.*

And yet...

On her pad of paper, Samantha had previously written 'Erskine' in a box. Under it were three more boxes labeled,

'Robber A', 'Robber B' and 'Getaway man'.

Samantha ripped off that sheet of paper and drew three boxes on a fresh sheet.

Little, spaced-out Donny Zimmerman had seen what was almost certainly Paula Winters and Eleanor Strong walking out of the front entrance of the Flowers and Horticulture Building toward the armored car, just as it pulled up. Samantha has assumed Eleanor Strong was reluctant to acknowledge their presence because they had seen the faces of the robbers.

Samantha wrote the women's names in two of the boxes.

What if *they* were the robbers?

It would all fit: the deer repellent to clear out the teenagers in the park. The home-made, super-strength pepper spray encased in liquid detergent. The absence of guns.

And the fact that no one remembered seeing them.

Samantha wrote 'world's greatest grandma' in the third box.

Another fragment came hurtling from the back of her mind. She had just arrived at the fair and joined the Brookfield detective in the EMT van. There had been another woman, one who had fainted and been treated by the EMTs. The woman was gone by the time Samantha and Hoffman interviewed the guards. Hoffman had been handed the woman's chart by mistake. The EMT had said something when Hoffman handed the chart back.

"This one is for the heat stroke lady we treated," the EMT had said. *"Never had someone who was in such bad shape when we got her put up such a fight to say she was all right. I have a feeling she was afraid we'd take her to the emergency room and she'd be charged. And I thought all those Hardington people were rich... She didn't even want to give her name, but her Medicare card said she lives in Hardington. Said she was feeling fine as soon as we gave her something to drink. My guess is she's poor."*

Holy mother of mercy, Samantha thought. *Four of them. Two of them to commit the robbery, one to transport the cash out of the fairgrounds,* and one to create a human pileup on the fairway's main walkway to distract attention. The perfect crime, committed by the world's least likely suspects.

Samantha didn't know who this fourth woman was but she was certain she knew where the woman lived.

Samantha turned on the computer on the coffee table and connected it into the state vehicle insurance database.

Insured owner age = +60 -75

Insured vehicle = minivan

Insured status = handicapped notation + plate/decal

Insured residence = Hardington.

In thirty seconds, the insurance database replied:

10 records found. Print? Y/N

She printed the ten names and addresses. She next called the Brookfield Fire Department.

"Hi, this is Samantha Ayers at Mass Casualty. You did a treat-and-release on a heat-stroke lady yesterday afternoon. We're the fair's insurance carrier and we need to close the loop to make certain there's no claim coming. Can you give me a name and address for the lady? I know she lives in Hardington.... Yes, I'll wait.

A few minutes later, Samantha drew a fourth box on her sheet of paper. In it, she wrote the name 'Alice Beauchamp'.

* * * * *

Chief Ashton and Martin Hoffman watched the Channel 7 newscast on the small set in the chief's office. "What are those guys smoking?" Ashton asked with disbelief.

"Maybe it's not that far-fetched," Hoffman replied. He spread a large piece of paper on Ashton's desk and quickly drew a rudimentary sketch of the portion of the fairground where the robbery had taken place.

Hoffman pointed to the perimeter fence with parking beyond. "I've assumed that two guys threw the satchels over the fence to an accomplice. But neither of the women in the flower show building saw anything when they were out in back, and they were in exactly the right place at the right time. If that was the money cut-off, they would have seen it."

Martin now pointed to the Main Gate, less than 200 feet from where the robbery took place. "But now, assume you've got grandma ready to push the cash out of the fair in a baby carriage – say you've reinforced the frame and added special wheels…"

"Nobody's going to stop grandma," Ashton said.

They were interrupted by a knock on Ashton's doorframe. The second shift dispatcher from the Fire Department, which shared the Public Safety Building with the Police Department, stood with a clipboard in his hand.

Ashton nodded. "What do you need?"

The dispatcher held up the clipboard. "Fire Chief is gone so I thought I'd ask you. There's an insurance lady on the phone who says she needs the name and address of the old lady the EMTs treated at the fair yesterday. Is that OK by you?"

"The insurance lady," Hoffman asked. "Did she give you her name?"

The dispatcher looked down at the clipboard. "Samantha Ayers. Mass Casualty."

"Why did she say she wants the information?"

"She said she's the fair's insurance carrier. She needs to close the loop to make certain the old lady isn't going to file a claim."

"Give her the name," Hoffman said quickly, even though the request had been directed at Ashton.

When the dispatcher left, Ashton asked, "What's that all about?"

Hoffman put a large 'X' on the walkway leading from the fair headquarters building. "Alice Beauchamp is the key to this whole thing," he said excitedly. "When I spoke with her today, I knew something was off but I couldn't put my finger on it. I'll bet you a week's salary that Beauchamp and grandma were both on the inside. Why am I so sure? Because Samantha Ayers doesn't work for the fair's insurance carrier. She works for the courier firm. And I'll bet another week's salary Ms. Ayers just saw that same newscast and put two and two together. Beauchamp creates the distraction – she couldn't have done a better job if she had put up a fence across the road – and grandma collects the money from the robbers and strolls out of the Main Gate. God, it's perfect…"

"A pair of sixty- and seventy-something women planned this heist?" Ashton asked, his voice incredulous.

"I don't know," Hoffman said. "I need time to think. I need to figure out a lot of things." He began writing down ideas on the side of the sheet of paper.

"Well, while you're thinking," Ashton said, "I'm going to call my wife and tell her to have dinner without me. You want your pizza with sausage or pepperoni?"

* * * * *

At State Police headquarters in Framingham, Captain Moynihan and Detective Sergeant Woolsey watched the last of the five segments of the local newscasts featuring Woolsey's press conference in Brookfield.

"You've got regular star quality," Moynihan said, a smile on his face. "We may have to transfer you to the PR squad."

Uncertain of the sincerity of the remark, Woolsey ignored it. "I've also been thinking. I also re-walked the fairgrounds this afternoon," he said. "There was something in that Brookfield detective's notes about another old lady who collapsed and needed medical attention. Completely blocked up the main walkway for a couple of minutes. It got me to thinking: if one old woman was involved, why not two? So, I went to the spot where this woman – Alice Beauchamp, age 71, lives in Hardington – fell. It was perfectly situated and timed to pull attention away from the robbery; *too* perfect in my mind. It's going to be a while before we have enough tips to start culling them. I'm going to drive down to Hardington and talk to this Beauchamp woman right now. If she won't talk at her home, I'll bring her here for questioning. That ought to scare the truth out of her."

Moynihan leaned in and looked Woolsey in the eye. "You're sure about that Beauchamp woman? Does this mean I've finally got something to tell the brass upstairs?"

Woolsey nodded. "You give me two minutes with her in an interrogation room. She'll spill everything."

Moynihan sat silently for a moment, drumming his fingers on the desk. "I think your intuition is right – that woman is involved. But you're not going anywhere. Beauchamp will keep until morning. First, follow up on the tips."

Woolsey was surprised by the adamant response. He started to protest when the phone rang. Woolsey answered, listened for a moment, then hung up and smiled. "We've already got twenty calls to the tip line," he said. "I think we're about to crack this case wide open."

17.

Gordon McLeod was seated at the dinner table with his wife and family when he heard the cell phone chirp from the den. He wiped his mouth with his napkin and started to rise.

His wife looked at him with pleading eyes. "Gordon, you promised…"

He shook his head. "That's the contractor. If I don't take that call, he's going to call the next customer in line and that's going to be the end of your new kitchen for this year."

He saw his wife's eyes relent, just for a fraction of a second.

"I promise I won't be more than a minute. Just long enough to say 'yes' to the price and get a timetable from him."

In the den, McLeod listened but said nothing until he knew the reason for the call.

"We just caught our break," the voice at the other end of the line said. "The woman in the state police sketch is definitely considered a suspect, not just a witness. She pushed the money out of the fair in a baby carriage. My source doesn't know who she is yet, but we've got a link from that woman to another one who was at the fair yesterday. She collapsed and was treated at the same time as the robbery. My source thinks she was a decoy. Her job was to pull a crowd. She was in on it."

"Go after the one whose name you have," McLeod said. "I don't give a damn if it's some old lady. Go after her hard and use muscle. I want that money recovered tonight. Before the police get to it."

"Tonight?"

"Hell, yes, I said tonight," McLeod said.

"Erskine said he didn't make the second deposit this afternoon. He said the place was crawling with police and TV cameras."

"Erskine is an idiot. You tell him he makes the second deposit tomorrow or he'll wish he had never been born."

McLeod snapped shut the phone. He took several deep breaths to regain his composure. *Relax,* he thought. *This thing is nearly over. You're past the crisis.*

McLeod went back to the dining room table less than two minutes after he left, just as promised.

McLeod smiled and put two thumbs up as he spoke. "The contractor says he can do the job within the budget and he can start Tuesday after Labor Day."

"Yay, daddy!" his children said in unison.

18.

The four women sat in Eleanor's living room as the clock struck eight o'clock. They watched yet another replay of the six o'clock news, always freezing on the sketch of the 'woman whom police believe can help with the investigation'.

"It doesn't look a thing like me," Jean said each time. "That woman has a fat face and beady eyes. I don't have a fat face, do I?"

Everyone agreed the woman in the sketch bore little resemblance to Jean, and that's Jean's face was lean and her eyes were kind and not the least bit beady. Moreover, her hair was silver and not gray.

"Who even saw me?" Jean asked. "Except for that ticket-taker who wanted to stamp my hand, I stayed completely out of sight."

"Paula and I didn't think anyone saw us," Eleanor said. "But it didn't stop that insurance woman from coming up with a witness who spotted us coming out of the building."

"And it didn't stop that detective from tracking me down at my garden plot and insinuating I had something to do with it," Alice said.

"Which leaves us with just one course of action over the next few days," Eleanor said, freezing the sketch on the screen as she spoke. "We all have a simple story. Paula and I went out the back of the exhibit. It makes no difference who *thinks* they saw us go out the front of the building, we say we went out the back and we didn't see anything. No one can break that story so long as Paula and I stick to it."

Eleanor continued. "Alice, you collapsed from the heat. You

had been in the Grange Building. If you had asked me this afternoon if I thought it was a good idea to go back to the fair and risk being seen there, I would have strongly discouraged you from doing so. But you went and now you know, at least, that it isn't a 'Grange Museum' but, rather, the Grange Building and it houses a kind of history of farming exhibit. So, no one can break your story and it doesn't matter if no one remembers seeing you there Sunday afternoon because no one ever remembers little old ladies. As Jean pointed out when this got started, we're invisible."

"And, Jean, you were never at the fair. You were working in the garden or making cookies or doing any of the innocent things that women do on a Sunday afternoon. You don't own a tee shirt that says 'world's greatest grandma' or a twin stroller and you threw away that handicapped card after your husband died. I don't care if the FBI comes knocking at your door. You don't look like the woman in the sketch and you don't like fairs. They're too crowded. Tomorrow morning, we're going to cut that stroller into unrecognizable pieces and take it to the town landfill, and you'll cut that tee shirt into rags."

"Any questions?" Eleanor concluded.

The women looked at one another.

"Why do we still hear that same $127,640 figure?" Paula asked. "Why hasn't anyone upped it to the real amount? And, whomever the rest of that money belongs to, aren't they looking for it, too?"

Eleanor nodded her head, affirming that this was a serious question. "The only people who know about that money are the ones who put it there and the ones who expected it to be deposited. We agree – although we have no way of knowing – that it's laundered money of some sort. And the people who put it in the bags aren't talking to the police about it."

"We have to assume the people for whom it was being

laundered are looking for it," Eleanor continued, "but they have the same leads as the police. And, as long as the police don't know who stole the money, neither do the criminals who arranged for it to be laundered. I'm not naive enough to think they'll write it off as a cost of doing business, but they also can't afford to attract a lot of attention. If we lay low, we'll be OK. As long as we stick to our stories, we're fine."

* * * * *

Night had fallen.

The notion that the old lady lived in some kind of a senior citizen's apartment complex did not especially alarm Frankie Tomkins. What troubled him was the awareness from previous burglaries that such places had two drawbacks: first, the neighbors were easily panicked and quick to call the police. The second was that the construction of such places was invariably cut-rate meaning walls were thin and noises carried easily from apartment to apartment.

But it was nearly nine o'clock on a warm evening and old people turned in early or else had their air conditioners blasting. There was no way in hell they'd be out on a humid night like this, admiring the moon or playing shuffleboard. He figured he could get in, get the information, and be out in fifteen minutes. Just the threat of physical violence would be sufficient to make the old lady tell him everything he wanted to know.

He tried the door. It was locked, but it was one of those flimsy lowest-bid, public-housing-quality locks and he was inside, silently, in under a minute.

The front door opened into a darkened area that apparently served as both a living and dining room. The whole apartment had an old-lady smell to it. To the rear on the right was a small kitchen, to the left was a door that probably led to a bedroom. No light showed under the door. The old woman was likely asleep.

He walked quietly to the bedroom door and tested it for noise. It opened soundlessly. With his eyes adjusted to the dark, he looked at the bed. It was made up neatly and unoccupied.

"She ain't here," he muttered to himself. He was disappointed that his night was going to be longer than his first estimate.

Tomkins busied himself with the rest of his task, which was looking for anything of value he might steal for himself and information that might lead him to the woman in the police sketch. Better yet, he might find the money, which he was told was enough to fill five large satchels.

From his back pocket, he extracted a small flashlight and began opening drawers and cabinets. After looking in two or three such spaces he concluded that there was nothing worth stealing in this apartment. The old lady was poor and the things she collected – ugly little ceramic things – were of no interest to a fence. The jewelry was cheap, costume pieces that had no street value.

Neither was the money here. There were only a few places where satchels could be hidden and he checked carefully in the apartment's lone closet, under the bed, and in the kitchen. She didn't have it, which meant the other woman – the one with the stroller – was holding the loot.

It didn't surprise him that women had committed the theft. His girlfriend of the moment was an accomplished shoplifter and hustler. She could walk into a Macy's wearing nothing but a halter top and short skirt and carrying a tiny purse, and walk out fifteen minutes later with a thousand bucks in watches, perfume and gold chains.

Nor was it a revelation that an older woman could be involved in crime. His mother had been collecting social security and disability under two names for as long as he had been cognizant that such a thing could be done. To Tomkins, crime had always been an equal-opportunity situation at which any gender could excel.

After twenty minutes, he had been through every inch of the apartment. All he could do now was wait for the old lady to show up. Once she did, he would have the element of surprise on his side. He figured five minutes, tops, to tie her up, stuff a rag in her mouth, let her know in no uncertain terms that the first words she uttered had better be the name and address of the lady with the stroller or else they would be her last.

But, despite being dark and it being an old lady who probably wore thick glasses, Tomkins was uneasy about leaving behind a witness who could identify him later, especially once she gave up the name of the person who had stashed the money. Twice in the last five years he had yielded to pleas for mercy from people he had beaten up and robbed. Twice he had allowed that good angel sitting on his right shoulder to persuade him that the person was speaking the truth when they said they would swear to the police or in court they had never seen their attacker or the person burglarizing their apartment.

Both times he had let them go with just a beating and a warning. And, for about three days, he had felt pretty good about it. Then, the cops had come around and put him in a lineup, and the little old lady and the gimpy old man had picked him out. Twice he had gone away because he had listened to that damned angel. Six months for the first one; nine months for the second.

Well, no more. He was sick of little old ladies lying to him about keeping their mouths shut. Whether he had to beat the crap out of this woman to get her to give him the name, or she coughed it up at the sight of his fist, it was going to be the last thing she said. He wasn't getting paid enough to go to prison again. He was going to leave behind a corpse.

Tomkins carried no weapon. Guns and knives made it

impossible to talk your way out of encounters with law enforcement agencies. Moreover, his hands were all the weapon he needed against little old ladies. He was strong and quick and had no compunction about choking or even giving a hard snap to someone's neck. And besides, there was something satisfying about watching someone die slowly.

Less than two minutes later, he was rewarded with the sound of jingling keys and a hand on the door. Tomkins smiled and got ready.

* * * * *

Samantha Ayers had narrowed the list of 'probables' to four. Insurance files indicated three of the women who otherwise met the description of the woman with the stroller were ambulatory only with the aid of a walker. Two vehicles were brightly colored. One was a minivan outfitted with a wheelchair lift, something anyone who had seen the car would have quickly recognized. Of the four remaining, one had a second, summer residence on Cape Cod. Samantha felt it unlikely this was the right person. The other three, though, were all logical: the right age and the right color car.

Samantha made the drive to Hardington and knocked at the door of the first woman on her list. Katherine Portman was five feet tall and gray haired, but she probably tipped the scales at two hundred pounds. Samantha asked if this was the Ayers residence and quickly excused herself when she was told that it was not.

There was no one home at the second name on the list, Jean Sullivan, but Samantha had a good feeling about the house. To judge from the perennial beds surrounding the house, Mrs. Sullivan was apparently a gardener and the two women minding the flower show were garden club members.

The third door was answered by an elderly man who said that, yes, his wife drove a minivan but that it could not have clipped Samantha's car in the Stop and Shop parking lot because Delores' eyesight had deteriorated during the past year to the point that she no longer drove. Samantha thanked him and left.

The last door on which she knocked – the one with a second home on the Cape – was answered by a woman her own age who viewed Samantha with immediate suspicion.

"I'm not selling anything," Samantha said and offered the woman her credentials. "We think your mother's minivan may have been in an accident."

"My mother's minivan is parked in the long-term lot at Logan," the woman said. "She's been in California for the past two days."

Which brought it all back to the woman named Jean Sullivan and the 1960's-era house set back on the long driveway. She must be the woman being sought by the state police. Of course, it was all predicated on Samantha's theory being right. Otherwise, this was all a wild goose chase built on the flimsiest of premises.

Samantha had a choice of watching the Sullivan house, which would involve sitting in the driveway across the street and hoping that the family didn't either come home and find a strange car in their driveway or else call the police to report her.

Her alternative was to pay a call on Alice Beauchamp and perhaps talk her into being the one to acknowledge that four women had successfully robbed the armored car. It was only a quarter past nine. Plenty of time to locate the Beauchamp woman and then re-pay a visit to Jean Sullivan.

It took several minutes to find Hardington Gardens. The project was tucked in behind the town's public works buildings, sharing an entry road with the town garage and, according to a sign at the street entrance, a sewage treatment plant. Samantha saw a half-dozen identical rectangular buildings arranged in a grid, a relic of "what-were-they-thinking?" 1960's-era planning. *What a depressing place*, she thought as she walked toward Apartment 118.

Here, at least, was a motive for robbery: an escape from what amounted to a storage warehouse for old people. She had been inside Eleanor Strong's home, which had been bright and cheerful. Her quick look at Jean Sullivan's house plus her knowledge of real estate values told her that Sullivan was sitting on a gold mine. Multi-acre properties in a town like Hardington were highly desirable even in a depressed home building market. Jean Sullivan might be house poor but she had ample alternatives to robbing a bank. The fourth woman, Paula Winters, was apparently young enough to still be working.

So, why had they robbed an armored car? Samantha asked herself that question as she approached Alice Beauchamp's door. Her father would have had a quick response: 'Bunch of rich white women with nothing else to do'. Samantha's generation did not see the world through the same prism. She imagined she would find out their motive soon enough.

She had stopped outside Alice Beauchamp's apartment and noted there was no light on in the living room. An elderly woman might well spend her evenings in her bedroom with books or television. Samantha was about to knock on the door when she saw the flicker of the flashlight inside.

She stood silently, listening and peering through the opening in the curtains. Whoever was inside was opening kitchen cabinets, roughly pawing at whatever was inside. The flashlight's arc occasionally swung in the direction of the living room.

Her police training, coupled with years of living under the same roof with two generations of law enforcement officers, came alive. She knew senior citizen complexes were low-yield targets for burglars. The residents had little worth stealing. Moreover, the odds that a burglar would have chosen this apartment on this night were too high to be sheer chance.

Whoever was in Alice Beauchamp's apartment right now was

there because they, too, believed the woman was part of the robbery. Were it a legal search by state or local police, the door would be open, the lights blazing, and multiple officers would be involved. Mass Casualty was the only non-police organization with a legitimate interest in finding the money and she was the only Mass Casualty employee involved. Therefore, the person inside the apartment was a criminal.

Which brought back the whole question of what had really been in the satchels. If the four women had committed the robbery, then Samantha's original theory was wrong. Erskine might have skimmed money from the deposit but there was definitely money in the bags. She was still certain Erskine had lied to her. Perhaps the person inside was Erskine or someone hired by him to get rid of the robbery's evidence.

She could call the police and she considered that option for a moment. The police would come and arrest a burglar. The burglar would be booked, arraigned, make bail, and never say a word about why he was there. She had worked with various suburban police departments during her time with Mass Casualty and she was not impressed by the caliber of the officers and their ability to look beyond what was immediately evident.

Moreover, if Samantha was to find the money, she needed answers. The person inside that apartment might give her those answers in return for a free pass away from the scene.

She needed a weapon. She didn't own a gun and hadn't time to find one. She walked quickly and silently back to her car and inventoried what might be useful. A tire jack, a can of mace, a dirty rag she had used to wipe her shoes during a week-earlier rainstorm and fifty feet of rope. Her lone other weapon was the element of surprise.

She walked back to the apartment, counting on the burglar not having had the presence of mind to lock the front door. She jingled her keys and then opened the front door.

But instead of stepping into the room she shoved the door back with her shoulder, feeling the resistance of someone who had been standing behind it. She then dove, head first, into the room, rolling sideways as she did. She heard the grunt of the man who had been behind the door and felt a hand grab for her arm as she dove.

Now she was in the room with the man. In the semi-darkness, he appeared to be at least six feet tall and built on a big frame. He shined his flashlight on her and she heard him mouth an obscenity. She lunged at him, holding the pepper spray in front of her. When she was a foot away, she pressed the nozzle.

But the man's reactions were quick. He stepped to the side and grabbed again at her arm, this time finding cloth and her body. The can of mace sprayed only the man's hand before it was smacked away, hitting the wood floor. Samantha was jerked by her arm and she saw the man's fist being raised. Her free hand held the tire iron and she swung it hard, catching him between the neck and the shoulder.

The tire iron made a satisfying 'thunk' as it hit muscle and bone. The hand released her and the man screamed, the flashlight flew out of his hand. Samantha swung again, smashing the man's right hand.

"Bitch!" he screamed and lunged for her.

Samantha dropped and rolled and, as she did, she felt something small and cylindrical under her leg. She felt for and found the mace with her left hand. The man thudded to the floor beside her. With her right hand, she swung the tire iron again, connecting with the man's knee cap.

"I'm gonna kill you, bitch!" he screamed and, as he did, she sprayed the mace in his eyes, nose, and mouth. The man immediately gagged and instinctively put his hands in front of the eyes. Samantha pulled away his injured hand and held down the sprayer button a full five seconds. She then shoved the sharp end of the tire iron into the man's belly. He sat bolt upright, suddenly unable to speak, gasping for what little breath his mace-filled lungs could take in.

Samantha took the rag from her back pocket and shoved it into the man's mouth. The rope had been coiled around her waist and she quickly wound it around the man's hands, then secured his hands to his midsection. The man swiveled his head sharply, a demand to have the rag removed.

Samantha had only a moment to think and to act. She had subdued the man but he had screamed several times. Neighbors may have called the police. She needed to get the man out of the apartment to a place where she could question him. And she had to do it quickly.

She leaned over the man's face, holding the mace inches away from his eyes. "Listen to me, you asshole," she whispered. The man stopped wriggling. "We're going to walk out of this place right now. We're going to go to my car and you're going to get into that car. The first time you do anything other than walk in a straight line, you're going to get a face full of this." She shook the bottle of mace to demonstrate it still had ample reserves. She then brandished the tire iron. "The second time, you're going to get this across that ugly skull."

She saw comprehension and fear in his eyes. It was probably the first time in his adult life that an African-American woman had ever threatened him. She wondered if the events of the past few minutes would cause him to have greater respect for women or to lash out for revenge at the next opportunity.

At that moment, Samantha made the decision that she could not free this man after hearing his story. He needed to be jailed. He had lain in wait in the apartment to get information out of Alice

Beauchamp and his method of extracting that information would have involved physical pain, possibly delivered with a degree of enjoyment.

She pulled the man to his feet, indicated the door and held the mace to his face. He turned his head as far as possible away from the canister but began walking toward the door.

This is going to work, Samantha thought.

But as soon as they reached the outside the man broke into a run. Through he would have likely outrun Samantha under most circumstances, he had the twin handicap of his bound hands and arms and the lingering effect of the well-placed tire-iron smack she had given his kneecap back in the apartment. She caught him in under ten yards, placed a leg between his feet and watched him sprawl forward and fall, face-first, into the hard-packed dirt and grass.

She rolled him over and he shook his head in fear.

"I told you what I would do the first time you disobeyed me," Samantha said and sprayed his eyes and nose. He stamped his feet but his muffled scream carried no more than a few feet.

"Now, let's get moving again," she said. "And just in case you forgot, next time, it's the tire iron." She waved it in front of his face.

They were a few feet from her car when an idea came to Samantha. She stopped and slapped the man's pockets until she found the one with keys in them.

"Let's take your car," she said, fishing the keys from his front pocket. The key ring included a fob with a door lock button and she pressed it until one of the cars in the apartment complex's parking lots made an obedient beeping sound.

It was a black Lincoln Navigator, which contrasted with Samantha's Honda Accord. "Don't you guys have any imagination?" she muttered.

She pushed the man into the back seat, lying face down, and used several yards of her rope to bind his feet. Unless the man was a magician, he would remain immobilized until she decided to release him.

She breathed a deep sigh and started the car.

* * * * *

Eleanor felt the crisis had passed. Jean was now comfortable that the sketch would lead no one to her. Alice had answered a barrage of questions about the Grange. Paula looked tired and Eleanor was all too aware that her friend was to check into the hospital Tuesday afternoon for her Wednesday surgery.

Then, the doorbell rang. Eleanor looked at the clock on the fireplace mantle. It was nine thirty. No one rang doorbells at this hour of the evening.

They all looked at one another, thinking the same thoughts. *It's the police.*

Eleanor put a finger to her lips.

She went to the door and opened it a crack. It was the young, African-American woman from the insurance company. She looked as though she had been in a fight with her hair disheveled and clothes askew.

"Please come back another time," Eleanor said firmly and tried to close the door.

The young woman pushed back, preventing Eleanor from latching the door. "Mrs. Strong, we need to talk and, I mean, we need to talk right now."

Samantha pushed her way into the doorway and stood in the foyer of the home. To her right was the living room and, in the living room were three women. To the youngest one with brown hair, she nodded and said, "Mrs. Winters, my name is Samantha Ayers." The woman's eyes widened with disbelief.

There were two shorter women, both with gray hair, but one

was almost pixie-like. Samantha had seen the light green Plymouth Voyager in the driveway. She nodded at the woman. "I assume you must be Jean Sullivan. I'm pleased to meet you. The last woman was the oldest of the group. "And you're Alice Beauchamp. Hi, I'm Samantha Ayers, and I'm with Mass Casualty."

She saw the look of shock on the women's faces.

"Ladies, I need your help, and I think you need mine." She turned to Eleanor. "And, Mrs. Strong, if you have a Diet Coca-Cola or something like that around the house, I'd love a glass right now."

Wordlessly, Eleanor walked back to the kitchen and was back in a few moments with a can of Diet Coke and a glass.

Samantha opened the can, poured it into a glass and took a long drink.

"Thank you, Mrs. Strong. I can't tell you how much I needed that." She then turned to the group. "Mrs. Strong, I think you may want to take a seat because the five of us need to have a serious discussion."

She took another drink of the soda. "Mrs. Beauchamp, I just came from your apartment where I fought with a man who was hiding there, waiting for you to come home. He left your place in kind of a mess but, right now, he's even more of a mess. I've got him tied up in a car outside. He's not a burglar, although that's probably what the police would have concluded. He wanted the money. The money the four of you stole. He was there to beat information out of you and, once he had that information, he would probably have killed you in order to ensure you couldn't identify him at a later date."

Alice put her hand to her mouth to hide her gasp.

Samantha let the words sink in.

"I figured it out," Samantha said. "The problem is, somebody else has also figured it out, or at least part of it. They fact that they're not here right now means they don't know who all of you are. But whoever they are, they're pretty smart and they've got the same clues that I had. Which means we've got to get this thing resolved now, because the man they sent around to Mrs. Beauchamp's apartment is one very scary person. I only got the best of him because he saw a young, black woman and, being a black man, he underestimated me. I wouldn't care for a re-match. I also wouldn't care to meet the next person they send around, because that one might have a gun and be prepared to use it."

She saw that they were listening and they understood.

"Like I said, I'm with Mass Casualty. We insured the armored car company. All I care about is not having to pay a claim on that shipment. I'm not with the police and, despite coming from two generations of police officers, I don't care much for them."

"What I need to know is, what exactly happened?"

She looked at Eleanor when she asked the final question, but it was Paula Winters who, to her surprise, answered.

"It was my idea," Paula said. "I talked them into it."

"You didn't talk me into anything," Jean said. "Lord, I wished the idea were mine right from the start."

"Ladies," Samantha said, shaking her head, "I'm not looking for confessions. I need to know what happened."

"That's what I said," Paula continued. "It was my idea. I saw an armored car picking up money at the Barnstable Fair last month and realized how casually it was all done. I had just found out that my breast cancer is back and I began thinking that I could die and that I had never taken a risk in my life. We're all part of the Hardington Garden Club. We started talking after the monthly meeting in July. Eleanor worked the flower show at the Brookfield Fair…"

Samantha held up her hand. "Wait," she said. "That's good

information for a different time and place. What I need to know is what happened Sunday afternoon. I know you and Mrs. Strong threw the pepper sauce at the guards and walked away with the money. I know Mrs. Beauchamp pretended to faint and, in the process, tied up all the foot traffic. I know Mrs. Sullivan got the money out of the fair in a baby carriage. What I don't know is why someone is on your trail; why someone wants to hurt you. That's what I'm asking when I say, 'what happened?'."

Jean raised her hand.

"We don't need to raise our hands, Mrs. Sullivan," Samantha said.

"The newspapers said there was $127,000 being picked up by the armored car. That wasn't true."

Erskine was skimming. He's got to get the money back before anyone finds out. I knew it, Samantha thought.

"There was nearly half a million dollars," Alice added.

Samantha's mind spun.

"I think I have the exact number," Jean said. "It was $477,640. Mostly in hundreds."

Oh, my God, Samantha thought.

"Where is the money right now?"

"In my attic," Jean said, pointing up toward the living room ceiling. "Except for eight hundred dollars that Eleanor took out. We each took two hundred dollars. But except for me, I don't think we've spent any of it."

"You ladies have half a million dollars in Mrs. Sullivan's attic," Samantha said. It wasn't a question. It was her way of trying to come to terms with the implications.

"We assume the fair was being used as a money laundering operation," Paula said.

"But as long as we stuck to our stories about where we were and what we saw, no one could pin anything on us," Eleanor added.

"Until now," Alice said softly. "I guess your being here and that man being in my apartment changes everything."

"Ladies, this is where we put our heads together and come up with a plan," Samantha said. "We don't leave here until we know what we're going to do with that man and the people who sent him."

19.

It was 10 p.m. Detective Sergeant Woolsey looked with disbelief at the log of calls. It was a quarter of an inch thick.

"More than eight hundred," Captain Moynihan said, flipping through the pages. "And they're still coming in at the rate of a hundred an hour. That's just the people who watched the early news. You're going to get a whole new crop after eleven and then again tomorrow morning when it shows up in the newspapers..."

"I know," Woolsey said sharply. "What I need is a quick name check to compare against my master list. By tomorrow morning, if I can get a few dozen positive cross-matches, I can check each one individually. By noon, we can have our suspect in custody."

"And all I have to do is turn the entire shift over to listening to the responses to your plea for help." Moynihan's voice was laced with sarcasm.

"Captain, this is going to work," Woolsey said with exasperation. "And I'm not going anywhere tonight."

"It had better work," Moynihan said, dropping the sheaf of papers on Woolsey's desk. "Otherwise, I'm the laughingstock of the state police. Chasing after a sixty-something grandmother for an armored car robbery. And you're damned right about one thing: you're not going anywhere tonight."

* * * * *

In Brookfield at that same moment, Detective Martin Hoffman swirled his cold coffee in a cup, sniffed it, and decided that it was beyond being microwaved. Two remaining slices of pizza were congealing in the box.

"The department could spring for a fresh pot, you know," Chief Ashton said.

"It's just the two of us," Hoffman said. "And I don't know how much longer I'm good for, anyway."

Before them was the large sheet of paper Hoffman had sketched after the newscast. Now, it also held handwritten theories and suppositions coupled with arrows and circles connecting people and events.

"Alice Beauchamp is the key," Hoffman said.

"You said that four hours ago," Ashton said. "We're agreed on that."

"And the sixty-something woman in the minivan," Hoffman added.

"You said that right after you spoke with the couple in Acton," Ashton said, yawning. "Your buddy Woolsey also seems to agree. I'll bet he's got a thousand calls on his tip line. I'd hate to be that bastard tonight."

"I keep coming back to two theories," Hoffman said. "First theory: let's say someone paid Alice Beauchamp a couple of hundred bucks and told her to fall down. Didn't tell her why. Just said, 'here's the money.' What should she have done when I confronted her? Denied everything or confessed everything?"

Ashton yawned again. "Depends on the person."

"No," Hoffman said. "She's at least seventy so she was raised in the thirties and the forties. Back then, if a policeman asks you a question, you answer it truthfully. It's drilled into you as a child and you never forget. If you're ten or fifteen years younger, you're part of the 'don't trust the pigs' generation and you can lie with a straight face. But not her. She's the wrong generation."

"We've been here before," Ashton said, looking at his watch.

"No," Hoffman replied. "I had assumed someone paid her. I *asked* her if someone paid her. That allowed her to answer the question the way she did: she told me the literal truth. I slipped up and didn't ask the question a different way because of the vehemence with which she responded to the first question. That's part of our generation's upbringing: be kind to sweet little old ladies and don't do things that might give them heart attacks."

"I'm going to get sweet Mrs. Beauchamp in here tomorrow and we're going to have a very different kind of talk," Hoffman said, dumping his coffee into a wastebasket. "But, under the heading of 'be careful what you wish for' – and this is the second theory – what if it turns out she's part of it?"

"She and the world's greatest grandma?"

"We already assume that the world's greatest grandma is in on it," Hoffman said.

"Alice Beauchamp, criminal mastermind?"

"If we get those two, then we get the rest of the crowd and I bet we recover the money," Hoffman said. "Besides, do you have a better theory?"

"Yes," Ashton said, yawning again. "Six hours of sleep followed by a trip to Hardington to put some serious questions to the criminal mastermind, including the identity of the world's greatest grandma."

* * * * *

At 10:30 p.m., the five women were still in Eleanor's living room, deep in discussion. Several pots of coffee had been brewed and consumed as had three Diet Cokes.

"We're going to question Franklin Tomkins," Samantha said, looking at the license in the wallet she had taken from him. "Assuming that the license wasn't stolen along with the car. A man like that is good for maybe three or four minutes of answering questions, after which he figures that his best course of action is to shut up until his lawyer arrives."

The women nodded. 'Lawyering up' was something they knew well from the police shows on television.

"What he has to understand is that no lawyer is going to ride to the rescue," Samantha added. "He has to believe that we're going to boil him alive unless he tells us the truth. And assume that he'll lie at first because it comes naturally to him."

"Literally boil him alive?" Alice asked.

"Or something equally inventive."

"Bury him alive," Eleanor suggested. "There's some nice, soft dirt around the side of the house where I figure we can get down at least two feet before we hit any rocks. If that doesn't scare him, nothing will."

* * * * *

Frankie Tomkins, despite being bound and gagged, had managed to fall asleep in the back of his car. He reasoned that if the Amazon bitch queen who had done this to him hadn't killed him by now, she wasn't going to. Like any woman, she lacked the quintessentially male quality of a willingness to take another's life when it was necessary, or even just because it was expedient.

Instead, she'd turn him over to the police where it would be his word against hers, and he was the one who could prove he had been kidnapped. Once he was out on bail – if it even got as far as a bail hearing – he'd go back, finish off the old lady, and make her and the Amazon bitch queen pay for every indignity he had suffered during the past hour. Despite the insistent pain in his own knee and hand, and the lingering effects of mace on his eyes, he had fallen asleep to the thought of the lethal punishments he would inflict.

He was roused out of his sleep as someone grabbed his bound feet and dragged him out of the car. He hit his head and shoulder on the way down, the same shoulder where the bitch queen had struck him with the tire iron and which now ached miserably. A cloth bag was thrown over his head. Now he was being dragged across grass but, between the darkness and the bag, he could not see by whom. Worse, with his hands bound and tied to his waist, he was helpless. The person or persons who dragged him made no noise.

After a minute his feet were dropped. Someone reached under the bag over his head and yanked out the gag.

He listened to the sound of shovels – several shovels – digging.

"What the fuck is going on here?" he screamed.

There was no answer. Only the sound of shovels. A sharp, insistent pain had developed in his head where it had hit the door frame as he was pulled from the car. There was no give in the rope that bound his hands and feet. Tomkins decided that perhaps belligerence wasn't the best tactic right now.

"Who are you?" he asked. It wasn't a scream this time. It sounded like a real question.

The sounds of the shovels continued.

"That's deep enough, Lou." It was the Amazon bitch queen's voice. "Get the bags."

A moment later, he felt what he was certain was a plastic garbage bag sliding up his legs. He kicked furiously but the bag slid on easily.

"Sam, help me put him in," the bitch queen said.

Hands grabbed his ankles and shoulders and he was dropped several feet on his back. He could feel the cool, damp dirt and small rocks under him.

"Got any last words?" the Amazon bitch queen asked.

"Why the hell are you doing this? I got a wife and kids."

"Those aren't the words I wanted to hear," the woman said coolly. "Plus, you're lying. You're not married. Guys like you are never married."

"What do you want to know?" His voice betrayed a pleading note.

"Who hired you?"

"Nobody hired me. I work for myself."

"That's two lies. Sam, fill the hole. Let's be done with this piece of garbage."

Two shovelfuls of dirt promptly landed on the garbage bag that covered his legs.

"Wait!" he screamed.

Another two shovelfuls of dirt went into the hole.

"Boz hired me. Boz told me where to find her."

"Boz who?" the woman asked.

More dirt went into the hole. Tomkins felt the weight of the dirt covering his legs. He could no longer move his feet or his knees.

"He's just Boz. Lives up in a huge house over in Concord. He's a rich gangster. Runs all kinds of shit. He's Puerto Rican or Nicaraguan or something."

The shoveling stopped. "How does he get in touch with you?"

"He gave me one of those throwaway phones."

"The one in your glove compartment?"

"That one."

"What were you supposed to do after you killed the old lady?"

"Wasn't gonna kill her," he lied. "Just find out where the money was and get it. Boz said she'd tell me. All I had to do was scare her so she's talk."

"And when you got the money?"

"Call him and arrange a drop."

"Where did you make your drops in the past?"

"He's got an office. On Route 9, in Framingham."

"Describe it."

"Old house. Sign out front says 'Madame LaRue, Palm Reading'. Always got a 'closed' sign on the door."

"You've got one chance to live, Franklin," the woman said.

"You're going to call Boz. You're going to tell him you got the money. All of the money. The whole half million. You tell him you need to make the drop tonight because there was trouble at the lady's apartment and you have to leave town for a while. You tell him you'll be there in an hour – right at midnight. You tell him exactly that, in exactly those words, and you have my word you'll be alive in the morning. You tell him anything else, and you have my word that Sam and Lou are going to finish burying you alive."

"I got to get that phone."

"I have it right here," the woman said. "I'm hitting 'last number dialed'. Catch your breath because here we go."

* * * * *

After the call was made, Samantha, Eleanor and Paula dragged Frankie out of the hole. The bag over his head was replaced by a blindfold and ear plugs.

"Alice and Eleanor," Samantha said softly. "Your job for the next two hours is to get this guy drunk. Knowing his kind, you should be able to just hold a bottle in front of his lips and he'll drink, but if he says he's had enough, just keep pouring it into him. I want him four-sheets-to-the-wind plastered before midnight. Eleanor, use a funnel if need be. You need to get at least two bottles into him. And whatever happens, don't talk to him. If he remembers anything, it's going to be me plus two guys named Sam and Lou. Let's keep it that way."

"Jean," Samantha continued, "You need to get one of those bags of money. Make it as close to the $127,000 as possible, but you need to have it back here and counted in under two hours. We'll need the satchels, too."

Paula said, "She can't. I cut them up into pieces."

"Do you still have the pieces?"

"They're in the garbage in my garage."

Samantha looked at Jean and shook her head. "You'll have to

retrieve them, Jean. Pieces are better than nothing. I'm going to need Paula with me."

Samantha and Paula left in the Lincoln Navigator after locating more rope, duct tape, and a baseball bat from Eleanor's garage.

Framingham was twenty minutes away. Samantha said they should arrive well in advance of 'Boz'.

"We do have a plan, don't we?" Paula asked as they drove the darkened suburban streets.

"We do," Samantha said. "We're going to find out what this is all about. I don't know if Boz is the ultimate guy or if he's the middleman. My guess is that he's the middleman, doing somebody's else's dirty work in exchange for a piece of the action."

"And why did you send Jean to get part of the money? Are we giving it back?"

"I'll tell you if you'll tell me about your surgery," Samantha said.

Paula was silent. Then, she said, "That's kind of personal."

"I've got breast cancer in my family," Samantha said. "My momma died of breast cancer when I was sixteen."

"Do you get mammograms?"

"You're not supposed to need them before you're thirty-five," Samantha said. "I've got a couple of years before I'm supposed to get them."

"If your mother died of breast cancer, you need one now."

"You don't worry about the radiation from those X-rays?"

"Your body absorbs more radiation on a cross-country airplane flight than it does from a mammogram."

"What are they going to do to you?" Samantha asked.

"I had a lumpectomy plus radiation nineteen months ago. I was clean until two months ago. This time I'll lose my right breast and they'll reconstruct it at the same time."

"What do you mean, 'reconstruct it'?"

"It means that after the surgeon is finished and I've healed, you'd have to see me undressed to even know I had surgery and, even then, you'd have to look very hard to see the scar. Not that I expect to be undressing in front of anyone anytime soon."

"Sounds expensive," Samantha said.

"That's why I have insurance. And the alternative is that the cancer spreads. Then, there's nothing they can do for me."

"So, why did you wait the two months?"

Paula was silent again, wondering how to explain her actions to someone who hadn't been through what she had experienced. Then she said, "It took a month to get a confirmation of the diagnosis. And it took a month of planning to do something that made me feel like I had done something extraordinary with my life."

"Robbing an armored car counts as extraordinary?" Samantha glanced over at her passenger.

"Better than gawking at zebras in Kenya, which was the alternative."

Samantha pondered Paula's answer for moment, then said, "I think my daddy is smarter than I give him credit for sometimes."

"Pardon?" Paula asked.

"Your husband must have died and left you a lot of money," Samantha said.

"My husband left me for a woman about your age. But, yes, he was so anxious to get divorced and re-married to his bimbo – and probably to start a new family – that he signed over half his business and most of his assets. I suppose I should feel grateful but for some reason, I don't."

"How about the others? Eleanor, Alice and Jean. Are they all divorced, too?"

"Alice and Jean lost their husbands. Eleanor's husband is in a nursing home. Alzheimer's." Changing subjects, Paula said, "I noticed that when you first started talking to us this evening, it was all 'Mrs. Winters' and 'Mrs. Beauchamp'. It switched to 'Eleanor' and 'Alice' somewhere along the way."

Samantha nodded. "Put yourself in my shoes. I'm half your age and my skin color doesn't automatically win me any friends in a town like Hardington. Plus, my momma raised me to be deferential to anyone older than me until they proved they weren't worthy of it. I needed for you to understand that I knew who you were and what you had done. I assume the four of you thought you were going to get away with it."

"We didn't plan on getting caught, if that's what you mean," Paula said.

"You would have, you know," Samantha said. "Gotten away with it. Any suburban police department would have poked around for a couple of days looking for clues. If they didn't find an eyewitness or you didn't start spending the money on cars, they'd give up and declare it a cold case. The state police are a joke. They can find more ways to screw up a case than I can count. What I'm saying is that the four of you pulled it off without leaving any clues behind. Unless you had messed up afterwards, you'd be home free in a week."

"As for me, I wouldn't have cared much one way or another," Samantha continued. "Mass Casualty can afford the hit. But Erskine – the fair manager – was lying through his teeth and I was convinced it was an inside job. Erskine – or whatever his real name is – didn't exist except as a name and a social security number until a couple of years ago, which is usually a sign that someone did something highly illegal and was forced to create a new identity."

"At first I thought Erskine had decided to skim a lot of money off the top of the fair's gross. Instead, it turns out you ladies just happened to hit a money laundering operation right in the middle of a deposit. Well, somebody else is interested besides me. Somebody ready to play rough. I don't know who this 'Boz' character is, but if he employs low-lifes like Tomkins to go after people like Alice, he's someone who thinks other people's lives are cheap."

"So, you're going to turn us in after this is all over?"

Samantha looked over at Paula, surprised. "If I were going to turn you in, we'd be at a police station right now. As far as I'm concerned, if we recover those gate receipts, I'm happy and Mass Casualty is happy."

"Won't the police keep looking for us?"

Samantha shrugged. "We'll see."

The drop point was as Frankie Tomkins had described. It was a small, 1930's-era house that, when built three-quarters of a century ago, had been on the then-bucolic turnpike that linked Boston and Worcester. Now, it was hemmed in by strip shopping centers and small office buildings. Apparently on too small a parcel of land to interest a developer, it sat shoehorned between a quick-oil-change franchise and a vacant video rental store. A faded, painted sign in front of the house invited travelers to consult Madame LaRue – Spiritual Advisor. What had once been a front lawn had been paved for parking, but weeds poked up between cracks in the macadam. Overgrown yews and junipers hid the windows.

"It was probably a lot nicer back when Madame LaRue was reading palms and holding seances," Samantha said, looking over the house and property. "It's not what I had in mind, but I guess it will have to do." She turned to Paula. "I may have dragged you along for nothing. I hope I can get the jump on this Boz character the same way I did on Tompkins. But if I don't and there's a fight, it's going to be very close quarters. Way too close for three people."

Even in the dark, Samantha could see the disappointed look on Paula's face.

"Look, Paula, when the other car gets here, just get in the driver's seat and sit tight. I don't want you to get hurt. I'm pretty sure I can handle it. I'm strong. I know judo and a lot of dirty fighting techniques."

"What are you going to do?" Paula asked.

"Kidnap this Boz character, more or less. Make him talk. Find out whose money that $350,000 is and then figure out what to do next."

"Why can't I help?"

"Because it's too tight a space," Samantha said. "I can't hide you. I don't think he'll be carrying because, as far as he's concerned, this is just a money drop from a reliable freelancer. He's going to see a car he recognizes. When he sees me, he'll probably think I'm the girlfriend – or worse. You were going to be my backup in case of trouble, but in this small a space there's no element of surprise. He's going to spot you from the get-go…"

Samantha's words were cut short by the appearance of a set of headlights turning into the parking area. It was 11:40 p.m.

"Damn it, he's twenty minutes early," Samantha said, unbuckling her seat belt. "The man must be anxious." She wrapped the rope around her waist and pushed the duct tape into her pants pocket. "The baseball bat stays here as a last resort and I'm leaving the keys in the ignition. If something happens, your orders are to get the hell out of here and fast. Drive over him and smash hell out of his car if you have to, but whatever happens, don't stop. It's not your car and any damage you do to it isn't going on your insurance."

Samantha looked out the side view mirror. "Looks like one guy only. He's getting out of the car. Here I go. Wish me luck."

Samantha got out of the car and walked over to where she saw the silhouette of a short, heavy-set man. The man leaned against his open car door – it appeared to be a Hummer - neither advancing to meet her or retreating into the car. The man's face was dimly lit by the cigarette he smoked; his bulk apparent from, the dome light cast by the vehicle. Paula watched through the side-view mirror, uncertain if the Navigator's smoked glass made her invisible to someone outside.

Samantha was gesturing, indicating the Navigator. She was apparently trying to get the man – presumably 'Boz' – to help her unload the satchels. The man continued to smoke, not moving. It was too dark to make out his facial expression or to interpret body language, but the fact that he did not move from the car door was disturbing. Samantha continued her animated gestures for several minutes, getting no closer than five or six feet from the man. Finally, getting no response, Samantha gave an exaggerated shrug and began walking back toward the Navigator.

In the instant her back was turned, the man pounced, closing the distance between them in two, cat-like steps, bringing his fist down like a hammer on her head. Samantha dropped to the ground, trying to roll away. The man – extremely agile for someone who appeared to weigh at least 250 pounds – then kicked her in the back.

Paula has been told to drive out if there was trouble. She could not do it. But neither could she be trapped in the car. Instinctively, she gripped the baseball bat tightly and opened the door. The man was kicking Samantha, who kept rolling away from him, lessening the impact of his blows while keeping him from getting a solid footing. The man, intent on inflicting pain, paid no attention to the dome light from the Navigator or to Paula.

Paula had never hit anyone in anger nor had she ever had to defend herself against a bodily attack. She weighed 122 pounds fully clothed and her upper arm strength came entirely from working with a trowel and shovel on her perennial beds. She did not even know if she could bring the bat down with any force.

In the few seconds it took to race to where this man and Samantha struggled, Paula determined that what she would *not* be was one of those women in the movies who stood by, cowering, while a life-and-death fight took place in front of her.

She raised the bat over her head. She brought it down with all of her strength and it hit the man on his right shoulder, a few inches from his neck. He fell to one knee and screamed in pain, then turned to see his attacker, the sudden movement adding to the pain. He winced but directed his attention to this new woman. Samantha rolled away, out of the range of his kicks.

Paula raised the bat again. This swing would not have the power of the first and so she aimed for the head. The man instinctively covered his head with one hands and the bat hit it square on. Paula thought she heard the crunch of bones. The man, however, had not been knocked out or even stunned. With his undamaged left hand, he reached out for Paula, grabbing her by her leg. He had huge, claw-like hands that completely encircled her thin legs and his grip on Paula inflicted immediate pain.

Samantha, free at last and no longer on the defense, rose to her feet and executed a kick to the man's groin. He let go of Paula's leg and threw himself at Samantha, screaming something unintelligible as he did. Samantha dropped and rolled out of the way and yelled for Paula to give her the bat. Paula, instead, swung the bat again, hitting the man in the back. If her first two swings had been powered by muscles, this third one was fueled by adrenaline.

The man howled in anguish and fell to the ground. But he rolled away from the two women and stumbled to his feet. Now, though, he was holding a knife. He assumed a stance that could have allowed him to lunge at either woman.

"The bat!" Samantha screamed and, this time, Paula tossed it to Samantha. With one motion, Samantha grabbed the bat and wheeled around. The man lunged at her, knife-first. The fat part of the bat slammed into the man's hand and the knife flew away, disappearing beyond the headlights' beam into the dark of the asphalt. The man screamed again, as much in rage as in pain, and continued his lunge toward Samantha.

Samantha flipped the bat back to Paula in the split second before he landed atop her. Paula deftly caught and swung the bat, aiming for the man's head but hitting him between the shoulder blades. She raised the bat to hit him again when she saw the man freeze and heard Samantha shout, "No! Don't hit him!"

The man slowly raised his arms, the hurt of doing so obvious in his movement. "*No mas,*" he whispered.

Paula saw the reason for the sudden cessation of hostilities. Samantha's right arm was between his legs, her hand squeezed around his crotch.

"Get the tape from my pocket and tape his hands together," Samantha instructed. Paula did as she was told. "Now the legs. We've got to get him out of here before we start attracting attention."

Samantha had a pronounced limp but she held the bat steady as they made their way to the Navigator. The man was pushed flat in the back seat and Samantha tied his hands to his feet.

Samantha went back to the Hummer and rummaged around through the car, returning with a paper bag full of items.

"You drive," Samantha said, getting into the front passenger seat. "Boz and I are going to have a little conversation. We're headed back to where we started from." Paula understood. No names, no locations.

"You're Boz," she said.

The man said nothing. Samantha jabbed at his shoulder with the end of the baseball bat.

"I go by Boz," he said in his thick Hispanic accent. "And who are you, in case we met again?"

Samantha jabbed his shoulder again.

"Cut it out!" he yelled.

"I ask you simple questions, you give me simple, truthful answers, and we'll drop you at the nearest emergency room," Samantha said. "Make me angry, or get me thinking about you kicking me like that, and we're going to drop you in the woods somewhere and let the coyotes get first crack at you. What's it going to be?"

"What do you want to know?"

"What was the other $350,000 in the fair receipts bag?"

"So you've got the money," Boz said.

As hard as she could within the confines of the car, Samantha jammed the baseball bat into his crotch. "Shit!" he screamed, his face contorted with pain.

"You're not listening to me," Samantha said. "I'm thinking those coyotes are going to find you an awfully tasty morsel. An awful lot of fat, a lot of meat. I hear coyotes like that. You'll feed a whole pack of coyotes for a day or two. And the way they work, it may take you five or six hours before you die."

"How do I know you're not going to kill me anyway?" Boz said.

"Because we're reasonable people. All we want is information. An emergency room can patch you up, good as new, in a couple of hours. You can have breakfast at home at that big mansion of yours. Now, what was the other $350,000?"

"Money Erskine was depositing as a favor."

"Now we're getting somewhere," Samantha said. "I presume he was laundering it for someone who couldn't afford to have bundles of cash around. Was it all done at once or are there multiple deposits?"

"Four deposits, one-point-four million, total."

"Good man. And for whom was Erskine doing this favor?"

Boz hesitated and Samantha lifted the bat.

"Gordon McLeod," he said.

"And who, pray tell, is Gordon McLeod?"

"Selectman in Brookfield. He's also an attorney."

"Did Mr. Gordon McLeod hire you to get back the money?"

"Yeah."

"You and Mr. Gordon McLeod have had previous dealings?"

"A couple."

"You had a snitch. Someone who tipped you to what the police were learning. Who was that?"

"It isn't important," Boz said. "You know who hired me."

"You've been so cooperative," Samantha said in a chiding tone. "I would hate like hell to feed you to the coyotes..."

"Sam Ashton," Boz said. "Chief of Police in Brookfield."

Samantha was pleased it wasn't Detective Hoffman. She had liked him. "Do you have something on Ashton or does McLeod?"

"I do. I bailed his daughter out of a jam a few years back."

"He supplies you with this kind of information regularly?"

"I don't need to know what happens in Brookfield. No one gives a crap about Brookfield. He was in reserve for something like this."

"What kind of hold does McLeod have over Erskine that Erskine would do McLeod this kind of favor? Seems to me that Erskine wert out on a quite a limb for his town selectman."

"Erskine is an assumed name," Boz said. "He did time for something back a few years ago. McLeod said he knew all about it because he was in charge of checking the guy's credentials. McLeod said he thought Erskine would be useful for a couple of 'side deals' whenever he needed assistance."

"Other money laundering deals?"

"McLeod didn't say. That's my guess."

"And now for the last question. Who, exactly, was willing to fork over one-point-four million dollars to Mr. Gordon McLeod? And please don't tell me you don't know because I'll jam this baseball bat into your *cojones* so hard you'll be singing soprano in that heavenly choir after the coyotes finish chewing your ass."

"FreshMart," Boz said without hesitation. "McLeod is the 'go-to' guy for the zoning commission. He pushed through a thirty-acre rezoning package. FreshMart paid up a couple of weeks ago when they got the construction permits for something called 'pads'. McLeod was bragging, saying FreshMart earned back its money just on a couple of the fast food leases."

"You mean PADs," Samantha said. "'Planned Area Developments' for the uninitiated. You're a businessman, Boz, you ought to know this stuff. Big old FreshMart gets a thirty-acre PAD and then turns around and sublets rights to every junk food purveyor who'd never stand a chance in hell of getting their building approved on its own. For a million four, Gordon McLeod sells the soul of a quaint New England town. Which of course is chump change for FreshMart."

Samantha pondered her newly acquired knowledge for a moment. "I would ask you why, if you've got the goods on Mr. Gordon McLeod, you don't squeeze him for everything he's worth, but I promised you that was my last question. Unless you feel like answering."

Boz was silent.

"Well then," Samantha said. "I need to factor this information into my thinking, but I'm pretty sure what we're going to do with you."

"You said you were going to take me to an emergency room,"

Boz said angrily. "I told you what you wanted to know."

"And you are going to an emergency room, honey," Samantha said with a smile. "We just need to make one stop."

She wrapped duct tape around Boz's head, covering his eyes, ears and mouth but leaving his nose clear.

"Do I want to know what the 'one stop' is?" Paula asked.

"We just have to put all the pieces together," Samantha said. "Then we can all go home and get a good night's sleep. Besides, you've got to be at a hospital tomorrow."

20.

It was midnight. Chief Sam Ashton went through the diagrams and notes left behind by Hoffman. To Ashton, Hoffman's idea of a scheme that involved two elderly ladies – one to divert attention from the crime and another to transport the money out of the fair – had seemed preposterous. But the state police were also looking for the 'world's greatest grandma', which lent greater credence to the idea.

There was another old lady in the mix, Ashton remembered, and he went through Hoffman's written crime scene synopsis from Sunday evening. There had been a sixty-something woman who ought to have been an eyewitness to the robbery but who said she saw nothing, even though she was also behind the building when the transfer of the money from the robbers likely took place.

Ashton found the name, plus that of another woman who had been minding the exhibit.

All three lived in Hardington.

In both his typed and his handwritten notes from earlier in the day, Hoffman had called the two women a dead end.

Ashton was much less certain.

From his briefcase, Ashton pulled a cell phone. Not the one issued to him by the department and not the one he was known to carry for personal use. This one had been given to him two years earlier by Enrico 'Boz' Boscales. Before this week, he had never used it. Indeed, before this week he had willed himself to forget he even possessed the phone.

But Sunday evening while he was working through the preliminary report on the robbery his personal cell phone had rung and, by habit, he had answered it.

"You still got the cell phone I gave you?" The voice asking

the question had a thick Hispanic accent. Though he had heard it only once before, it was immediately familiar to Ashton. "You get yourself someplace where you can talk and you call the number programmed into it."

It was the one time in his life he had ever made a deal with the devil. His daughter, then a student at Boston University, had been caught in a drug raid. She had sufficient pills, including Extasy, to constitute intent to distribute. The college's zero tolerance policy would have meant her expulsion. His daughter had called him, crying, from the police station where she had been taken. She was in the process of being booked and would need bail.

As Ashton collected his car keys, the phone rang a second time. A man who introduced himself only as 'Boz' said he had just heard of Ashton's daughter's plight and he believed he could intercede. "I can make the booking go away," Boz had said. "Your daughter has no record. I can keep it that way."

Wary, Ashton asked what he needed to do.

"For now, nothing," Boz had said. "I promise. Maybe nothing ever. But one day I may need a favor. Maybe someday some other police chief's good daughter may need to get out of a jam. But I need to know now if you're willing to maybe help me someday." Boz's voice had not been menacing. There was no threat of retaliation for refusing to agree. Boz's voice had sounded reasonable; businesslike. Almost pleading to be allowed to be of service to him.

Well aware of what would happen to his daughter otherwise, Ashton had agreed. An hour later he had arrived at the Boston PD precinct where his daughter was being held. To his surprise, she was outside on the sidewalk. "They said it was a mistake and they let me go," his daughter had said.

A week later, the cell phone arrived with a single number

programmed into its memory. It was one of those throwaway phones with a hundred minutes of air time on it. Ashton knew what it was for.

The arrest had been a wake-up call. His daughter had foresworn drugs and had graduated. She was now in law school, something that would have been impossible without Boz's intervention.

Ten minutes after he received the call, Ashton went into his office, retrieved the second phone from the back of his desk drawer and called the number programmed into it. Boz wanted a 'simple favor'. 'A friend' asked to be kept abreast of developments in solving the Brookfield Fair robbery. As Ashton became aware of any leads, he should relay them to Boz.

The request was, of course, as unethical – and illegal – as it was simple. On the one hand, Ashton had tipped reporters to investigations when it suited him, but reporters were interested only in meeting story deadlines. The information Ashton was being asked to provide could help someone thwart the investigation. Ashton had no way of knowing to whom the information he provided would be relayed or what consequences it might have.

But it was a deal on which he dared not renege. After the cell phone arrived two years earlier, Ashton had quietly inquired as to what kind of weight Enrico Boscales pulled in the Boston area. What he learned was chilling. Boscales had a hand in drug trafficking all across New England. Moreover, he had powerful friends. One of those friends had apparently tipped off Boscales that the daughter of a suburban police chief was about to be booked for drug possession. It was easy for Boscales to ask his tipster to lose the paperwork. He was a man whom you did not cross. All Ashton could hope was that whatever 'favor' Boz might need was inconsequential.

Ashton hit the "1" on the phone's speed dial. He would tell Boz that Eleanor Strong and Paula Winters, both of Hardington, likely played a role in the robbery and that he was sending his detective to question them in the morning.

The phone on the other end rang but did not answer. After twenty rings, Ashton hung up. He pulled a pillow from a closet in the lunch room and lay down on the sofa in his office. He would call again in a few hours.

* * * * *

Both Samantha and Paula heard the phone ring. It was coming from the paper bag of items Samantha had retrieved from Boz's car before they left the house on Route 9.

"Should I answer it?" Paula asked.

Samantha shook her head. "He's closed for business for the night, though we're going to want to see what numbers our friend has been calling."

After twenty rings, the phone went silent. Paula scrolled through the call list. There were more than thirty names and numbers in the telephone's address book, including 'McLeod'. The call log showed that several had been made to McLeod since Sunday evening. Frankie Tomkins was in the directory and three calls had been made to him since Sunday evening, including one just a few hours earlier, presumably setting up the break-in at Alice Beauchamp's apartment. Tony Erskine, however, was not in the directory, indicating that someone else, some crony, had made those calls or contacts with Erskine were made on yet another cell phone.

They pulled into Eleanor's driveway at 12:30 a.m. In Eleanor's garage, Frankie Tomkins reeked of rum and babbled incoherently.

"Drunk as a skunk," Eleanor said when the four of them were back in the house and out of Tomkins' hearing range. "He put away a bottle of Tanqueray without any fuss. We had to switch to rum because that's all I had in the house. I don't even think he noticed. The first half of the bottle went down easily. We had to force down the rest."

Samantha nodded but was more interested in the fragments of the Bay State Transport Service satchels. It took eight fragments to create the blue 'BSTS' crest.

"Paula, you did a real good job on these, Samantha said. "I hope it wasn't *too* good. The police don't like jigsaw puzzles. All we can do is make it easy for them to put them back together, but we're talking people with short attention spans."

"What if we just staple enough of the pieces together to let them know what they have?" Paula asked.

"If it's the best we can do, then we'll do it," Samantha said. She then called the four women into Eleanor's living room.

"This can all be over in a little more than an hour," Samantha said to them. "I have a plan. If that plan works, you can go on and live your lives without fear of some smart detective knocking on the door some day. If it doesn't work, well, I'm in just as deep as you are, and I've got the bonus of a couple of kidnapping charges."

"Each of you has a mission. When your part of the mission is over, you go home, you go to bed. Your alibi is that you were sound asleep. None of this ever happened. You never met me, you don't know me. Our drunken companion, Frankie Tomkins, has no idea where he is and, assuming you never spoke to him, he has no idea who you are. He'll remember what I look like but, unless he sees me some day, he has no idea who I am. Same thing with Boz, who is hog-tied out there in Tomkins' car."

"So, let's go over the plan."

* * * * *

The Middlesex Detective's Bureau is based at the state police headquarters on Route 9 in Framingham. It is an old, brick-front colonial building that could just as easily have been a 1930's-era schoolhouse. The detectives are housed in cubicles in the basement of the building.

At 1:45 a.m., Detective Sergeant Woolsey, having reviewed more than five hundred phone logs and feeling no closer to a solution to the identity of the woman in the minivan than he had four hours earlier, had laid down for an hour's rest in a cot in the state police barracks. As he was getting comfortable in the cot, he heard a screech and a crash and thought to himself, 'That one's going to be an easy one to investigate.'

He had been asleep fifteen minutes when he felt hands on his shoulders, shaking him.

"Woolsey!" someone said. "You got to get out here and see this!"

Woolsey quickly pulled on his boots and followed a trooper upstairs and out the front of the building. Three state police cars, their full array of lights flashing, were on the scene. There was a wail of an ambulance in the distance.

A black Lincoln Navigator looked as though it had attempted to climb a telephone pole in front of the state police headquarters building. The front end was badly damaged, indicating an impact speed of better than forty miles per hour. There was only a minimal skid mark.

The trooper pulled Woolsey by the arm to the side of the car and opened the rear door.

Three things were obvious. First, there was money everywhere. It was as though a money bomb had burst in the car. Hundred dollar bills covered every surface. Second was the smell of alcohol. Third was the man trussed and gagged in the back seat, squirming. From the driver's seat, another man babbled incoherently about being buried alive. He was so drunk that he could not even hold his head straight.

The trooper pointed to a piece of paper taped to the base of the rear view mirror. On the paper was written a name and address and a time, 3 a.m.

"It looks like our friend was on his way to keep an appointment," Woolsey said.

"Then this is what you've really got to see," the trooper said. He pointed to a patchwork of canvas pieces one of the troopers had assembled on the ground outside the vehicle. "These were in a paper bag in the front seat."

The patchwork formed several of the distinctive blue BSTS logos of the Bay State Transport Service.

"Holy mother of mercy," Woolsey said. "Get a video team out here before you touch anything else."

* * * * *

Also at 1:45 a.m., at the Brookfield Police Department, the night dispatcher on duty gently tapped Chief Ashton on the shoulder. Ashton had slept uncomfortably for an hour and was grateful for the interruption. He really needed to go home.

"I just got handed this envelope, Captain," the dispatcher said. The envelope was marked *'Capt. Sam Ashton – Personal'*.

"Who delivered it?" Ashton asked.

"Some short woman, probably in her sixties though I wouldn't swear to it. All I really saw was a big floppy hat and sunglasses," the dispatcher said. "She just walked in, put this on the counter and walked back out. I really just saw her back as she was leaving."

The dispatcher left and Ashton opened the envelope. Inside was a sheet of standard typing paper and a handwritten message:

Captain Ashton,

Tonight, your debt to Boz was repaid in full. With luck, your name will not be linked to him. Whether you use this opportunity to retire is between you and your conscience.

Ashton re-read the unsigned note several times. When he had memorized its contents, he tore the sheet of paper into fine confetti and flushed it down the toilet in the men's room. He was sixty-three years old, but at that moment he felt more like ninety-three.

* * * * *

Tony Erskine sat uncomfortably in front of the darkened house. It was a few minutes before 3 a.m. and he was, if not frightened, very apprehensive. There had been no misinterpreting the call from the woman who identified herself as Gordon McLeod's secretary.

All afternoon, Erskine has wrestled with his impossible situation. McLeod, through his hired goon, demanded that he complete the final three deposits as quickly as possible. The police and insurance investigator were certain he was part of a scam to make a theft appear as a robbery. His staff was watching his every move and it was impossible for him to change the amount of the deposit slip or fill the money bags himself. Yet, he had been threatened with death if he did not do this and he was certain that the people McLeod worked with would make good on that threat.

Then, ninety minutes earlier – at 1:30 in the morning – he had been rousted by a telephone call. "Mr. McLeod recognizes that recent events have made it impossible for you to complete the task you were assigned," the woman had said. "In recognition of that, he asks that you return all uncompleted work to his home and he will relieve you of responsibility for it. He realizes that asking you to do so this evening is extraordinarily inconvenient but he asks if you can be at his home at 3 a.m. He will meet you at the door."

"Uncompleted work" could mean only one thing: the $1.1 million that was still in his office safe at the fair. From the vague language McLeod's secretary had used, it wasn't clear she even knew what this 'uncompleted work' consisted of.

"You're certain he wants me there at 3 a.m.?" Erskine had asked.

"He was very specific about the time. Not earlier and not later." Then the line had gone silent.

Erskine hugged the suitcase with the money. His watch said 3 a.m. It was time to get this whole wretched business over with, and if he never saw or did business with McLeod again, it was fine with him. And if McLeod threatened to expose him... well, he could move on. He had found a new identity once. He could do it again.

* * * * *

Gordon McLeod watched out the window of his den at the car waiting outside. It wasn't the Hummer that Boz had driven the last time they met but then Boz could presumably be discreet when it was to his advantage. The car outside was some kind of a small sedan, the kind that attracted no attention. That was good.

The goddam cell phone had rung at 2 a.m. He had heard it instantly. His wife had mumbled but had not awakened and, fortunately, the children were on the third floor. He had dashed downstairs and gotten the phone on its fifth ring.

"Boz found the money. All of it." The voice wasn't Boz but, rather, a woman. Possibly African-American by the sound. "He's also got a solution for getting the rest of the money deposited. He's going to come around to your place at 3 a.m. It will only take a few minutes. Meet him at the front door."

"Can't we do this by phone?" McLeod asked, looking at the watch on his desk.

"Boz says this has to be done in person. Plus, he's got the money he recovered and he thinks you'll want it back."

"But I..."

The line was dead.

McLeod spent the next fifty-five minutes sitting in his office, wondering what Boz would demand in return for his 'solution'. McLeod had already agreed to a twenty percent 'recovery fee' if Boz succeeded in getting back the initial $350,000 before the police captured the robbers. If he demanded the same twenty percent on the full $1.4 million, McLeod would be giving up $280,000. McLeod had decided he would offer a flat ten percent. And screw Boz if he thought he was going to get paid a penny more.

The whole damned thing had been screwed up from the get-go. The project development crew from FreshMart had pussy-footed around for six months, feeling him out. McLeod knew how badly they wanted the site. Big Box stores and Planned Area Developments were an anathema to towns attempting to retain their small-village feel. The site, where Brookfield touched an I-495 interchange, was ideal for retail development. When the FreshMart people finally broached the subject, he had made it clear that his support for the site could be had for the right price, payable to several dummy corporations he had set up for this and similar purposes with other firms seeking to do business with Brookfield. But the fools from FreshMart had insisted that there be no paper trail, which meant a cash transaction.

Cash! What the hell could he do with a suitcase full of cash? Deposit it at a string of ATMs with his photo being taken every time? And then explain where the cash had come from? And then pay taxes on it? FreshMart had been adamant: cash or no deal. And, to make matters worse, FreshMart insisted on no payments until zoning variances and building permits were in hand, and pilings were being driven.

McLeod had taped the final payoff and the discussions leading up to it, of course. If anything ever happened, he had one of the biggest fish – and one of the most loathed corporations in America – to offer in return for his freedom.

But it was a good deal all the way around. McLeod's fee was cheap for what FreshMart got. The FreshMart Superstore and its parking area would use just twenty of the thirty acres. The balance was leased out to banks, fast food chains and other stores that did not compete directly with FreshMart. Not one of those chains had ever gotten a foot in the door in Brookfield or any surrounding town. Now, they had their presence in a prestigious community. It was a win-win situation.

Depositing the cash through the fair had been a stroke of genius. A mountain of cash was generated in just ten days. Nobody understood fairs or fair economics. So what it if took in three million dollars or four million? Nobody cared. Just like no one cared to which organizations the fair wrote checks to with those gate receipts. The fair made the same amount of money either way and it all happened so quickly. Who was Legacy Management or Appleton Distributors? What did they do for the fair? No one gave a damn.

Because Erskine owed him – because he could break Erskine any time he chose – it was easy to talk him into making the deposits. Four crummy deposits. A week from today the checks would be in his accounts. Instead, some asshole robbers had loused it up – at least for a while. But Boz had come through. Boz would show him the cash and explain how it was all going to be converted into electrons in his accounts.

The glowing dial of the clock showed 3 a.m. In the darkness outside, McLeod saw a car door open and the shape of a man emerge with a suitcase. McLeod walked to the front door, deactivated the alarm, and opened the front door, not turning on the porch light.

"We probably ought to talk outside," McLeod said, closing the door behind him.

Those were the only words he spoke before all hell broke

loose. Sirens and flashing lights approached from either end of the street, converging on his house. Spotlights from three police cars shined on the front door of the house. McLeod squinted and put out his hands to try to block the glare of the lights.

Which is when he saw that the person standing next to him, equally dumfounded, was not Boz, but Tony Erskine.

What the hell was he doing here?

From one of the cars – they were all state police cruisers – emerged a tall man in full trooper regalia. Because of the lights behind the man, McLeod could not see the face until he was a few feet away. It was the idiotic trooper who had been on the evening news talking about that damn stroller-pushing grandmother in a minivan.

The man smiled, and McLeod noticed that at least one of the bright lights behind the trooper appeared to be mounted atop a video camera carried by a man who was most decidedly not a trooper.

"Gordon McLeod," the trooper said. "I am arresting you for conspiracy to commit robbery and for soliciting and accepting bribes while in the performance of public duties. You have the right to remain silent…"

THREE MONTHS LATER

It was elegant for a suburban restaurant. The exterior of the building was a grand Victorian dating from the 1880's, yet it was freshly painted and well maintained. The interior décor made clear to diners that this establishment was not part of any chain. The walls were pastels, the linens were a soothing yellow and the artwork adorning the partitions was original. Around the room, women in autumnal chic spoke in animated tones while sipping colorful drinks.

It was the sort of restaurant that Detective Martin Hoffman had avoided all his life, but it was also the place suggested by Paula Winters. He had dutifully made the reservation and, after making a couple of drive-bys over the preceding week, determined that his best blazer and a new tie were in order.

Paula Winters looked wonderful. Her color was back and her clothes no longer hung loosely on her. She wore a brightly colored sweater and black skirt. Her cheeks were blushed and her smile bright. She had been candid with him about the reason for her absence and extended convalescence. Cancer was a disease that could be stopped. It *had* been stopped at the cost of a breast. Now, she was getting on with her life.

It was their third date in as many weeks, though neither of them would have called it such and would have strenuously objected to such a label regardless of its accuracy. They were two people who had met under unusual circumstances and found points of common interest. Their get-togethers – for surely people over fifty did not go out on dates – had consisted of lunch, dinner, and now lunch again. They were becoming comfortable with one another. Any stiffness was long gone, replaced by a dawning awareness that there was a physical and emotional attraction between them. Perhaps even something more than just an attraction.

"You're probably already packed for Washington," Hoffman said as they were seated.

"I wish," Paula said, a wisp of exasperation in her voice. "I've spent four hours on the phone this morning with my daughter, walking her through every step of making a Thanksgiving dinner. She's a nervous wreck. I've told Julie to relax and everything will be fine, but this will be her first time and my suspicion is that she thinks the fate of the world rests on how well her stuffing turns out."

"And your son is still coming?"

"Knock on wood," Paula said. "Perry is flying out of Seattle and there are tickets waiting there for him. Both Julie and I are holding our breath that he actually gets on the plane." Paula looked at her watch. "Which ought to be in exactly twelve hours. I think Julie will be heartbroken if he doesn't show up. I'm just happy to have heard he's all right."

"So, is there going to be a trial?" Paula asked as they studied menus.

"Which one?" Hoffman replied, pointing to half a dozen imaginary defendants around the room. "Tomkins got offered the minimum on the kidnapping and robbery in return for his testimony on Boscales. He should be the happiest thug in New England right now, but he still sticks to this incredible 'two guys named Lou and Sam and an Amazon of a black woman tried to bury me alive' story. It's pathetic and the DA has tried to talk sense to the public defender, but Tomkins won't let go of it. He still claims he has no idea how Boscales got into the back seat of his car and it was the Amazon, Lou and Sam who poured two fifths of liquor down his throat."

"He says he has absolutely no idea of how he came to be on

Route 9, blind drunk. He has no clue how the fair's gate receipts and the bags came to be in his car." Hoffman shook his head in disbelief. "Given the evidence and his record, it will take a jury about ten minutes to convict him. So, yeah, it looks like there's going to be one very short trial for that one."

"Boscales is a real piece of work. He claims McLeod paid Tomkins to kidnap and/or kill him and he tried to trade his knowledge of McLeod's deal with FreshMart for a walk on the robbery charge. When you start looking at who-called-whom on all those phones, it's fairly clear that Boscales had the niftiest scam of all: he knew Erskine was making the first deposit on Sunday and he set up the robbery to get both the fair receipts and the first part of McLeod's bribe money. Then he goes to McLeod and offers to 'find' the money before the cops do. We have no idea of what went south between Erskine and Tomkins, and we don't care. They're both going away for a long time."

Hoffman took a sip of water. "Is it a trial or a deal? I think they ought to just lock up Boscales and throw away the key. But he has enough stuff on enough people – and especially public officials – to thoroughly muck up the system of justice. He's got a team of thousand-dollar-an-hour lawyers with a stack of proffers, and I'm not sure there's a law enforcement agency in the state that he hasn't corrupted at some point along the way. Of course, there's also the question of what Boscales did with the $350,000. We assume it's in some safe deposit box, ready to be claimed when he gets out of prison. I'd even go out on a limb and say it's probably helping to fund his defense. I wouldn't hold out any hope of recovering it."

Hoffman tried to signal a waiter to take their order. "If there's an innocent party in this whole rat's nest, it's probably Erskine – or rather, William Marsh, to use his real name. It turns out Marsh had been a principal in a PR firm out in California, living the good life. Then, five years ago, he made the mistake of lying for a client in court, got caught, and pleaded out to a perjury charge. He served one year of a three-year sentence and was released on parole but couldn't get a job doing anything but flipping hamburgers because of the prison record. Apparently in the world of PR, it's OK to lie, but not to get caught doing so."

"To try to get back some semblance of his life he found a grave marker for an infant born in the same year he was, got a duplicate birth certificate and used that to find the dead infant's social security number. Marsh came east, became Tony Erskine, grew a beard, invented a resume's worth of credentials and started looking for a job. With his management background he could do the fair manager's job with one hand tied behind his back and he applied."

"As a selectman, McLeod sat on the town's personnel and hiring committee. He spotted the resume as a phony but approved the town's hiring of Marsh as the fair manager. Then, McLeod turned around and demanded ten grand a year from Marsh as 'hush' money. That went on for three years. Then, a few weeks before the robbery, McLeod coerced Marsh into participating in McLeod's money laundering scheme."

Two glasses of wine appeared at the table. Paula and Hoffman each took a sip and Hoffman continued. "Marsh was in a lose-lose position and, personally, I feel sorry for him. But it's still criminal conspiracy, plus he violated his parole every way possible. His testimony on McLeod will be useful if that ever goes to trial but Marsh is going back to jail. It's a shame, really. He ran the fair decently, he made money for the town and he had some good ideas. He just got caught up in it: a small fish in a net meant for much bigger fish."

"McLeod is the most pathetic case of the four. At first, he claimed he had no idea that Marsh was going to show up with the rest of the bribe money and he claimed he had no idea what the money was for. I suppose he just happened to be fully dressed at 3 a.m., standing by the door, waiting to answer it in case someone came by. After we showed him Boscales' phone log, he changed his story twenty times trying to cover all the bases. Then he offered up FreshMart, except that we already had that from the first search warrant. Yeah, he'll go to trial. He's got money – no doubt the bounty from a dozen other bribes – and his attorneys will fight it through every court. McLeod will lose, but he'll lose in about seven years when he's bankrupt and there are no more attorneys willing to take the case on some vague notion that McLeod is going to recover his expenses from someone. The ones I feel sorry for are his family. A wife and two young kids and they had no idea what daddy was up to."

Salads arrived. "Is there any new word on the chief's job?" Paula asked.

Hoffman dabbed at his chin. "All I know is, I'm on the list. I don't hold out a lot of hope, though. Sam says he's gone as of the end of the year. I still don't accept the thing about his heart, but it's his decision and I wish him well. He's pulling for me, but that only goes so far because the town's personnel committee is short one member and McLeod's replacement won't be elected until next month. The new selectman may want a chief from the outside, and you can believe that they'll be checking credentials carefully."

"And you have a skeleton in your closet?" Paula asked.

"Well, let's see: I had the biggest case in Brookfield's history taken away from me by the state police after just sixteen hours," Hoffman said. "And Woolsey cracked it wide open just eighteen hours later. What does that say about my detective skills?"

"But you were still working on the case," Paula said.

"As soon as the state police made their arrests – for which, by the way, they gave us no advance warning – Sam and I shredded everything we had worked on since Woolsey and his boss waltzed into the station. The record shows I handed off the case at 9 a.m. Monday morning. Anything else I did that day was other Brookfield business."

When they had finished their salads, Hoffman said, "I have a confession to make, Paula. It's difficult to tell you, but it's something you need to know and I'd rather you heard it from me than from someone else or, worse, read about it one day."

Paula looked at him with curiosity but said nothing.

Hoffman breathed a sigh. "There was a point in time when... you were a suspect. I had this theory – completely idiotic but my theory all the same – that you and Eleanor Strong were the robbers and that you had handed off the money to whoever the woman was in the 'world's greatest grandma' tee shirt. And I had Alice Beauchamp pegged as a diversionary plot – falling down deliberately to distract the crowd."

"It was dumb. I was desperate for leads and I was grasping at straws. For a few hours, it all seemed to fit. I was going to bring you and Alice and Eleanor in for formal questioning the next morning. Then I went home and slept on it. Well, slept on it until Sam called me at four in the morning to say the staties had just arrested McLeod and that Tomkins' SUV had been found hemorrhaging hundred dollar bills out in front of the state police headquarters. But you need to know that, well, I had this wacko idea that the three of you plus the 'world's greatest grandma' had pulled off the robbery."

Paula laughed. She reached her hand across the table and took his. "I'm honored!" she said. "You must have thought I was brilliant to have planned and executed such a perfect robbery. Why, Martin, I couldn't be more pleased."

Hoffman was thrilled by her hand on his and the way she gently squeezed him. "Well, there was the deer repellent and the home-made pepper spray..."

"Oh, it all makes complete sense," Paula said. "I guess I would have suspected me, too, if I were you. Oh, that makes my day! I love it that you'd think I was that clever." She squeezed his hand tighter and laughed, attracting the attention of curious diners at nearby tables.

"Just so you know," Hoffman said, relieved that she had not been angry.

"I am duly warned," Paula said, smiling broadly. "No more planning robberies. I swear. Cross my heart. That was my last heist."

* * * * *

At the same moment at another restaurant, this one a loud and noisy one in the cluster of anonymous chain bistros around the Natick Mall, Eleanor Strong and Samantha Ayers also met, and talked. A carafe of wine was on the table between them.

"I hear Alice has her condo," Samantha said, taking a drink from her glass. "I'm pleased for her."

Eleanor nodded. "Well, Paula gave Alice her share, which is what made it all possible and then Jean and I contributed some, too. Paula said she didn't need the money, which is certainly true. Alice hated that senior citizen's place. Getting out of there will probably add ten years to her life. She's also off crutches now. Her foot surgery went perfectly and her doctor said she was a model of healing."

"What about Jean?" Samantha asked.

"She took her cruise," Eleanor said, shaking her head. "None of us had any idea how many cruel restrictions her husband had put on his estate. He must have been a terrible man, and horrible to put up with all those years. Jean didn't say so, but the rest of us had the idea her goal on that cruise was to find a new husband. She didn't, but there's always next year."

Eleanor set down her glass of wine and looked at Samantha directly. "You know, I still don't know why you helped us… why you took those risks when you could have just called the police and closed the case. We're all grateful, but…"

Samantha waved her hand. "It all happened too quickly to say it was planned. I went to Alice's apartment with the intent of talking her into cooperating. Had she been there – and had she talked – I suspect I would have just taken a statement and given it to the police the next day."

"But she wasn't there," Samantha continued. "Frankie Tomkins was there, waiting for her. And if Alice had opened that door instead of me, I'm certain she'd be dead now and there's a good chance Jean might be, too. Because Frankie Tompkins had two things on his mind: get the money and leave behind no witnesses."

"I guess I made up my mind when I took his car instead of my own. The four of you had planned it all beautifully, but you couldn't have known about McLeod and what he was doing. When Boz told me this was all about bribe money to build a shopping center – and I knew that two of you would have been killed to protect McLeod's little scam – I knew that not only was I not going to turn the four of you in, but that I was going to do my best to make certain that McLeod went down and you kept the money. A lot of what happened after that was pure luck, but it all worked out."

"You didn't ask for a share," Eleanor said.

"I didn't want a share," Samantha said, shaking her head. "It wasn't my plan. I didn't have the bright idea to rob a fair and then just go back to some flower show and watch the police arrive and run around in circles, chasing their own tails. I'm not that smart." Then, Samantha smiled. "Besides, I don't need the money."

"But you certainly deserved it," Eleanor said.

Samantha poked at her salad, trying to find the right opportunity. It seemed to be now.

"What about you?" Samantha asked. "Did the money come in handy for you?"

"Oh, I need every dollar of it," Eleanor said. "My husband's care is going up another thousand dollars a month effective the first of the year and the insurance won't pick up an additional penny. It's outrageous. I don't know if Phil is going to live one more year or ten, but I owe it to him to give him the best care as long as I can afford it. Before the..." Eleanor lowered her voice, "... robbery, I was looking at being out of money in a little over a year or having to sell the house. Now, I have some options. You made those options possible for all of us, and we'll always be in your debt."

There was a moment's quiet, then Samantha said, "I have a thought. I want to try it out on you."

Eleanor looked at Samantha but said nothing.

"I've just been assigned a new case," Samantha said, pouring Eleanor another glass of wine, filling her glass to the top. "Suspected insurance fraud. There's a car dealership up on the north shore. Mass Casualty has gotten four claims in the past year. Two for cars that were ostensibly torched by 'eco-terrorists' and two for cars supposedly wrecked while on test drives by uninsured drivers. All these cars, interestingly, were gas hogs that had been sitting on the dealer's lot for six months without a taker. The dealer had been paying out a couple of hundred a month in carrying costs. Now, he's got cash equal to full retail value. We've paid out more than two hundred grand, and we're just braced for the next claim."

Eleanor had an interested look in her eye and so Samantha continued. "Right now, I can't prove anything. What I need is to get someone on the inside – maybe two people that the owner would never suspect – and then plant a couple of decoys who could agree to help out the dealer in exchange for..."